TAMARA LEMUS

From the Top Rope

Book 1 of the Wrestling with Love Series

First edition

ISBN: 979-8-9917849-1-7

Editing by Allison Meloni
Cover art by Mackenzie Gimben

This book was professionally typeset on Reedsy.
Find out more at reedsy.com

To all the girls out there who watch wrestling and whisper, "Now kiss," whenever the wrestlers get all up in each other's faces—this one's for you.

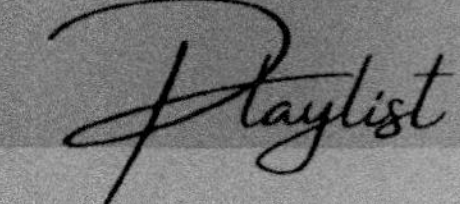

Busy Girl - Tove Lo & SG Lewis

Villain Era - Bryce Savage

Girlfight - Brooke Valentine

Ouchies - Doja Cat

Pretty Girls - Reneé Rapp

Can't Get You Out of My Head - Kylie Minogue

I Kissed A Girl - Katy Perry

If I Didn't Know Better - Mack Lorén

Girls Like You - Cloudy June

Behind These Hazel Eyes - Kelly Clarkson

Thinking of You - Katy Perry

He'll Never Love You (HNLY) - Hayley Kiyoko

Adore You (Cover) - Brittany Broski

Feels Like Home - Beau Miller & Jessie Reyez

Strangers - Halsey & Lauren Jauregui

Say it First - Sam Smith

0:44   3:45

1

Amaya

"Are you ready?"

"You ask me this every time, Sid, and my answer is always the same. What do I say, Sid?" I scream over the roaring crowd.

"You were made for this." He rolls his eyes.

"Exactly. I was made for this." I pat him on the back as my entrance music blasts from the speakers.

I love Sid. He's been my family's manager for years, but he can be a pain in my ass. The crowd goes insane, giving me goosebumps all over. I sway my hips as I walk towards the ring. Over 42,000 people are singing along to every word of my song, sending chills down my spine.

I will never get tired of this feeling.

At this point, everything is muscle memory to me. I make sure to give high-fives as I make my way down the ramp, all while also giving the cameraman my best angles. As soon as I reach the ring, I slide under the bottom ropes.

Momma's home.

My championship belt fits snugly around my waist, where it has been for 522 days. Becoming a champion is my destiny. My family is legendary in this industry, but I'll be damned if anyone tells me that's why I'm in this position. You would think that would give me an advantage when it comes to designing the belt, but no, it's still this stupid bright pink color. Val is obsessed with the color pink and tries to tie it into the champ's look whenever she can. She swears the color is meant to convey authority, despite the rest of the world deciding to give pink a bad rap. I just think she likes the power she has to do whatever she wants. I unstrap the belt from my waist, letting it shine as the arena lights hit the rhinestones.

The cheering is replaced by a wave of boos as another theme song takes the place of mine. I looked towards the ramp, and there she was, attitude and all. Ravyn, the thorn in my side, the bane of my existence. She's been my arch-nemesis since training. We both got pulled into the main roster during the draft, and that hate followed us. The reason she hates me remains a mystery.

It's annoying how my biggest hater is also one of the hottest women on the roster.

I talked to my dad about Ravyn when I realized it wasn't just an act for the camera. He just told me to shake it off; it's one of the prices to pay for being a part of the Acosta family. Even though she's the bane of my existence, she's fucking incredible at what she does. I'll give her credit where credit is due. She has a commanding presence.

She enters the ring with an air of unshakable confidence. Her olive skin glistens under the harsh lights, and her hazel eyes are locked onto my green ones with such intensity that I want to look away, but I don't. Her long, straight jet-black hair flows behind her, the strands moving like a dark river, with a single silver streak framing the sharp angles of her face.

She towers over my petite frame, but that has never intimidated me. I've taken down bigger. Her body is covered in intricate tattoos, whereas mine is a blank canvas. From her arms to her thighs, the tattoos twist and coil like dark serpents and add to her badass image.

The crowd erupts as they usually do when we're in the ring together. It's the mixture of awe and fear from them that gets my adrenaline pumping. Ravyn and I in the ring means they're in for a show. We're a force of nature.

The fans love me and love to hate her, but what they love the most is us going head-to-head. Social media goes insane during our matches; we are always the number one trending topic. Are most of the comments about how hot we are? Yes, but hey, any publicity is good publicity.

They aren't wrong. We're hot and aren't afraid to flaunt it. Our job is physically taxing. The constant working out and taking bumps on the mat. Everyone thinks they're cut out to take that bump until they realize it's the equivalent of being in a car crash. After all that hard work, hell yeah, we show our bodies off in our gear. We're going to be sexualized either way. This is a man's world after all, so we might as well use the sex appeal they love so much to our advantage.

"Are you ready for me to take that belt from you, Amaya?" A smirk curls at the corners of Ravyn's lips.

I kiss my belt before handing it over to the referee. "Over my dead body, Ravyn."

"That can be arranged." Her index finger pops me on the nose, and it takes everything in me not to rage out on her before that bell rings.

I can't afford to lose control. I can't risk ruining my reputation as the babyface of this company. Your goal as a baby face is to be liked by the audience. EWC relies on me to be their sweet, good girl, the girl that everyone loves. I've never been a heel like Ravyn. I would be hated by most and only loved by people who love the bad guy. There have been times when I've been curious about it, becoming a villain, but that's not the Acosta brand. It would certainly piss Ravyn off if I did, because of how much better I would be than she is at her own game. The bell rings, and we're like moths to a flame. We gravitate towards each other, ready to fight for the right to call ourselves the best in the game.

2

Ravyn

"That's a bullshit call, ref, and you know it! That was three!" I yelled out to the incompetent man in the black-and-white striped shirt.

Okay, incompetent might be a strong word. The referees are important in the wrestling business. They have earpieces to communicate with the schedule director. They let us wrestlers know what moves to do and when to wrap things up. They deserve respect, but that doesn't mean I have to like it when they take their sweet time to count to three. My pin was flawless; I had both Amaya's shoulder blades perfectly laid out on the mat.

Tonight was supposed to be my night; it was in the script that I was finally going to win.

"I'm sorry, Ravyn, they're in my ear." The ref whispers.

Before I could even process his words, my feet were knocked out from under me. My body slammed to the mat. Now here I am, flipped onto my stomach.

This bitch!

It's a well-known fact that my ankle has been fucked up since the last pay-per-view match, yet here she is, about to attack that ankle. I scream out in pain as she positions my ankle in an ankle lock. The amount of pressure on my ankle has me in excruciating pain, not to mention the embarrassment of being at Amaya's mercy right now. I don't want to tap, I want to fight off this pain with everything I've got, but dammit, this bitch is going to break my ankle if I don't tap. I slammed my hand hard multiple times until the ref called my tap out. Amaya had the nerve to slap my ass before letting go of my ankle and grabbing her title belt.

I'm going to kill her.

"Maybe next time, Ravyn. Good try though!" She winked at me as I cradled my ankle.

Her stupid entrance music was blasting in my ear as I limped backstage.

Amaya fucking Acosta. I know hate is a strong word, but it's the only word I find fitting enough for my feelings towards her. Everything about her makes my skin crawl. Her fair, freckled skin always glows under the bright lights. The way her piercing green eyes stand out against the intensity of the match. Her stupid, natural strawberry red hair gets in my face every time and constantly smells like lavender. Her worst trait is her cocky confidence. With the last name Acosta alone, she commands attention, whether in the ring or on the mic, using her natural charm and good looks to connect with fans while navigating the pressure of living up to her family name.

As soon as I entered the locker room showers, I crumbled to the ground. Ravyn in the ring is a completely different person from Ravyn outside of the ring. Don't get me wrong, I'm still a badass through and through, but when there are no cameras around, my feelings take over. I've worked hard to get where I am, yet after everything, it still feels like it's not enough. Like I'm not enough. I made it through training, I've been on the main roster for five years now, and I'm still stuck in the same position. When will it finally be my turn to have the Women's Championship Belt? Everyone in Creative says I have what it takes to hold the title, yet here I am losing to Amaya again. I'm tired of hearing the word undisputed before her name is announced. The Acosta family has run the game since before she was even a thought. I'm just as good, maybe better than Amaya.

"Are you crying?"

She sounds concerned, even though her voice hits my ears like nails on a chalkboard.

"It's called being in fucking pain after a bitch decided to target my bad ankle." My words spew out like venom, and I watch her flinch.

"Just get your ass up. Sid and Scarlett want to see us in Val's office."

What was I thinking? Amaya is never concerned about anyone but herself. *This is not good.*

"I'll be out in a sec." I roll my eyes.

I can feel her eyes staring me down as I wash the suds off my body. "This isn't a peep show. If you'd like, I can take a picture for you, but it'll cost you more than you can afford."

"You've never seen one of my checks. I could buy this stadium right now if I wanted to."

I hate how true that statement is.

Her wicked laugh echoes in the hallway as the soap I throw at her hits the wall next to her face. What the hell could Val want with us, and why do I have a bad feeling that this meeting will end in a brawl?

3

Amaya

Valerie Archer is not the kind of woman who accepts the word "no." In fact, I'd bet that if anyone tried, they would be annihilated on the spot. Her mother, Melanie Archer, founded the Epic Wrestling Corporation, and when she stepped down two years ago, she handed her empire over to her only child, Val. Melanie's known for being a kick-ass businesswoman who's never needed a man. Hell, she used a sperm donor because she was 'tired of waiting for a man to get what she wanted.' I'm honestly shocked that someone as cutthroat as Melanie decided she wanted to reproduce, but I guess EWC being her baby wasn't enough.

I took deep breaths, trying to calm myself before stepping into Val's office. Did I cross a line when I ankle-locked Ravyn's bad ankle? Yes, I did. That move wasn't in the plans we discussed, but I couldn't help myself. In the moment, all I could focus on was retaining my title, but seeing Ravyn's breakdown in the showers made me feel ill.

Val's massive office could make the biggest wrestler feel small. I find her rolling her eyes as she listens to whoever is on the other end of her phone. She holds up a finger in warning, as if she thinks I would dare to interrupt her call. Sid is typing away on his phone in the corner, far away from Val's wrath. My eyes scan her office; no matter how many times I've been invited in here, I will always be in awe of all of the awards that hang on her bubblegum pink walls. Like I said, her obsession with the color is strong.

I loathe the color pink, but I love that she can have her office this color and still be feared by everyone in this company. I'm proud that my family is a part of EWC instead of any other wrestling company because the women here actually get respect. It's no secret that wrestling is a male-dominated sport, but in EWC, Melanie made it her mission for the men and women to be treated equally.

Ravyn takes a seat next to me in front of Val's desk, and I can't help but look her way. Her hair is still damp from her shower, but all of her makeup has been removed, and her freckled olive skin is flawless.

"I understand where you're coming from, but frankly, I don't give a fuck. Make it happen." Val slams her office phone so hard that I'm sure the person on the other end felt like it like a slap to the face.

"Hello, beautiful ladies. I am so proud of you two. Another amazing match. Ravyn, I wish you had held out more before tapping, but overall, the fans ate it up."

A pit forms in my stomach as I see Ravyn bite back the words she wants to say. I'm sure they are along the lines of cursing me out in the multiple languages I know she can speak. From experience, I know she can curse me out in Spanish, French, and Italian. Instead, she forces a smile, and I swear I see steam coming out from the top of her head.

"Thanks, Val," Ravyn said through gritted teeth.

"All in a day's work, boss," I replied.

"I am so sorry I'm late." Scarlett bursts through the door, short of breath and typing viciously on her phone.

"Honestly, Scarlett, when are you ever on time? Ravyn, it's a miracle you've gotten this far in your career with a manager like her." Val rolled her eyes.

Scarlett was going to speak before she received a death glare from Val. She stood silent, deciding it wasn't worth losing her head over.

"Now that everyone is finally here, we can discuss why I brought you here."

Val has a thing for dramatics, and her exaggerated pause was slowly killing me.

"We're introducing some new meat to the roster, Tashi Williams. Have you heard of her?"

Shit.

Everyone in the EWC has heard the name Tashi Williams. She's the hotshot making a name for herself in the indie leagues. She has a strong online following and has called out EWC for a while now, trying to get into our ring. Last Val told me she wasn't EWC material. What the hell changed?

"Anyone who has social media and is in this business has heard of Williams. She's been trying to get your attention for years. Why now?" Ravyn asked.

The tension was thick. Ravyn started bouncing her leg up and down, a tick that I noticed she does when she is anxious. I'm sure she's worrying about what this means for her place in the EWC. I, on the other hand, was completely unbothered.

I am a fucking Acosta, Tashi can get in line with the rest of these bitches that have been trying to take my belt.

Val's eyes shot from Ravyn's to mine as she answered.

"Andres Acosta is what happened. He came into my office, highly suggesting that we take in Ms. Williams."

Double shit.

4

Ravyn

Of fucking course.

The Acostas tell EWC to jump, and they ask how fucking high. I can't help my leg from bouncing around like a madwoman. Word vomit is threatening to spew out against every word that Val speaks.

"So when exactly did my dad talk to you about Tashi?" Amaya asks.

"Sometime last week, I think you guys were in Indianapolis? He came unannounced, demanding I hire her."

"Did he say why?"

Amaya looks genuinely shocked. I guess Tashi wasn't a topic of conversation in the Acosta family group chat.

Val sighs deeply and responds with frustration in her voice, "Amaya, the man is your father; take this up with him."

"Fine. Great for Tashi, but what does her joining the EWC have to do with us?" Amaya asked.

She is acting so calm, I want to rip her face off. Of course, she's calm. She doesn't have to worry about her title being in jeopardy. Doesn't have to worry about this new girl overshadowing her. What the hell was Mr. Acosta thinking, telling Val to recruit Tashi fucking Williams? That woman's a complete beast; her muscles have muscles. Not only is she strong, but of course, she's gorgeous too. The last thing I need is another woman trying to one-up me, and so help me God if she gets her hands on Amaya's belt before

I do. My thoughts were cut off by the feeling of nails digging into my thigh. Amaya's hand was trying to stop my leg from bouncing.

"That's fine. Ravyn and I will be there." Amaya replied to Val.

Fuck. Did I just miss that whole conversation?

"Yeah, sure. Can't wait." My chair made a horrible screeching noise as I stormed out.

"Ravyn, wait." Scarlett's heels echoed in the hallway as she races after me.

"Scarlett, I'm not in the mood. I suggest you leave me alone. I'm sure whatever you have to say can be sent via email." I spit out.

Her heels stop clacking just as my phone goes off. An event has been added to my calendar courtesy of Scarlett.

9:00 am Meeting with Tashi & Amaya at the training facility.

I push open the door to the locker room and toss my phone onto the bench, the screen cracks as it bounces off and lands on the floor.

"Fucking fantastic," I say as I shove all my crap in my bag.

"I'm not happy about this either, you know." Amaya picks up my phone, hands it to me, as she raises her left hand in a gesture of peace.

God damn, how the fuck does she just appear out of thin air?

"You can be unhappy all you want. It's not like this will affect you as much as it affects me. Your father is the reason I have Williams as a problem to begin with. Tell Daddy that I send my thanks." I throw my duffel bag over my shoulder, wincing as pain shoots through it.

Great, something else I'll have to get looked at sometime this week.

"I can be put on the back burner just as much as you can. My life isn't easy just because my last name is Acosta."

I scoff, "Oh, that's rich. Do you honestly believe that?" I ask.

"I work hard just like everyone else."

"No one is questioning your work ethic, Amaya. You can work hard and still be privileged. The facts are that your last name has *a lot* to do with why you're in the position you're in."

Amaya stands there quietly.

"You're in denial." I scoff. "You might work just as hard as everyone else, Amaya, but people like me had to work harder to get through those doors.

You rode in here on your daddy's back while the rest of us trekked through the mud."

Amaya opened her mouth, getting ready to object, but I cut her off before she had the chance.

"I'm not finished."

Amaya bit her bottom lip, and I swore I saw it tremble.

"Tashi Williams is a threat to what I've been working towards. I want your belt, and my chances have become even slimmer because of her. I'll be damned if she takes what's mine."

"Now look who's in denial. My belt will never be yours," she scolded.

"Say you are right, you aren't, but let's pretend. No other woman on the roster is more deserving of that belt than I am. We know it, the fans know it, and so does your father."

"What are you trying to say, Ravyn?" Amaya asked.

"I'm starting to think he wants Williams to take that belt from your grubby little hands."

5

Amaya

"Watch your tone when you're talking to me, girl. You think because you have a belt around your little waist, you're the champion of this house, too?"

Andres Acosta. The man, the myth, the legend, and the man who's about to body slam me into this dinner table.

"I'm sorry," I whispered as I looked at his red face.

I couldn't get the conversation with Ravyn in the locker room out of my head.

Is my dad trying to sabotage my career?

"Can you believe what your daughter is asking me?" Andres looked over at my beautiful mother. The woman who makes family dinner mandatory whenever we have shows back home I swear, if she could, she would follow us all over the world.

It still baffles me that my parents ever got together, let alone stayed together. They met at EWC. My mom was a ring announcer. She announced his name for the first time, and the rest was history. They are complete opposites. Dad is seven feet of complete hard ass. The only time he tells me he loves me is when there is an award of some sort in my hand. Failure is never an option in his household, and everything must be done his way or it's wrong. Mom, however, is five feet nothing, and she can't go five minutes without giving me praise and love.

"Anabella, please tell your daughter to watch her tone with me," he said, around a mouth full of mom's famous ropa vieja.

"Honey, she apologized." Mom mouthed the words "I love you" as soon as he looked the other way.

"Dad, I just don't understand what could've possessed you to tell Val to hire Tashi Williams."

I'll admit that Ravyn's words stuck. Did my dad want me to lose my title? It made no sense since he's the one who has pushed me to become a champion.

"I ran into the girl. I like the girl. Therefore, I vouched for the girl. Simple as that, and I don't have to explain my actions to you. I have to do that enough with this one." He points to my mother, and he almost loses that finger as she snaps her teeth at him.

I love coming home and seeing them together, but my heart can't help but ache. My relationship status only has two settings: single or complicated. Men are usually intimidated by me or flatter me to get close to my father. Women are just as bad. They shame me for not being just into women and constantly question my faithfulness since I am surrounded by naked women in locker rooms. Being on the road the majority of the year is no help in the love department either, but those are the sacrifices you make being in this business. It's why most wrestlers get involved with someone in the industry, so they can have that quality time together when we have those days off in whatever city we're in that day. I refuse to get romantically involved with anyone I work with. The chances of it turning into what my mom and dad have are one in a million. The awkwardness I've witnessed with other failed couples being on the road together in this industry is one I refuse to experience myself.

"Listen here, Amaya. You're going to meet with Tashi Williams tomorrow, and you're going to welcome her to the EWC with open arms. What is it I always tell you?"

"You never know who's going to be your ally or your enemy in the ring." All three of us spoke in unison.

Our laughter fills the mansion my parents call home.

The front door swings open. "Sorry to interrupt all the fun, but I'm part of this family too. Did you forget?"

"I'm sorry, the help isn't welcome during family dinner time." I throw a maduro at my big brother, which he easily catches.

"Ha, ha, you're so funny. No wonder we kept you around after fishing you out of the dumpster." Aiden speaks with his mouth full of the sweet plantain I tried to assault him with.

Aiden has always been rough around the edges. He's tall, just like Dad, covered in tattoos, and is constantly sticking out his pierced tongue at me whenever I win an argument. His long hair is always a different color, so much so that I can never keep track of what his hair color of the week is.

"Purple again, I see." I reach for his violet locks, and he swats my hand away.

"Thanks, you should try it out sometime. Aren't you bored of looking at the same thing every day when you stare at the mirror?" Aiden ruffles my naturally red hair. I punch him as hard as I can. He doesn't flinch.

Aiden claims he gets easily bored with his look, and that's why he's always changing his hair, but I secretly think he hates looking so much like dad.

"Do you know how many people would die to have hair like mine? Plus, some people like what they see when they look in the mirror. It's called confidence. You should try it sometimes."

Before I knew it, I was choking on the yellow rice I had just shoveled into my mouth, and my head was placed under Aiden's armpit.

This fucker is putting me in a headlock right now. How mature.

"Let go of your sister right now, Aiden Angel Acosta. It's always the same shit with you two." Mom ordered.

"No, honey, let them fight it out. Let's see who wins." My father smirked as he took a sip of his beer.

Once again, my pain is my father's entertainment. I struggled to swallow the food that was currently lodged in my throat. Damn, Aiden, for being so fucking strong. Dad knows I'm never able to get out of his clutches, and I've passed out once or twice. I don't care if I lose to Aiden because I have a title and he doesn't. That will always make me my dad's favorite, and he knows it.

It's not like he doesn't try, but Val is always giving him a hard time, and his storylines never connect with the viewers.

"Just tap out, sis. It's painful seeing you struggle," he grunted as he applied more force.

I will never give Aiden what he wants. I put my hand in front of his face, and just when he thinks I'm going to tap, I flip him off instead.

"Can you let her go before she passes out again?" Mom sighed, knowing I would never tap out against him.

"Saved by Mother Dearest once again," he kissed my forehead before letting me go.

"Such a disappointing battle between the Acostas," my father sighed.

"How? I didn't even tap out!" I complained.

"Yes, but you found no way to free yourself. Disappointing." He shoveled more ropa vieja into his mouth, and I'm not proud of it, but I prayed for him to choke on it…. Just a little.

"I'm not sure if you're aware, but I'm currently the reigning EWC Women's champion. Does that not give me any recognition around here?" I asked.

"No." My family said in unison.

The house once again filled with laughter.

6

Ravyn

"Again!" Eddie screams over the music that was blaring in my headphones.

I've always loved music. It calms me, which I desperately need right now.

My right glove hits the punching bag again at full force. Sweat drips out of places I don't think it could drip from. After the meeting in Val's office yesterday, my mind can't stop racing. There was no way I was getting any sleep, hence me beating this punching bag since 5:00 am, pretending it was Amaya's face.

"Still don't want to talk about it, huh?" Eddie asked, his pale skin as red as a tomato.

"If I'm hurting you, just let me know and I'll take it down a notch, you big baby." I huffed.

Eddie was the first friend I made when I signed my contract for EWC, but he's also the biggest pain in my ass, other than Amaya, of course. With his blonde hair and blue eyes, he's beautiful to look at, but as soon as he opens his mouth, I want to sew it shut.

"Oh, honey, nice try, but you cannot deflect with me. Spill it." He let go of the bag, his hand landing on his hip.

"I don't appreciate the sass, Edward. Can't a girl just come to the gym and punch out her frustration without her trainer giving her the third degree?"

I barely dodge the punching bag that Eddie swings at me.

"Do not full government name me and no, she can't. Not when she's also my friend. Is it Amaya again? Why don't you two fucking kiss already and get it over with?"

"Eddie, we've been over this. I do not swing that way, and even if I did, I wouldn't touch that woman even if you paid me."

"Just because you kissed one girl when you were sixteen does not mean that you are fully straight."

Technically, it was two times. There was this other time when I went with Mariana to a college party, but does it even count if I was giving mouth-to-mouth?"

"Oh, really? I recall you telling me that you had sex with one woman and 'would never dip your penis in that pond again.'"

"Touche," he shrugged.

"Plus, I'm offended that you think she could handle me."

"A bit cocky, don't you think?" Eddie raised an eyebrow before sitting next to me on the bench.

"Not cocky, confident, there's a difference."

"Okay, then, Ms. Confident. Are you ready to tell me what has your panties in a twist?"

"Bold of you to assume I'm wearing underwear." I winked at Eddie, earning one of his famous eye rolls before he gave me a look that would scare the Devil himself.

I gulped down some water before giving him the bad news. "Fine. Have you heard of Tashi Williams?"

"Oh yeah, she's insanely fit. Have you seen how she's built? I'm jealous."

"Lovely, she already has a fan girl in the EWC. Anyway, fucking King Acosta got into Val's ear once again, and now she's scheduled to debut on the main roster next week. I'm just worried about where I fit into this new narrative. I've worked my ass off to get to where I am, and I swear to God if this bitch gets a title before me, I will lose my shit." I jump at the noise of my water bottle being crushed in my hands.

"Okay, *She-Hulk*. I need you to chill. You've been in this industry long enough to know how it works. Wrestlers come and go. You've beaten all of them so far."

"Not Amaya." I sighed.

"Fine. Everyone but Amaya."

"Tashi feels different. I don't know how to explain it."

"Don't stress it, just keep doing what you're doing and you'll be fine," Eddie said, squeezing my shoulder.

"Can you make me as fit as she is?" I asked.

"Oh, honey, I'm not a miracle worker, but I'm blushing at the fact you think I am that good at my job."

"I just need to make sure she doesn't outshine me."

"Maybe a little wrestling in the bedroom will relax you enough so you don't overthink it." A smirk emerged on Eddie's face as he punched me in the arm.

"Hey, my toys work just fine. They are charged religiously for a reason."

"My hand also works fine, but nothing beats a good old…"

"Do not finish that sentence, please, or I will hurl. I do not need any distractions, Eddie."

The sound of the gym doors opening startled us both.

"Speaking of distractions," Eddie whispered in my ear.

Amaya came floating in wearing her bright orange workout gear and a matching duffel bag in hand. I'm not blind, I know she's attractive. Her ginger hair and green eyes make for a lethal combo. Even if I were curious, which I'm not, I couldn't go there.

"Oh shit, she's coming over here. Gotta go." Eddie started packing up his workout bag.

"Don't you fucking dare leave me alone with her, Eddie," I whispered.

Eddie ignored me as he zipped up his workout bag.

"Edward, I swear. If you love me, you won't do this!" I pleaded.

"That's where you're wrong. I do love you, and that's why I'm doing it." He kissed my forehead as he abandoned me.

Eddie waved goodbye to Amaya as he made his way out the door. I gave him the death glare as he started to make kissy faces behind Amaya's back.

"I see I wasn't the only one with the bright idea of getting here early. What did you do to run Eddie off?" Amaya's gym bag made a loud thud as she threw it next to mine.

"He couldn't handle my punches." I shrugged.

"I doubt that, but sure, whatever makes you feel better," Amaya said as she began to stretch.

I tried not to stare down her sports bra as she bent down, her cleavage on full display.

Just because you find women attractive doesn't mean you want to sleep with them. I can appreciate a good-looking woman without it meaning anything. Maybe Eddie had a point. I do need some time away from my battery-operated friends. Skin-to-skin contact is important for humans. I mean, that's why they make parents have that contact when a baby is born, right? Cause it's good for us.

Amaya turned around, full ass on display, and I made a mental note to re-download the dating app I deleted from my phone as soon as possible.

"Earth to Ravyn." Amaya snapped her fingers.

"I asked you if you're ready to meet Tashi?" she repeated.

"Tashi is just another new wrestler to me. She's nothing special. I'll beat her just like I've beaten everyone else." I shocked myself with the confidence in my voice. Who knew I could be such a good liar?

"Everyone but me, of course," Amaya smirked, and I fought the urge to smack it off her stupidly beautiful face.

"Oh, don't worry, your time is coming, sweetheart, don't you worry." I sipped on my water bottle, trying not to squeeze the life out of it again.

"Why don't you put your money where your mouth is? You and I, right here, right now."

Guess I don't need the punching bag anymore now that the real thing is here and wanting to get her ass beat.

"Stop talking and get in the ring," I smirked.

* * *

The silence in the training center is deafening as Amaya and I circle each other in the ring, each of us waiting for the other to pounce.

"At least there is no one around to see you lose, again." Amaya looked around at the empty training center.

I took advantage of her cockiness and lunged at her, knocking her to the ground. The mat made a satisfying thud noise as I flipped her body face down. I pulled her up slightly, my body weight holding her down as I sat on her back.

"Nice camel clutch." She mumbled as my interlocked fingers grabbed her chin.

Did she just compliment me?

Amaya pushed her arms out of the hold, and as she slowly got on her knees, I knew I fucked up. Before I could register that she lifted all 180 pounds of me on her back, she sprinted backward, slamming my body into the corner of the ring. Amaya doesn't give me the chance to catch my breath. She kicked me into the turnbuckles before dragging me to the middle of the ring.

"Come on. Get up, hotshot." She screams at me from the opposite side of the ring.

As soon as I planted both feet on the mat, she bounced her body off the ropes, coming at me so fast you would think she was flying. I collected myself, realizing the bitch was trying to spear me. I lifted my right leg and super-kicked her ass across the mat. I dragged her to the turnbuckle, lifting her onto her feet and hitting her with a corner clothesline.

"How do you like being slammed into the corner?" I hit her with another clothesline before moving her to the middle of the ring to pin her.

My whole body is pressed against hers as I lift her right leg, making sure her shoulders are flat on the floor. I start my count. Pinning without a ref always feels illegal.

"One. Two." She kicks out.

"Nice try, Silver." She huffed.

What the fuck did she just call me?

"Excuse me?" I questioned.

Amaya got to her knees, and before I could block her, she hit me with a backhand chop. Her backhanded swing lands perfectly on my chest, the sting barely registering when another blow hits my chest.

"I called you Silver." She said as she pushed me down onto the mat.

Amaya lies on top of me, grabbing my arm and placing it between her legs. Her grip tightens around my wrist as she pulls it upwards.

"Do you not like my nickname for you? I think it's pretty clever because not only does it reference your silver locks." She pulled harder on my arm, causing me to wince.

"It also references how you will always be second place to me. You can tap out whenever you're ready, Silver."

The pressure building in my arm was getting more intense by the second. I tried lifting my arm to gain control, but her grip was fucking tight. If I tap out now, it'll just prove her stupid little nickname for me is right.

"For the love of all that is holy, Ravyn, just tap out before you hurt something." The voice wasn't Amaya's.

"Oh, hey, Scarlett." Amaya nodded in her direction.

Oh great. When the fuck did she get here? Not only is my manager witnessing yet another defeat at the hands of Amaya, but right next to her is Tashi Williams.

Fuck my life.

"You heard the nice lady. Tap." Amaya grinned as she pulled once more on my arm.

I reluctantly tapped out, Amaya untangling herself from my body.

"That, ladies, is the difference between gold and silver. Gold never taps. A for effort."

I am going to take that analogy and shove it so far up her ass she won't be able to tell the difference between gold and silver.

"Don't call me Silver." I huffed before leaving the ring.

"Beat me and then I'll think about it." She slung her arms over the top ropes, a smug look across her stupid face.

"Well, that put some pep in my step. Williams, I have some energy left in me. Wanna go at it?"

The videos and pictures I've seen of Tashi Williams do not do her justice. She is gorgeous. Her body reminds me of the sculptures in Italy that depict the Gods. She towers over me, which is a rare occurrence, and I hate how small she makes me feel. Her beautiful, chocolate brown skin is glowing, and not one piece of curly hair on her head is out of place. As she laughs at Amaya, her perfect hair bounces on her head as her white teeth blind me.

"I usually don't like to fight on the first date, but I'll give it a go."

Is she flirting with Amaya?

"That's too bad, I love rolling around on the first date." Amaya winks.

Is Amaya flirting with Tashi?

It's no secret that Amaya is Bi; she's out and proud, and I love that for her. What I *don't* love is her flirting with the enemy.

Tashi started to shed her jacket before Scarlett stopped her. "There will be plenty of time to feed both of your egos. Right now, you both can help out by giving Tashi a tour."

I'm in no mood to be hospitable, especially after the embarrassment of being bested by Amaya in that cross-arm bar. Plus, if I have to see these two flirt anymore, I might throw up. "Giving a tour of the facility isn't a two-person job. Amaya practically grew up here, so she's the best person to give you the tour anyway. I'm gonna head out, I don't feel well anyway."

Scarlett gave me a stern look that screamed, "We'll talk about this later". I threw my bag on my shoulder and as I walked out the door, all I could hear was Tashi and Amaya laughing. Of course, they would hit it off; Amaya could wrap everyone around her finger.

Everyone but me.

"Feel better, Silver," Amaya shouted before the door slammed shut behind me.

* * *

"You need to get your perfect little tight ass back in that training center, NOW!" Eddie screamed into the phone.

I walked out on Amaya and Tashi over an hour ago, but I couldn't bring myself to leave the parking lot. I've been sitting in my car just staring at the double doors of the training center, waiting for them to finally leave.

How long does a tour take anyway? I don't remember my tour being this long.

Amaya's brother, Aiden, had shown us around, and Amaya was on her phone the entire time because she knew this place like the back of her hand.

"Eddie, you don't understand. I was humiliated. The first impression that Tashi has of me is Amaya having me on my damn knees in the ring."

"Honey, she's seen it before, I'm sure. Did you forget that you constantly lose to Amaya in front of millions watching at home?"

"Eddie, you're no help. Why did I even call you?"

"You called me because I tell it how it is. I say this with love in my heart. Who gives a shit, Ramona!" Eddie's voice went up multiple octaves.

"Hey, you know better than to call me that," I scowled.

Eddie had gone out one night with me and my best friend, Mariana, and learned my legal name. It was one of the worst nights of my life.

"Payback for you calling me Edward."

I sighed, "Fair. enough."

"Do you *really* want Tashi and Amaya alone *together?*"

"Scarlett is there," I mumbled.

"Love Scarlett, but you think she's paying attention to what those two are gossiping about?"

"Fuck, you're right. They could be planning my demise as we speak." I slouched into the driver's seat.

"I have to go, Ravyn, get back in there and show Tashi why you aren't to be messed with."

7

Amaya

"Thanks again for the tour. This place is nicer than any other training facility I've been to." Tashi said.

I gave Tashi the best tour I could, leaving no stone unturned. I spent hours talking to her and hated how much I enjoyed her company. As much as I want to be upset with my dad for vouching for her to be hired by EWC, I can see why he did it.

Does the bastard always have to be right?

She's sweet and knowledgeable about what we do. It doesn't hurt that she's a flirt and has the face of a goddess.

Do not go there, Amaya. We do not sleep with our coworkers.

"No problem. I know this place like the back of my hand." I shrugged.

"Never doubted it, I'm going to sound like a complete fan girl right now, but I love your work."

Dammit, now I have to like her.

"You look surprised, do you not know how amazing your wrestling is? There's a reason you're the champ." Tashi questioned.

"I just wasn't expecting you to compliment me. I'm used to the newbies gushing about my father, not me."

"Oh, don't get me wrong, when I met him, I turned into a six-year-old again. He knows how I feel about him and his work." Tashi laughed.

Here's my chance to ask what I've been dying to know.

"How did you meet my dad again?"

"He sent an email saying he wanted to meet and discuss a possible future in the EWC. It was weeks old because I barely check my email, and I thought it was spam, but as I was getting ready to trash it, I got a phone call from an unknown number, and it was him."

Lying asshole.

He said he ran into her, more like he slid into her email. Not only did he reach out to her, but he lied about it. Why?

I fake a smile, something I have plenty of practice doing. "That's nice of him to reach out to you. You're going to make a great addition to the roster."

"I appreciate that, especially since I'm terrified of being the new girl. Ravyn's bad reaction is the first of many, I'm sure. So this is refreshing."

It wasn't the best move for Ravyn to up and leave. I'm sure Scarlett is going to give her a mouthful. I couldn't help but smile thinking about her getting in trouble. 'Not feeling so good,' my ass, more like she couldn't handle getting her ass beat by me again.

"Ravyn is… actually, I don't know how to finish that sentence."

"You can say Ravyn is beautiful, smart, a badass bitch, all of the above are acceptable answers." Tashi and I turn towards the double doors to find Ravyn leaning against the wall.

"Well, look who feels better," I smirk.

"Yeah, sorry about that, Tashi. I get bad migraines sometimes, but I took some medication and a little nap, and I feel so much better."

Bullshit.

"That's alright, I'm just glad it wasn't anything I said. I'm sorry if I came off a little strong. I was going to ask if you two are…"

"No." Ravyn and I both said in unison.

"I'm straight," Ravyn said.

The way you check me out makes me question that statement.

I smirk at her response, which earns me a look from Ravyn.

"I'm sorry, there was just a vibe in the air, but what do I know? I just got here." Tashi shrugged.

"I can assure you there is no 'vibe'. The tour is officially over if you want to get in the ring. I still have some steam in me after beating Ravyn."

"You did not beat me. We were interrupted." Ravyn rolled her eyes.

"Yeah, by *your* manager, who thought you couldn't handle it and told you to tap."

Ravyn looked around, no doubt looking for Scarlett, who was long gone.

"How about a triple-threat match?" Tashi smirked.

Ravyn and I looked at one another and burst into laughter before we spoke in unison, "Hell yeah!"

* * *

People constantly ask me in interviews how it feels to wrestle in front of a crowd. The answer is always the same: it feels amazing. There's truth to that statement, but nothing beats the feeling of wrestling when no one is watching. When it's just you and your opponent in the ring and not a soul is eyeing you, watching for your mistakes, and no titles are on the line. I love wrestling, and I'm grateful that I get paid to do something I love, but damn does it feel good to be able to do it freely and without judgment.

The three of us are just going with our instincts, a beautiful dance where no one misses a step. Even the bumps we're taking are perfect. This feeling is euphoric, and I'm not even mad when Ravyn chokeslams me. Honestly, I'm proud of the move.

I hate to admit that I'm also a little turned on.

The wonderful bubble we're in bursts as *his* voice echoes.

"Amaya, come on, I taught you better than that. You couldn't reverse that?"

There goes my relaxation.

"Hi, Mr. Acosta." Tashi quickly abandons the ring to greet my father.

And there goes Tashi, turning into a fan girl.

She extended her hand out to him in greeting, which he refused. "I'm a hugger, Tashi, bring it in."

Dad drags her by her arm and envelops her in a tight hug. Tashi immediately disappears into his arms.

"Uhm, hello. We were in the middle of something." Ravyn calls out to her, annoyed.

"I'm sorry, but when an Acosta is in the room, everything stops," Tashi mumbles into my father's chest.

"You were just wrestling in the ring with an Acosta." I wipe the sweat off my face.

"Oh, sweetie. You cannot compare yourself to me. I'm a legend," my dad winks.

He finally releases Tashi, "Nice work, Ravyn."

"Thank you, sir." Ravyn's response is so dry I feel it in my throat and reach for my water bottle.

I know Ravyn hates me, and that's most likely why she's never starstruck around my dad, but damn it's refreshing. Every friend I've had is in the industry; it's the only way I know it's genuine, and they aren't just becoming my friend for free tickets, but even they act like their brains turn to mush around my dad. Some of them even talk about how dreamy he is, and if he and my mom ever divorce, they would want to be my step-mom. Those conversations end with me threatening all of their careers if they ever mention how hot they think my dad is again. I know my dad is considered attractive, half my looks come from him, and I'm drop-dead gorgeous, but a girl does not need to know her friends have the hots for her dad. Aiden was pissed when I told him my friends would rather bone our father than him. A chill goes through my body at the thought of anyone touching either of them, and I feel myself becoming queasy.

"I'm gonna head out. See you around, Tashi, thanks for the workout." Ravyn grabs her things, leaving me alone with Dad and his current number one fan and draft pick.

Seeing them interacting together is boiling my blood. I've never been the jealous type, especially when it came to other wrestlers talking to my dad. I'll always be my dad's number one, or so I thought. Knowing that he personally reached out to her to join EWC is eating me up inside, and I'm dying to ask why.

You know why, Ravyn is right.

I shook that idea out of my head before running after Ravyn. "I'll be right back. Hey, Ravyn, wait up."

"I'm about to pee and I don't need an audience."

"Not a kink of yours?" I wiggle my eyebrows.

Ravyn ignores me as she keeps her stride.

"You know, I was also in the ring, right? Why didn't you thank me for the workout?" I ask.

Ravyn smirks, "Oh, I know. I never forget those who I put in a chokeslam."

"Do that often then?" I ask.

"It's my favorite hobby," she replies.

"I thought your favorite hobby was hating me." I teased.

"It's a close second," she said with fire in her eyes.

"I'll have to fix that. I am never second place."

Ravyn laughed, and dammit, it was a beautiful sound. "You have to have at least one second-place trophy. I'll ask Aiden to check around the Acosta mansion and send me a picture. Better yet, I wonder if he would steal it for me so I can have it."

"Of course, you would be friends with my brother." I roll my eyes.

"What can I say, Aiden is a special case," she shrugs.

"Please tell me you aren't fucking my brother." I groan.

"Oh, please, I wouldn't touch an Acosta with a ten-foot pole." Ravyn locks herself in the bathroom stall.

The feeling is not mutual.

I strip my sweat-drenched sports bra off my body, and as I reach down to do the same to my leggings, Ravyn comes back in and immediately redirects her eyes. "Not gonna hit the showers?" I ask.

"I'm good, I have somewhere to be, and I'm running late," she replies, still refusing to look in my direction.

"Why are you being weird and not looking at me? We've seen each other naked before, Ravyn. We've been working together for years. I have no interest in us eye fucking each other in the showers."

Liar.

"I'm not so sure about that. You lingered too long for my liking yesterday when you walked in on me."

Can you blame me? You have an ass like a peach.

"I'm sorry about that, by the way," I apologize.

"It's fine, I'm used to getting ogled at. Part of the job, remember." Ravyn hauls her duffel bag over her shoulder.

Let her think that's what you meant. Don't be vulnerable, don't show weakness.

Ravyn's halfway through the door before I correct her.

"That's not what I'm sorry for. I'm sorry for targeting your bad ankle. It was a dick move. I won't do it again. You have my word."

Ravyn's body stiffens, her hands flexing around the handle of the door. She takes a deep breath before she turns to face me. I can tell she's trying to keep eye contact with me as I stand there naked in front of her. I hold my breath as I wait for her to speak.

"Keep being nice to me, and hating you is going to move down to my third favorite hobby."

"A simple thank you would've been the proper response."

"Amaya, you should know better than that. Nothing about me is proper." Ravyn winks before walking out.

Ravyn Ramirez left me naked, alone, turned on, and in desperate need of a cold shower.

8

Ravyn

I winked at her. I fucking winked at Amaya Acosta. What the actual fuck has gotten into me? It's been a week since Amaya, Tashi, and I wrestled each other in the training facility, and all I can think about is how tempted I was to look down at Amaya's naked body. Why was I acting like a hormonal teenage boy? You've seen her naked plenty of times before. I blame Eddie for putting those stupid fucking thoughts in my head about us banging one out. I wouldn't know what to do if I even entertained that idea.

Things have been back to normal between us since then. Flying from city to city, getting matches together, wrestling our asses off, and I lose, again. Tashi made her debut on the main roster in her hometown of Philadelphia and was exactly as expected. The crowd went wild as her entrance music blared from the speakers. She walked out after one of Amaya and I's matches ended and challenged her to a title match. Her hand was wrapped around the mic, tight as she told Amaya how she was "going to show her what a real big dog looked like."

She's been fighting another big dog this whole time. I've been here, dammit.

It's no secret that wrestling is scripted; it's why people over the age of thirteen constantly get bullied for liking professional wrestling. I remember when I would get shit in foster homes from other kids.

"You know that's not real, right?"

"Does it look like I give a shit?" I would spit back at them.

Then I would hit them with a spear that was very much real. Even though parts of this world are fake, the words spoken still can feel very much real. It's hard not to take things personally, and people have been known to go off script. It's why I have never spoken to anyone about my past, even Val has no idea where I came from. I didn't want to give them any ammo to use against me in the ring. Everyone in EWC knows my parents are dead, but they don't need to know the pathetic details of my life. Like how my mom was a drug addict who loved coke more than she loved me, or how I don't know who my dad is because my mom would whore herself out for drugs and didn't use protection.

The only person I consider family is my best friend, Mariana. She's the definition of a beauty queen. I might be the "celebrity," but she's the one who has an undeniable presence that turns heads wherever she goes. People barely notice me whenever she is around. Her blue eyes shimmer and are framed by some of the longest and thickest lashes I've ever seen. I swear I have never seen a pimple on her smooth, perfect skin that is somehow always glowing. Her blonde hair constantly feels like silk and cascades in beautiful, soft waves. Not only is my best friend stunning, but she's funny and smart as hell. I always tell her that she was no doubt Miss America in her past life. Her response to that statement is always the same: "I wouldn't want to represent this corrupt country in any other way than by becoming president so I can fix all the shit that's broken." We connected in foster care. I met her in the last home I was ever in, and we've been inseparable ever since. We're roommates, but with the EWC crazy schedule, she basically has the apartment to herself. A detail she has no problem with since she and her boyfriend like to hump like bunnies. Thankfully, whenever I am in town, she tells him to stay away. It's not that I don't like Ethan; he's just not what Mariana deserves. Also, the sound of his grunting is vomit-inducing. I never want to hear that noise again, and I also would prefer not to see his pale ass, but that is exactly what I get an eyeful of as soon as I walk through my front door.

"Dude!" I scream, making both him and Mariana jump apart.

Ethan runs to Mariana's room, his hands covering his manhood.

"I checked your location and it showed you were still at the airport." Mariana tries to fix her sex hair.

"Yeah, my phone died at the airport. I know I'm barely here bitch, but I use that couch when I am."

"I'm sorry, it was a heat-of-the-moment thing. You remember how those go." Mariana blushes.

I don't remember the last time I was touched by another human other than in the training ring.

"I'm going to drop off my things in my room, disinfect my eyes, and then come back out to disinfect that couch."

"Yes, ma'am. Ethan will be out of here by the time you're done. I promise."

I walk into my room, greeted by the plain white walls and a bed that was less comfy than all the beds I sleep on at the hotels the EWC provides. Another perk of working for EWC compared to other companies was that they did not require their wrestlers to have to pay out of pocket for their accommodations; it was covered in every wrestler's contract. All that I have in my room is a single bed and a dresser. I take out my contacts, scrubbing my eyes after seeing Ethan's ass. A single knock on my door has me quickly put on my glasses before heading towards my bed to lie down. Mariana pops her head inside.

"Sorry about that. Permission to come into the jail cell?" she asks.

"Are you fully clothed?"

"Yes. I will never understand why you are so weird about seeing me naked. You know, some best friends are so close they shower together." Mariana plops herself next to me.

"Good for them. That will not be us, ever. I see enough naked women in my day-to-day life. When I'm home, the only naked female I want to see is when I look into a mirror. Also, when will you stop calling my room a jail cell?"

"I guess you're not watching any porn. Unless you're into guy-on guy which I won't judge. I tried, and it does nothing for me."

"MARIANA!" I yell.

"I'll stop calling your room a jail cell when you finally decide to decorate it. Honestly, I'm pretty sure there are jail cells out there that are better decorated than this room. We've been living here for two years, and it still looks how it did the day we moved in."

"I don't see the point in decorating a place I'm barely in."

"Or you're scared to make a place feel like home because you're so used to being moved between homes from growing up in the foster care system."

"Mariana, what did I tell you about psycho-analyzing me!" I slap her on the arm.

"I'm just putting my education to use."

"You want me to put my education to use?" I ask before putting her in a headlock.

"You can put me in a headlock all you want, but you know I'm right,"

I start to tickle her, and Mariana flails around, trying to get out of my grasp.

"Please, stop, I'm going to piss myself."

"Will you stop trying to fix me?" I threaten.

"Never, but I will buy all your drinks tonight," she wheezes.

"Deal." I let her go, blocking the pillow that she threw at me.

"FYI, Mariana, I think my mental issues make me interesting."

"Yeah, I'm sure that's what every man I've seen coming in and out of your life thinks. Oh, wait, they don't exist."

"Not everyone can be you and find the love of their life in their freshman year of college."

"You're right, but everyone needs a little plaything, and no, your sex drawer doesn't count."

"Why does everyone rag on my sex toys like they don't have their own!"

"Eddie?" she questioned, even though she knew the answer.

"Can we stop talking about my sex life and my amazing toys so we get ready for tonight already?" I roll my eyes.

"I'll get the wine, and you set up the music. Tonight is going to be so much fun, Ramona."

Unlike Eddie, I don't scold Mariana for using my legal name. She's one of the two people in the world who're allowed to call me by my legal name.

You'll never hear him say your name again.

Mariana snaps me out of that depressing thought, "Ramona?"

"Yeah?"

"I'm not trying to fix you because you're not broken." She kisses me on my forehead before getting up.

"I love you, Mariana."

"I love you, too, now let's go get shit-faced."

* * *

"We're so shit-faced," I yell over the music the club we're in is blasting.

"Not me, I'm fine." Mariana slurs her words as she trips over her heels.

"Should we call it a night?" I ask her.

The question gets ignored as Mariana drags me by the arm towards the dance floor. Mariana is dancing her heart out, grabbing at her red mini dress that keeps riding up her thighs. I'm dancing alongside her, letting the dance music seep into my skin. I've always loved dancing. I would beg my foster parents to let me take dance lessons, but they all laughed right in my face. Telling me I was crazy to think that they could afford dance lessons when they could barely afford to feed us. In reality, they had plenty of money coming their way; they just didn't want to spend it on us. Mariana and I exclusively go to gay clubs since our last visit to a straight bar ended in a brawl when a man did what men do best, got too handsy.

"Are you okay here alone? I'll be quick, I'm going to get us water."

Mariana gives me a thumbs-up as she keeps dancing in circles.

The crowd around the bar was massive, and the idea of being back with Mariana quickly vanished. I tried to push my way through the crowd, praying that I wouldn't fall on my face since Mariana refused to let me leave the house in my favorite sneakers. I felt my body swaying from the mixture of alcohol in my system and the heels that Mariana forced onto my feet. If it's one thing any newbie to gay clubs should be warned of, it's that the bartender will always overpour their liquor. Finally, I was able to order our water. With one red solo cup in each hand, I tried to force myself between the crowd once more. I was almost back to Mariana when I was shoved so violently that I tripped over my heels, and the waters went flying. I was able to catch myself before falling flat on my ass, but the poor woman in front of me now had a back that was soaked. Her white crop top was now completely see-through, and the water was slowly rolling down to her ass, darkening her jeans.

"I am so sorry." I apologize, wanting the ground to open below me and swallow me whole from the embarrassment.

Her friend checks on her before turning to me.

"What's your problem?" She yells at me in a heavy Spanish accent.

Her skin is a deep, rich brown that gleams under the laser lights of the club. Tight, curly hair frames her face, which I would find beautiful if she weren't scowling at me.

Oh, come on. I like this club. I do not want to be in another club brawl, especially here.

"I said sorry. Someone pushed me and I tripped." I explained.

Her friend gives me a dirty look before asking her again if she was okay.

"Can I buy you a drink to make up for it? I'm honestly really sorry."

The woman whispers in her friend's ear, making her laugh. She looks me up and down before she answers. Her answer makes her turn around, and it feels like a slap in the face.

"I wouldn't mind a free drink, thanks, Silver," Amaya smirks.

9

Amaya

A tingling sensation moves through my body as I look at her. Honestly, I'm just as shocked to see her, but I'm just better at hiding it. Reina insisted I join her tonight, and I've never been happier that I listened to her in my entire life.

I'm going to have to thank her later because this is priceless.

"What are you doing here?" Ravyn asks.

"Apparently, I'm in the splash zone of the club. I didn't realize there was one before today."

She rolls her eyes, "I said I'm sorry. Have a good night."

Ravyn starts to walk away, but I grab her wrist.

"Not so fast. You owe me a drink."

Ravyn looks amazing. Her silky hair is in loose curls, and her lips are a bright red. Her cleavage is on full display in a black corset top. Her toned thighs look amazing in her black jeans.

"That was before I realized I was offering a drink to the *Wicked Witch of the West*."

"Now, Silver, if I were the *Wicked Witch of the West*, I would've melted by now." I cocked an eyebrow towards her.

She tries to fight off a smile, "*Wizard of Oz fan?*"

"Eh, more of a *Wicked* fan." I shrug.

There it was again, that beautiful look of confusion on her face.

What I wouldn't give to know what's going on in that head of hers.

"I have to go back to my friend," she tries to wiggle her wrist free, but my grip is too tight.

If she wanted me to go fishing, I would. I know the perfect bait.

"Oh, is it that cute friend who comes to see you when we have pay-per-view shows? I wouldn't mind introducing myself." I smirk.

"Hell no," she spits out.

Hook, line, and sinker.

Ravyn intertwines her fingers with mine as she pulls me towards the bar. Her other hand is busy typing away a message on her cellphone.

Note to self: get Ravyn's phone number.

"What do you want to drink?" Ravyn whispers in my ear, and the hairs on my neck stand up.

"I'm not picky, I'll have whatever you're having."

"I'm done for the night. Hence the water incident."

"Come on, have one drink with me," I plead.

I didn't notice that we were holding hands still until I squeezed hers, but as I did, Ravyn didn't flinch or try to pull away.

It's the alcohol; she probably didn't even feel me squeezing her hand. Don't overthink this.

"I will not have a drink with you."

"A shot?"

"That's still a drink."

"Yes, but it's a little one."

Ravyn rolls her eyes as I pout, but a sliver of a smile is on her fire-red lips.

"Fine," she caves as she waves down the bartender.

"Two lemon drop shots, please," she asks.

"No, I am not drinking that sugary shit. Do you happen to have any Havana Club?"

The bartender shakes his head no.

"Ugh, fine. Can we get two shots of tequila, please?"

"Any particular brand?" the bartender asks.

"The most expensive shot you have. She's paying," I wink.

The bartender gives me a thumbs-up as he walks away.

"What's Havana Club?" Ravyn asks.

"My whole family drinks it. It's a famous Cuban rum. Apparently, too good for this fine establishment to carry."

"So your alternative is tequila?" Ravyn looks puzzled.

"Don't tell me I give off the impression that I drink fruity drinks and take weak shots."

"Sorry, Red, yeah, you do." Ravyn winces.

"Red? You've never called me that before." I arch my brow.

Why do I find that so hot?

"Well, you want to call me Silver, so I figured it's just as fair to call you Red."

"I like it."

"Of course you do." She rolls her eyes.

"Is it the hair that makes you think I can't handle tequila?"

The bartender comes back with our shots. "Do you want salt and lime?"

"No." Ravyn said at the same time, I said 'Yes."

Ravyn raises an eyebrow, and I want to smack the smirk off her face.

"I'm good, thanks," I told him.

"You don't have to add hair on your chest to prove a point. It's okay if you need help with your tequila. Should I call him back and ask for a chaser?"

The challenge in Ravyn's voice is making my blood boil.

"If you can do it, so can I."

"God, of course, you would turn something as simple as taking a shot into a competition." Ravyn mocks.

"It was just a statement. If you want a competition, I'll give you one. Let's see who can take back the most shots."

"You have the advantage, you're barely tipsy. How is this fair?"

"How many drinks did you have already?"

"Including the pre-game… like four and a half bottles of wine."

"Jesus, Silver. Okay, I'll try to catch up, and then we'll start. Deal?"

"What does the winner get?" she asks.

"Not my title belt, that's for sure."

Ravyn finally lets go of my hand, just so she could smack me in the arm, and my hand already misses hers.

"The winner gets to decide what they want once they win." I raise my shot glass, and Ravyn follows.

"This is a dangerous game you're playing, Red." Ravyn clicks her shot glass to mine.

"Good," I say before downing the first of many shots.

* * *

I lost count of how many shots Ravyn and I have consumed. All I know is that I am having the time of my life right now, and I can't believe that I am enjoying Ravyn's company and she hasn't threatened to kill me once tonight.

I've only thought about how hot she looks three times tonight.

Her cute friend, who I've learned her name but has escaped my mind at the moment, joined us at my V.I.P. section and has been chatting with Reina. Apparently, they both go to the same college and are in the same psychology class.

I think her name starts with an M.

"I'm having so much fun, Ramona." Ravyn's friend yells at her.

"Who the fuck is Ramona?" I question.

"Oops," her friend hiccups.

"I'm Ramona, and if I ever hear you call me by that name, I will cut your tongue off and feed it to my cat. Understood?"

"Understood, Silver." I wink.

"You don't have a cat, Ramona." Ravyn's friend points out.

"Mariana, she didn't know that. My threat still stands. I'm sure I can find a hungry stray on our street that would be thankful for the meal."

Ah, that's her name. I knew it started with an M.

"Let's go back on the dance floor, Ramona, please," Mariana begs.

"I'm tired, honey, and I'm scared if I do, I will barf all over the dance floor."

"I'll go with you." Reina offers her hand to Mariana, and off they go.

I flag down the bottle girl assigned to our section.

"I'm tapping out, no more alcohol." Ravyn grabs a napkin from the table, waving it in my face.

"I'm ordering water, relax. Good to know that even out of the ring, I can get you to tap."

"I can tap because there is no way that you can catch up to me. I've been keeping score of our shots." She waves the napkin in my face again, and there it is.

"Is that lipstick?" I grab the napkin out of her hands.

"I didn't have a pen." She shrugs.

"Well, shit," I whisper.

She was right. I took ten shots and she took… wait.

"No fucking way you took sixteen shots." I gasp.

"I have witnesses." She points towards Mariana and Reina, who are lighting up the dance floor.

"When did you even take those extra six?"

Also, should I be worried we're both going to have alcohol poisoning?

"When you were busy flirting with your groupie."

I knew it! Her attitude had changed, and I knew it had to do with her.

Our bottle girl had come over to me earlier in the night, asking if it was okay if a fan came to the table to say hi. Of course, I said yes, even though the last thing I wanted to think about was wrestling tonight. In two days, I have my big title match with Tashi, and for the first time in a long time, I'm terrified of losing it. I've been watching her old matches and watching her backstage with the rest of the crew, and she is incredible. The fact that my father also vouched for her is getting to my head. He doesn't vouch for losers. The fan was very sweet, and I admit she's hot as hell. As we talked, I could see Ravyn from the corner of my eye bouncing her knee.

There's that tick again.

I leaned into the fan's neck, whispering my thanks to her again before she left. She handed me a napkin with her number on it, and I slipped it into my pocket. I had no intention of using it. I had one experience with a groupie turned stalker, and that was enough for me. Ravyn's knuckles went white with how hard she was holding her drink. She was jealous, but why?

"I wasn't flirting," I clarify.

"I don't care if you were. If anything, I'm grateful for her cause; now I can rub it in your face that I won."

I can tell you what you can rub in my face, more on my face, but...

"No one likes a cocky winner."

"Says the cockiest winner ever. Have you seen yourself in the ring?" Ravyn crosses her arms in front of her chest.

"That's different, and you know it. The person you are in the ring is a different person out of the ring."

Our water arrives, and we both chug like our lives depend on it.

"You've given me a run for my money plenty of times in that ring," I admit.

It wasn't a lie. Ravyn is the only other woman in the EWC who would deserve my belt. She's worked her ass off. I would go to the training center at three in the morning and find her there. Ravyn had no idea I was watching her, but how could you not? Her technique is amazing, she works the crowd, and she lives, eats, and breathes wrestling.

"Is that a compliment?" she gasps.

I move closer to her. Our thighs now touching, and I move a strand of her silver hair behind her ear before I whisper to her, "No. A compliment would be me telling you how amazing you are in the ring. Which you are."

Then Ravyn did something I didn't know she was capable of doing.

Is she blushing?

"That compliment better not be my reward for beating you. If so, I want a do-over."

"What I'm hearing is that you want to hang out with me again." I raise my eyebrow.

"You need to get your ears checked. That is not what I said."

"Sure, whatever you say, Silver."

"So what's my prize?"

"You tell me, remember the winner gets to choose their prize."

Ravyn laughs, "My memory is a little foggy due to all the tequila. Do I have to pick now?"

"You can do whatever you want, Silver." I play with a silver strand of her hair.

"You're giving me too much power, Red." Ravyn licks her lips, causing her red lipstick to smudge.

"With great power comes great responsibility."

"Did you just quote *Spider-Man?*"

"I did."

"Who's your favorite *Spider-Man?*" she asks.

"Tobey Maguire, duh."

"Oh my God, yes, finally someone who agrees with me. Don't get me wrong, no hate to Andrew Garfield or Tom Holland, but Tobey is top-tier *Spider-Man.*"

We both start to laugh so hard that we start to cry.

"What were we talking about?" Ravyn asks as she uses a napkin to dry off her tears.

"Responsibility," I answer.

"Ah, yes, great power blah, blah, blah. Well, what if I don't want to be responsible?" She leans closer to me, our lips so close that if we move even an inch, they would touch.

"What if I want to do something extremely irresponsible right now?"

10

Ravyn

My brain was telling me to run. My body, on the other hand, was hot and tingling all over, and I didn't want that feeling to stop.

Why are you feeling all hot and bothered over her? It has to be the alcohol mixed with the lack of dick in your life.

Amaya places her thumb on my lower lip, wiping off the smudge of red lipstick. A wave of electricity courses through me, and I pray that the club is dark enough for her not to see the goosebumps that formed on my skin from her touch.

"What do you want to do that's so irresponsible, Silver?" she whispers.

Snap out of it, Ramona. You hate that nickname, and you hate Amaya Acosta.

"Actually, I have to go to the bathroom." I need to get away before I do something stupid.

"I'll go with you." Amaya starts to get up, and I push her right back down into her seat.

"No, I'm fine."

"I don't care. I'm going with you." Amaya grabs my hand and starts moving through the crowd.

Curse the unspoken girl rule of going to the bathroom together in public spaces.

Once I find myself in a stall, I realize I actually do have to pee. Just as I was thinking how long I could possibly stay here before Amaya gets tired of waiting for me and leaves. She clears her throat.

"You can't stay in there forever."

I take a deep breath before opening the stall, walking past Amaya to wash my hands.

"So, are you going to answer my question or?"

"I want to tell you that I admire your wrestling skills."

Why did you just admit that you idiot?

"How is that irresponsible?"

I rip a piece of paper towel from the dispenser, aggressively drying my hands. "It's going to make your head bigger than it already is."

"Can I ask you a question, Ravyn?"

I think I'm going to throw up, and it's not due to the tequila.

"No, I don't want your autograph." I tease.

"Oh, you're getting one anyway. That's not my question, though."

I nod my head, afraid to speak. My throat is so dry I feel like *SpongeBob* in that one episode where Sandy invites him to her house for the first time. My knee begins to bounce, making Amaya look down and place her hand on it.

"If you admire me so much, why do you act like you hate me?"

Because you're a nepo baby and I'm jealous.

"I'm a heel. It's my job." I shrug.

"You're a heel in the ring. We don't have to bring that crap out into our real life."

"Wrestling is my life. It's all I have, it's not just a hobby that I picked up because of my daddy." I snap.

Amaya flinches, and I immediately regret what I said.

"I'm sorry. I —"

"No, don't apologize. You never have to apologize for how you feel, not with me. Do you think I don't know what people in the industry think of me? It's why I don't have many friends. They all believe I got a free ride because I'm an Acosta. It's bullshit, being an Acosta means that I have to work harder, be better, and I have impossible standards. I would rather have done it your way, be a nobody that had to make herself into a somebody."

"You think I'm a somebody?"

My heart feels like it's going to leap out of my chest.

"Of course, I don't have rivalries with just anyone." Amaya rolls her eyes.

"I'm sorry you have that much pressure on you." My eyes soften.

What is wrong with you? Why are you having sympathy for her?

I quickly change the subject. Not wanting Amaya to linger on the pain she's feeling. "Can you say that I'm a somebody again? I just want to record it so there's proof. Also, the acoustics in here are amazing."

"I'm happy to repeat myself, but I will not let you record that to use as blackmail," she smirks.

"Oh, come on. How else am I supposed to know that the tequila wasn't playing any mind tricks on me?"

Amaya laughs, "So is that what we're going to do? Blame the alcohol as the reason we're getting along tonight?"

"Most definitely. I blame tequila for all of my bad decisions." I shrug.

"Ouch." Amaya clutches at her heart.

Blame it on the tequila, Ramona.

"How hammered are you?" I ask Amaya.

"Hammered enough that I know I'll be kissing the toilet in the morning. You?"

"Hammered enough to know what I want as my prize for winning," I confess.

Blame it on the tequila, Ramona.

"What do you want, Silver?" she asks.

Blame it on the tequila, Ramona.

Amaya moves closer to me, and the smell of alcohol on her lips should have been a warning sign. Yet here I was getting intoxicated by how it mingles so well with her floral scent.

Don't do it, Ramona.

But as Amaya looks at me, I can't help but wonder.

Just do it, I'm sure it's going to be awful. You'll hate it just like you did when you were sixteen.

"You're killing me from the anticipation here, Sil—"

Fuck it.

I grab her face and place my lips on hers. This kiss isn't anything like the kiss I had when I was a teenager. Sixteen-year-old Ramona was curious after watching Natalie Portman and Mila Kunis go at it in *Black Swan,* so she made out with one of her school friends. It was extremely awkward, and we never spoke to each other after it. That kiss felt cold; there was no passion behind it, and we just clumsily kept hitting each other's noses; it was a nightmare. This kiss with Amaya is the complete opposite. We melt into each other; it feels like the club and the people in it vanished. Amaya's body is stiff at first, and so is mine due to the shock of what the fuck I was doing. For years, Amaya and I exchanged nothing but sharp words and bitter glares. Every encounter in and out of the ring was a battle, yet all of that ceased to exist at this moment. Hell, I forgot we were in a gay club bathroom that I'm sure has seen plenty of action. Our kiss changes from firm to tender as Amaya relaxes into it at the same moment I do. Even though I was the one who initiated the kiss, I'm giving her full control. Amaya licks my bottom lip, asking for permission to enter, and dammit, I let her. If I weren't already intoxicated due to the tequila shots, I would've been drunk on her. She deepens the kiss as she pulls the hair at the base of my neck. Our bubble bursts as the bathroom door swings open, Mariana and Reina's mouths gaping open.

I don't dare look at Amaya; the realization of what I had done settled in my stomach.

"I have to go," I cover my mouth, grabbing Mariana by the wrist as I run out of the restroom.

"That was so hot," Mariana yells as I pull her through the restroom door.

As soon as the humid outside air hits my face, my stomach gives out.

"It's okay, Ramona, let it out," she pats my back.

"I want to go home," I grumble as I paint the concrete street with the contents of my stomach.

* * *

I will never touch tequila again after last night; the world won't stop spinning this morning. My poor toilet is a wreck, and I'm pretty sure that Mariana and I took turns throwing up in it last night.

Now that I think about it...

"Did one of us throw up in the shower last night?" I ask.

"Yeah… we're going to have to deep clean the bathroom."

"By *we*, you mean me." I groan.

Mariana and I are both hanging on by a thread this morning. Neither of us remembers getting home, and instead of passing out in our own rooms, we woke up cuddled up on the living room floor. Thankfully, Mariana was the stronger of the two of us and made her way to the kitchen to get us Advil.

"Are we going to ignore the elephant in the room?" Mariana asks as she sips on her coffee.

Yes.

I wince, slowly sipping on the ginger ale Mariana gave me since I hate coffee.

"Do we have to do this?" I ask.

"I'm just saying. I know I had fun last night. Clearly, not as much fun as you did, though," she smirks.

It feels like a dream. One minute, I was casually talking to Amaya, and the next, our tongues were mingling. I woke up with my bottom lip sore because I'm pretty sure she bit me. I don't know how I should feel, and I'm so confused about what this could mean. The one thing I am sure of is that it can't happen again. Mariana takes my silence as permission to continue talking.

"My best friend made out with a woman last night. Let's not forget that woman is Amaya freaking Acosta."

"People drunkenly make out with the same sex all the time." I shrug, trying to make last night's situation as nonchalant as possible.

Mariana is *not* buying my bullshit.

"We've been wasted plenty of times together. You've never made out with me. Honestly, I'm offended."

"Mariana, are you really trying to start a fight about me not making out with you when I'm drunk?" I scold.

"I just feel like I would've been a good choice, that's all."

"Oh my God, are you jealous right now!" I can't help but roll my eyes at how ridiculous she's being right now.

"I'm the best friend. You know how many times I've been asked if we're dating, and I would say, 'No, she doesn't swing that way. If she did, I know I would be her first choice, and then I would have to break her heart.' Well, look at me now. Booboo the fool."

She raises her voice, making me wince and pray the pills would hurry up and do their job.

"Can we just forget that happened?" I beg.

"Absolutely not. I need to know everything. Who made the first move?"

"Tequila did."

"So you. Got it." Mariana smirks.

"Hey!"

"Ramona, you blame every bad decision you've ever made on tequila. Even when you aren't drinking tequila."

"So you agree it was a bad decision." I point at her and smile as though I've won the argument.

You foolish girl, you never win arguments with Mariana.

"Yeah, a bad decision to choose her over me," she mumbles.

"That's it, I'm telling Ethan you have the hots for me and want me to suck on your face." I pull out my phone, pretending to bring up his number.

"Oh, please. That's every man's wet dream. If you call him, he'll be here in a heartbeat to see it happen."

"Touche."

"All joking aside. No, I don't think kissing her was the worst decision. You could've brought her back home to finish the job." Mariana nudges me.

"Oh, so you could be standing at the other side of the door, glass in hand, trying to listen?" I scoff.

"Duh."

"You're such a creep. Let go of that dream because it's never going to happen." I roll my eyes.

"Why not? You looked like you were enjoying yourself, and don't you dare blame that on the tequila, Ramona, or so help me God, I will scream." Mariana stomps her foot.

"It's true. I was drunk."

"Drunk minds speak sober thoughts. In this case, drunk minds make out with the people that they want to make out with when they're sober. Did that make sense? I'm too heartbroken to make sense right now."

"If I kiss you right now, will it make you shut up?" I sigh.

"No, it'll lose all meaning." Mariana pouts.

"You're so dramatic. It meant nothing," I said.

I know the only way to end this conversation was to leave, so I do, leaving Mariana on our newly disinfected couch. As I close my bedroom door behind me, I hear a knock at the front door and her mumbling as she gets up to answer it.

"Didn't mean anything, my ass. I know my best friend. She felt something."

I sit on the floor of my room, my back pressing into my door. Amaya's big fight with Tashi is happening tomorrow, and I'm supposed to come in and interfere. What was I thinking, kissing her last night? How can I face her tomorrow? Maybe I'm overthinking it; she might not even remember anything from last night.

"Ramona, you have mail." Mariana slides the manila envelope under the door.

The envelope has no return address or stamps; my legal name is in cursive on the front.

"Are you on the other side of the door, still hoping to hear something?"

"Maybe," Mariana whispers.

"Go away before I file a restraining order."

I open the envelope, and what I see makes me run to the bathroom to puke.

Mariana knocks on the bathroom door.

"I'm good, I don't need help," I yell out.

Once I'm done heaving, I look down at the photo in my hand. Amaya's green eyes were piercing into mine. Her bright smile is on display, her championship belt on her right shoulder, and strawberry-red hair in two French braids. She's wearing gear that shows her cleavage, and I keep finding myself staring. On the bottom right is her signature, accompanied by the words, *For my secret admirer.*

There goes the doubt I had about her remembering what happened last night.

11

Ravyn

I'm not sure how it happened, but I found the strength to peel myself off the floor and make it to the gym. The whole time I was getting ready, Mariana was chirping my ear off about the photo Amaya mailed me.

I knew I shouldn't have told her about it.

Mariana is taking it as a declaration of love. She's delusional, and I see this for what it is, which is a power move. Amaya will *never* let me live this down, and she'll mention it every chance she gets. Knowing her, she'll use it to her advantage, trying to throw me off my game, but I refuse to let that happen. I will not let the actions of tequila Ravyn affect sober Ravyn.

Eddie's face says it all as he looks at me, but in true Eddie fashion, he speaks anyway. "You look like shit."

"Well, not everyone can look as hot as you," I roll my eyes before stretching.

"Rough night last night?" he questions, and there's a knowing gleam in his eye.

He's about to torture me physically, so why not do the same to him mentally? It's only fair.

"Nope, a pretty chill night. Had a movie marathon with Mariana."

"Hmm... okay." He squints his eyes.

Oh, this is going to be fun.

Eddie and I go through our usual drills, like the sergeant he is, the whole time he pesters me about my movie marathon night with Mariana.

"What movies did you watch?" he asks.

"*Twilight*, all five movies," I answer.

"What snacks did you eat?"

"The usual. We're both on our periods, so a lot of chocolate."

The thought of us shedding our uterine lining grosses Eddie out enough for him to stop with the questions. I'm on my last set with battling ropes when I see her. Amaya's wearing bright red workout gear, the same fucking workout set that I'm currently wearing. Usually, this wouldn't bother me, but after last night, I do not need to add this to the list of things Amaya can tease me about.

"Okay, all done, Eddie. I'm going to head out." I start to power walk towards my belongings, but Eddie has other plans.

His strong chest stops me right in my tracks," No, you don't. We aren't done yet."

Oh God. She sees me.

"For the love of all that is holy, Eddie, move."

"Are you sure you're feeling okay? You look like you're about to be sick, and if that's the case, I'll gladly move. These are new sneakers, and if you puke on them, Ravyn, I'm going to be pissed."

She's walking over here. Maybe Eddie is right, I'm about to be sick all over the gym floor.

"Hey, Eddie." Amaya hugs Eddie before giving me her full attention.

"Nice outfit. Stalking me already, Silver?" she smirks, her eyes trailing down my body, making me feel like I'm on fire.

Don't respond, that's what she wants. She wants you to lose your shit.

"Did you get my gift?" she asks.

I nod, scared that if I open my mouth to talk again, all of the ginger ale I drank this morning will come out instead of words.

"Good, it's 8x10 in case you want to frame it," she winks before walking away.

Eddie crosses his arms across his chest, and I know what's coming, but before he can bombard me with questions, Amaya yells across the gym.

"Silver, check the back of your gift before hanging it."

I pinch the bridge of my nose, praying that the pressure will stop the headache that's starting to form.

"Oh, bitch. Consider our workout done, we're going out for smoothies while you spill the tea on what the fuck that was." Eddie loops his arm with mine, grabs both our duffel bags with the other, and pulls us out the door.

* * *

"You whore, I'm proud." Eddie sips on his overpriced smoothie.

I told him everything that I could remember in my fuzzy memory about last night.

"I don't want to say I told you so, but..."

"Then don't, Eddie. I'm glad that my confusion about my sexual identity is entertaining to you." I snap, tears threatening to spill out.

Eddie puts his smoothie down on the table, handing me a napkin.

"Oh, honey, I'm sorry. You know I'm just teasing you. It's been so long since I've come out that I forgot how life-changing it is. Talk to me, I'm here for you."

"There's no coming out, Eddie. It was a drunken mistake; it meant nothing. The only thing I felt after that kiss was embarrassment for letting my curiosity get the best of me."

Eddie stays quiet, but I can tell he's racking his brain for the right words to say, but the truth is, there aren't any. I kissed Amaya in a drunken haze, and yes, the kiss wasn't completely terrible.

Who are you trying to fool bitch? It was the best kiss you've had in a while.

Great kiss or not, it doesn't mean anything. It isn't validating that I like girls.

Does it?

"I've already had this discussion with Mariana. Plenty of girls get drunk and kiss their girlfriends all the time, Eddie."

"Yes, and unfortunately, their gay guy friends too." He shudders as he recalls a memory from a bachelorette weekend.

"But… Amaya isn't one of your girlfriends. You guys aren't friends at all, and I'm sure that's what's adding to your confusion. Do you think you would want to try that again sober?"

Yes.

"NO!" I yell, making everyone in the cafe turn in our direction.

"Okay. If you did, there's nothing wrong with that. Sexuality is confusing, and it isn't all black and white. There's a shit ton of gray area, and once you figure everything out, it's a colorful fucking world out there." Eddie grabs my hand, giving me his annoyingly perfect smile.

"Thank you, but the next person I'm going to be hooking up with won't be Amaya Acosta."

"It doesn't have to be. Just make sure it's something with a pulse." Eddie mumbles and dodges the napkin I throw his way.

12

Amaya

I've been tossing and turning in my bed for hours. My inability to sleep is annoying the shit out of me, and there's only one person to blame: Ravyn. Who kisses someone like that and then storms out like a bat out of hell? At first, I thought it was all a dream until I woke up the next day to a text from Reina asking if I had ever caught up with Ravyn after that 'orgasmic-looking kiss'. I was right about how trashed I was because I indeed kissed the porcelain throne the next morning. Just because I was hungover, that didn't mean I couldn't torture my secret admirer from afar. I text my assistant with specific instructions for a special delivery. Once I received confirmation that it was delivered, I paced my apartment, patiently waiting for the text I hoped would come. Ravyn is most definitely looking at my beautiful autographed photo with my number written on the back, telling her to text me whenever she gets tired of pretending to hate me. Hours passed, and my phone only buzzed with notifications from my dating app, alerting me to new matches. I double-checked my texts; nope, no new texts from an unknown number. I could've easily gotten her number from someone at EWC, that's how I received her address, but what's the fun in that? I wanted her to willingly give me her number and text me of her own accord. She kissed me on her own accord last night, and what a hell of a kiss it was. I've made out with my fair share of people, but there was something about this kiss with Ravyn that I couldn't shake.

When I checked my phone for what felt like the hundredth time, I decided to blow off steam the only way I knew how.

I lost track of how long I had been at the gym, but the moment I saw Ravyn with Eddie, it was as if time stopped. There she was in the same outfit I was wearing.

This is too perfect.

How could someone look so beautiful while also looking like they're about to empty their stomach contents on the floor? After I gave her the hint to look at the back of the photo, I headed back to my apartment, playing the waiting game once again.

"I am not a fan of playing hard to get, Silver," I whisper to my phone.

Great, now I'm talking to inanimate objects.

"A cold shower. I need a cold shower."

Great, now I'm talking to myself.

I'm shampooing my hair when my phone starts to ring. The shock makes me jump, and I almost slip inside the shower. As I scramble to reach it, shampoo burns my eyes, and I flood my bathroom floor as I run towards the vanity.

"Hello?" I answer, without a clue who's on the other side of the line.

"Oh, perfect. You were in the shower." Reina snickers.

"Reina, I'm expecting an important call." I scold.

"More like a booty call. She hasn't called or texted you yet, has she?"

I stand quietly, the puddle of water under me growing larger by the second.

"I mean, if she did, you would've been taking an everything shower. Unless I interrupted your masterpiece of a landing strip."

That comment snaps me out of my thought process of how I could get away with her murder. This is a FaceTime call, and I'm standing here all exposed.

"Can you stop objectifying me?" I jump back into the shower, rinsing the shampoo out of my hair before I lose my eyesight.

"Oh, please. It's nothing I haven't seen before."

I love Reina, but that girl has no chill. Whenever I am in town, she takes full advantage. She's my cousin from my mom's side, but we're practically sisters. Even though Reina and I are complete opposites in every way, she will always be my 911 call, the first person I run to whenever anything major happens.

"Did you just call me to compliment my pubic hair, or is there another purpose for this call?"

"I just wanted to make sure you remember karaoke tonight at seven. Don't be late!"

"Are you talking to yourself, because I am never late?"

"A Latina is never late; everyone else is just early."

"That logic doesn't work when the other person you're talking to is also Hispanic, Reina!" I wrap a towel around myself before starting my skincare routine.

"Whatever, Gringa."

Just like a little sister, she knows how to push my buttons. I take a deep breath, trying to relax before snapping at her. Reina and I are different in so many ways. Where I have pale skin, she has beautiful olive skin. I have naturally red curly hair that I straighten any chance I get, and she has chaotic black curls that she wears on her head like a crown. My green eyes are piercing, while her brown eyes are ones you can melt over. Our upbringings were also completely different. My Tía and Tío focused on Reina getting the best education, making sure she spoke Spanish and knew how to cook all the essential Cuban meals. Reina is about to be the first person in our family to graduate from college, which is more impressive than any title I can hold in the EWC. My parents couldn't care less about any of those things; they focused on training me in wrestling, eating a balanced meal, and avoiding talking to the press about my father. Mom never spoke Spanish in the house unless she was talking to Reina's mom, and Dad was too busy wrestling to even care to teach us. When I was younger, I didn't care to learn; I didn't think it was important to, but as an adult, I regret that decision. I've never felt Hispanic enough, and my appearance doesn't help. Anyone who looks at me assumes I'm white. I would love to represent Cuba just like the other wrestlers represent their heritage, but it would feel fraudulent. Hell, I can't even roll my r's.

"Amaya, snap out of it, chica!" Reina screams.

"Yeah, sorry. Who's going to this thing?"

"Aiden will be there, and some other people. Don't worry about it. Listen, I gotta go, te amo. I'll see you later!"

Why the hell was she being so damn shady?

As soon as she hangs up, I check my text message notifications, only to find them still empty.

Fuck this.

I sigh as I reply to the messages on my dating app. If she doesn't want to talk to me, fine, I'll find someone who will.

13

Ravyn

I spent the entirety of my car ride home anxious, thinking about what Amaya could've written on the back of that stupid picture she sent me. I fling open the door to the apartment. I'm on a mission to head straight to my bedroom and fish out that crumbled photo from the trash. There's just one problem, Mariana. She has been chatting my ear off from the moment she saw me, about what exactly I couldn't tell you. I'm trying to be a good friend, but dammit, I can't concentrate on anything coming out of her mouth.

I need to get to that picture.

"So will you come with me?" Mariana asks.

"I'm sorry, can you repeat that?"

"Oh my God, you just drowned me out, didn't you!"

"I didn't mean to, I'm sorry. Ask me again."

"Come out with me tonight."

"No," I replied.

"Oh, come on. Please!"

"Why can't you take no as an answer? You taught me that no is a complete sentence," I scold Mariana, trying to pass her, but she refuses to move.

"Yes, but that advice is for telling men no, not your best friend that you barely get to see." She pouts her lip and gives me her best doe eyes.

"You said you would stop guilt-tripping me into doing things with you. If I remember correctly, your exact words were, 'I'll stop using you following your dream as ammo to get you to hang out with me.'"

Mariana opens her mouth to argue, but shuts it as soon as she realizes I'm right.

"I did say that, but it was right after a therapy session, and you know how I get over those."

"I do know, it's my favorite version of you. Mariana, drunk on all of this 'insight. '"

I head towards the kitchen. If Mariana won't let me escape her nagging, I might as well have lunch while she yaps. I take out the ingredients for a salad.

"Oh, can you make me one while you're at it?" Mariana asks.

"So not only are you going to nag me, you're going to make me prepare lunch for you, too, while you do it?"

"Yes, nagging is a sport that takes a lot of energy. I'm hungry."

I roll my eyes, which Mariana knows is a sign that I will be making her lunch. I start chopping the lettuce for what's now *our* salad instead of doing what I want... which is to push Mariana off the kitchen counter she's currently sitting on.

"Pretty please, Ravyn. I don't want to go alone, and Ethan said he has to study all night for some stupid test.'

"So, Ethan saying no to you because of something important is okay, but when I do it, all hell breaks loose? Sounds like a double standard to me."

"The match tomorrow isn't even yours. You're just there to DQ it. You'll be in the ring for about five minutes max."

I point the knife in my hand towards her, making her throw her hands up in surrender. "Those five minutes are still important. I need the disqualification to go well, and I need rest."

"What if I promise that we'll come home early? No later than midnight, and I won't even drink."

Mariana has puppy-dog eyes that always make me crumble. I don't believe a word she says. I love her, but she's a notorious party girl. She also studies hard and works not only one, but two full-time jobs to afford college. She's so close to graduating that she deserves to blow off some steam whenever possible, and her offer is tempting.

I sigh. "Not later than midnight, I'm serious, Mariana."

She squeals as she hops off the counter, squeezing my midsection from behind.

"You're the best. We have to be there by seven."

"Where exactly are you dragging me to?"

"Karaoke," Mariana sings off-key into a spatula.

"I know you said you wouldn't drink, but if you're going to force me to hear *that* all night, I'm going to need at least one drink myself."

Mariana slaps me on the ass with the spatula, and I hope that she will leave me in peace after we eat our lunch so that I can finally read Amaya's note.

* * *

Mariana did not leave my side. We ate lunch, and she forced me to watch *Love Island* with her. When I finally thought I could escape to get dressed for the night, she insisted we do that together in her room. Amaya's headshot was still living at the bottom of the trash can, and it was killing me. We decided to Uber to the karaoke spot since we both hate dealing with downtown parking. I knew from the moment I saw the gaudy sign outside the bar that this was a bad idea. The place is named The Tune Tavern for God's sake. Mariana and I stepped inside the karaoke bar, and as we did, all the middle-aged men turned their heads to ogle us. We aren't even wearing revealing clothing. I opted for loose-fitting cargo pants and a band tee while Mariana wore a floral jumpsuit. My black and silver hair is in two French braids with face-framing curls, and I refused to put on any makeup, knowing it would be caked on my face tomorrow night for the show.

"It's times like these I hate being a woman," Mariana whispers.

"Why are there so many men in this karaoke bar in the first place?" I question.

"Oops. I guess we picked the wrong night to come." Mariana points over to the chalkboard by the bar.

Guys' Night!
Sing it Loud, Sing it Proud!
Drink Specials All Night!
Bring your friends and show off your best karaoke skills!
Prizes for Best Performances!
Let's make some noise!

"A little overkill on the exclamation points, don't you think?" I chuckle as I examine the sign.

"Mariana, over here!"

Reina stands up from her seat, waving her hands above her head like a madwoman.

"Great, now every man in this bar knows my name." Mariana sighs.

"Don't worry, just say the word and I'll smack your ass and call you my woman." I wink at her.

"Oh, now you want me to be your woman." Mariana rolls her eyes.

"Mariana, please not this again." I plead.

"The wound is still fresh. Plus, you doing that would just turn these men on more. We'll go from 'Hey sweetie, what brings you around?' to 'So have you ever wanted a third?' So let's not have these men cream their pants."

As we walk towards Reina, my chest starts to feel tight.

This is not the time for an anxiety attack right now, Ramona.

The last time I saw Reina, I was sucking face with Amaya. I just hope she wouldn't bring it up tonight, and I breathe a sigh of relief when I notice Amaya's presence is being replaced by her brother, Aiden.

That feeling of relief doesn't last long as I notice Aiden checking out Mariana.

Oh hell no.

"I didn't know you would be here." I wrap Aiden in a tight hug, and as I do, I make sure to put the fear of God into him.

"Don't think I didn't notice how you're eyeing my best friend. She's happily taken and completely off limits. Try anything, and I will spear you right where you stand. You know I can, and you know I will." I whisper into his ear.

63

Unlike Amaya, I have no ill feelings towards Aiden. He's been kind to me since I joined the main roster and invites me to group outings. It's no secret that his sister and I have bad blood, so he always assures me she won't be around. Apparently, that's never been a problem since they didn't have the same social circle. There have been rumors of us hooking up, but I shut those down immediately. I might have grown up longing to be a part of a family, but there's nothing I would hate more than to be a part of the Acosta clan. He's a good time, a big party animal. Now that I'm thinking about it, he and Mariana *would* make sense. Nope, not gonna go there. I would still consider Aiden a friend, but not friendly enough to make a move on Mariana. I'm actually being a good friend to him right now by warning him before Mariana uses her methods, which are never a fun time.

Aiden laughs as I release him from my grip. "Nice to see you, too, Ravyn. Who's your friend here?" he smirks.

This mother fucker thinks this is a joke. I tried to warn him.

"I'm her best friend, Mariana." She holds out her right hand, no doubt looking for a handshake.

"Nice to meet you, Mariana, you look lovely today." Aiden takes her hand and kisses the top of it.

Here we go.

"Ugh, no." Mariana reels her hand back, and before I could tell her no, she smacks Aiden across his smug face.

Reina and I stand there in shock as Aiden starts to laugh, his left cheek now red from impact.

"Never gotten that type of response before." Aiden rubs his face before taking his seat.

"Yeah, well, I know a move when I see one, and I usually nip it in the bud. Speaking of…"

"Mariana, please, not the speech." I groan.

"Yes, the speech." Mariana clears her throat before proceeding.

"I have a boyfriend. Yes, it's serious. No, he would not like to share. Yes, I am happy. No, I don't want your number just in case things go south because they won't, and even if they did, you're not my type."

Aiden slowly claps, and Mariana takes her seat on the opposite side of the table. "Bravo, that's a pretty good speech. I give it an eight out of ten."

Mariana gasps, "Excuse me, you do not get to grade my speech. I'll have you know that I received an A+ in my speech class."

"I knew it, beauty and brains. Keep slapping me like that, and I might fall in love with you." Aiden winks.

Mariana's face begins to turn red, and before she can say anything else, the lights dim as a spotlight hits the stage in front of us.

"Look, the show is about to start." Reina claps as she sits next to Mariana.

I take the seat next to Aiden, making sure I jab him as hard as I can in the ribs with my elbow as I did. That's when I finally notice the empty chair between Reina and me. The crowd starts to cheer as the DJ grabs the mic, ready to announce the first performer for the night.

"Hey, Reina. Why is there an empty chair here? Is someone else—" The DJ cuts me off before I can finish asking my question.

"Gentlemen, you're in for a sweet treat, and I'm not just talking about the ladies that Aiden has brought to the function."

He finger-gunned Aiden, and I want to barf. Of course, he's the reason we're at this sausage fest.

"Give it up for our first performer of the night, Amaya!"

Oh, God.

There she is, the devil in red. Amaya is on the stage, dressed in a low-cut red top and jeans, microphone in hand. As our eyes lock, her smile drops. She looks towards Reina with pure rage. Aiden howls, making Amaya channel that rage she has towards Reina onto him.

Reina blows her a kiss before screaming. "You're going to do great, sweetie."

Kylie Minogue's Can't Get You Out of My Head starts to blare out of the speakers before Amaya can curse Reina out. At first, Amaya's tense as fuck as she sings; the anger of seeing me is still boiling in her. She's refusing to give me eye contact. I can't help but feel a little hurt.

She seemed fine earlier today at the gym; she was her normal cocky self. Did I do something to piss her off? Why do I even care if I did?

As the song continues playing, Amaya's anger slowly melts away. She bops along to the rhythm of the music and hits every note perfectly.

Is there truly nothing this woman can't do?

"Did you know she was going to be here?" I question Mariana.

"Uhm, not exactly. Reina asked if she could invite her, and it would've been rude to say no."

I take a deep breath as the music ends and the audience whistles and applauds Amaya's performance. My heart races as Amaya gets off stage, walking towards our table.

"I'm going to the bar." I stumble out of my chair before Mariana can complain that I was being rude for leaving before saying hi to Amaya.

One drink, just to calm the nerves.

The barstools are all occupied, so I stand in the corner, hoping that one of the bartenders will notice me waiting there. My mind's going a mile a minute, trying to find the perfect opening line for Amaya. I need to play it cool, but how does one play cool after drunkenly making out with your coworker?

"Fuck my life." I sigh.

"If you not having a place to sit at the bar, is that serious. You can have a seat right here, sweetheart." A burly man with a country accent pats his lap and winks at me.

Don't punch this dick head in the face. You cannot go to jail tonight.

"I'm good," I say in a monotone voice.

"You sure about that, sweet cheeks?" He licks his bottom lip as he eye fucks me.

Oh, this drink is about to be a double.

"Positive," I replied, stone-faced.

I wave down the bartender, finally able to put in my order while ignoring the gaze of the man sitting beside me.

"Okay, that's fine. I'm enjoying the view."

Before I can reply, a familiar voice does the honors for me. "Would you enjoy the view as much with a black eye?"

The man coughs before giving Amaya a deep chuckle. " A black eye wouldn't stop me from checking that fine ass out. Out of curiosity, who exactly would be giving me this black eye? Do you have a boyfriend, sweetie?"

Once again, Amaya replies for me."She doesn't need a boyfriend; she has me."

"Oh shit, we have some lesbians at the bar tonight, fellas." He screamed across the bar, making all the men hoot and holler.

The bartender hands me my double shot of vodka cranberry.

Amaya laughs before correcting him."Not lesbian, bisexual. So I enjoy both men and women… yet neither one of us would touch you. We're not into bestiality."

The men around him snicker, making his face turn red from embarrassment.

If there's one thing you can count on when it comes to men, they never back down from a challenge.

"Fuck off, fire crotch," he spits at Amaya.

"How original, never heard that one before." Amaya rolls her eyes.

"Have you heard this before? I'm going to fuck your bitch and make her forget you ever touched her."

"Oh, please. I have a strap-on bigger than what's in between your legs, and I know how to use it." Amaya winks.

He pushes himself off his chair, towering over her. Amaya doesn't back down.

Fucking hell.

"Enough." I put myself between the two of them.

Where is Aiden?

"Amaya, go back to the table. Please." I plead with her, knowing that her walking away from a fight would kill her inside.

With fire still in her eyes, she walks away.

"That's right, listen to your bitch." He yells towards Amaya.

She comes to a halt, her body stiffening and her hand balling into fists at her side.

Please don't turn around. Please, please, please.

Amaya's back rises and falls as she takes a deep breath before continuing towards the table.

I turn to the gross excuse of a man beside me.

"Let's get one thing straight. I did that for your benefit, not hers. She can kick your ass back to whatever dumpster you came from. Her punch clocks in at twenty miles per hour, so you're lucky you're not leaving with that black eye."

How do I know that? Did I subconsciously memorize one of her stats?

"I'm not scared of no female. Now walk away so I can watch."

He smirks, and something in me snaps. The drink in my hand is now dripping from his beard.

"Enough, Larry, get the fuck out." The bartender yells at the man, who now reeks of vodka.

"Are you fucking kidding me? The whore threw a drink at me!"

"Just because she won't fuck you doesn't make her a whore. You deserved that shit. Get out before I let Ravyn put you in a submission hold."

"Or before I fucking punch you and Larry, once I start, I don't know how to stop," Aiden interjects.

Fucking Finally. Where the fuck has he been?

Larry storms out.

"I didn't need your help; it was handled." I grab a napkin, trying to get the wetness and stickiness from the drink off my hands.

"I know, but Amaya threatened to cut my balls off and feed them to me if I didn't come over here."

"Big brother is scared of his little sister. Don't see that dynamic often."

"Not scared. Just a little cautious. Amaya is not your average little sister."

The bartender waves us both down. "She's good, Aiden. I got her from here."

I reassure him with a hug before taking a seat on what used to be asshole Larry's stool.

"I'll remake your drink." He smiles.

"Thank you. I'll pay for the one I threw at Mr. Jackass."

"Like I would make Ravyn pay for drinks, all of these are on the house.

What does Amaya drink? I can make her something too."

"Do you have any Havana Club?" I ask.

"We exclusively carry it for Aiden." The bartender winks.

"Remembering my drink order already?" Amaya replies as she leans on the bar.

"Didn't think you would want tequila again so soon."

"Good call," she smiles.

"You didn't have to tell Aiden to come over."

"I know," she replies.

The silence between us is suffocating.

"If you're here to receive praise for being my knight in shining armor, it's not happening."

"You'll praise me one day, Silver," she winks.

I try to speak, but I can't find the words. All I can think about is our kiss and the tingling that took over my body as it happened.

"Here you go, ladies, on the house. Unless you want to pay me in the form of telling me who is going to win the match tomorrow?"

"We love our fans, but we love keeping our jobs even more." Amaya lifts her glass in thanks to the bartender.

"Fair enough." He shrugs.

"Is what you said to that dickhead true?" I ask.

"Which part?"

"That you have a strap-on that's bigger than his dick."

Amaya chokes on her rum.

"You trying to find out?" she questions.

"Just curious," I shrug.

"I bet you are."

Silence once again fills the air between us. Both of us stare at one another as we sip our drinks.

God, she's gorgeous. Amaya has always been beautiful. I'd done some investigative research on her and her family. She's always had a spark about her, an energy that you could even feel through photos.

"Are you going to sing?" Amaya asks.

"I don't sing. I'm only here because Mariana begged me to."

Amaya raises an eyebrow, "Have you and Mariana ever…"

Now it's my turn to choke on my drink.

"No. I've never…"

I need to find a way to change the subject. I am not going to talk about my sexual history or the internal crisis I'm currently having about my sexual identity with her.

"So, about the other night, I —"

I interrupt Amaya before she can finish her sentence, "Do you and Reina usually do karaoke night during guys' night?"

Reina is now on stage, trying to stay on key as she sings to Ariana Grande's *No Tears Left to Cry.*

"You can thank Aiden for that. That dickhead thought it would be funny, and it's the perfect example of why I don't like to hang out with him outside of family functions or wrestling events."

"I like your brother, but just so you're aware, if he tries anything with Mariana, I'll kill him."

Amaya laughs, "Oh, I'm sure she'll murder him before you even get the chance to. I heard she slapped him."

"That's Mariana, my party girl with a loyal heart."

"Yeah, my idiot brother thinks he has a chance, so we'll see how that goes."

"It's his funeral." I shrug.

"I promise our karaoke nights aren't always this chaotic. Reina and I try to meet with friends for karaoke as much as possible. Growing up, I had a karaoke machine that had a camera so it would record our performances. We were delusional in thinking we would become the next Aly & Aj Michalka."

I gasped."Don't tell anyone at EWC this, but… I love them! *Potential Breakup Song* is my guilty pleasure song. Honestly, it's one of the best songs of our generation."

"It's a masterpiece. It was our favorite song to perform. Still is."

We both laugh as Reina cracks on the high notes.

"So you don't sing, but if you did. What song would you sing?"

"I'm not sure. I love music, but I've never listened to a song and thought,

'Wow, I would perform the shit out of that.' No song has ever spoken to me in that way."

Amaya's smile quickly turns into a devilish grin.

I'm not a fan of that look one bit. Okay, she looks fucking gorgeous, but in a scary way. I'm starting to see why Aiden is scared of her.

"Go over to the table with Mariana and Reina," she instructs.

Amaya throws back the rest of her rum before running towards the DJ, whispering in his ear. Whatever she's telling him is causing him to shake his head no profusely.

"I was going to head over there, but Amaya threatened both of our lives if we left the table," Mariana tells me as I sit down.

"True story," Reina said.

"It's because she asked the muscle to go instead." Aiden wiggles his eyebrows at Mariana.

"I suggest you shut your mouth before I replace your steroid shots with estrogen shots," Mariana replies.

"I'll help you." Reina high-fives Mariana.

As tempting as it is to give this interaction my full attention, my eyes don't leave Amaya.

What the hell is she doing?

After begging, pleading, and what I think is a slip of cash in his hand, Amaya makes her way onto the stage.

"Hey, what is she doing up there? It's my turn, DJ!" A guy shouts from the table next to ours.

"I know Tucker, but the pretty lady asked me for a favor and passed me a twenty. Are you going to pass me forty bucks?" he explains into his mic.

The man huffs, motioning for Amaya to continue.

She clears her throat, "I hope this song speaks to you. Hit it, DJ!"

No. She. Did. Not

An instantly recognizable and upbeat song floods the room.

She did.

Amaya opens her mouth, confirming that she, in fact, did. "This was never the way I planned, not my intention. I got so brave, drink in hand, lost my discretion."

This bitch is singing I Kissed a Girl by Katy Perry. Not only is she singing it, but she also dedicated it to me.

I look towards Mariana and Reina. Both bopping their heads along to the music, refusing to look at me.

"Ugh, she knows I hate this song," Aiden mumbles before leaving for the bar.

"Everyone, sing along!" Amaya commands the audience before belting out the chorus.

"I kissed a girl and I liked it! The taste of her cherry Chapstick. I kissed a girl just to try it, I hope my boyfriend don't mind it." The whole bar is joining in on Amaya's taunt to me.

Did I die? Did Larry kill me, and am I now in my own personal hell?

"Come on, Ramona, sing along. Don't be a party pooper." Mariana shoves my arm.

"You realize what she's doing. It's psychological torture, Mariana. You're a psych major, how can you not see it!"

Mariana stops swaying and singing to the music, a wrinkle forming between her eyebrows as she thinks.

"She is, but it's a crime to hear a Katy Perry song and *not* sing along." Mariana takes a sip of her drink.

When the hell did she get a drink? So much for no drinking.

"I gotta get out of here."

I walk towards the exit as Amaya calls my name into the microphone, asking me not to leave.

14

Amaya

"Amaya, what the fuck." Mariana scolds me as I jump off the stage.

I roll my eyes at her, "Oh, spare me the best friend speech, you were singing along too."

"It's not my fault Katy Perry's songs are so catchy!" She stomps her foot.

Was singing *I Kissed a Girl* the smartest idea? No. I didn't think it would piss Ravyn off that badly.

Can no one take a little friendly banter anymore?

"When we set this up to get you guys to talk, this is not what we had in mind." Reina sips her drink.

"You two did what?" I growl.

Reina winces, regret taking over her face.

"Dammit, Reina. So much for our top-secret mission." Mariana pouts.

I was ready to talk to Ravyn about the kiss. She's cut me off mid-sentence. How else was I supposed to get her attention? The song was a stroke of genius; it practically screamed Ravyn's name at me.

"Come on bitches, let's go find her." I huff.

"Where are you taking the love of my life?" Aiden asks.

"Aiden Acosta, we just met. I am not the love of your life." Mariana yells.

"When you break up with Eric, you'll see."

"His name is Ethan, and he's the love of *my* life. It's not happening. Settle for friendship, or all you'll have is heartbreak, Aiden."

"Fine. Best friends, it is," Aiden smirks.

"Ramona will have your head if you ever call me your best friend again."

"Ramona, oh shit, that's Ravyn's real name. Do we get to call Ravyn by her real name now? Are we at that level of friendship?" Aiden questions.

"Can we fucking focus! God, Mom really should've had you tested. We need to find Ravyn." I slap Aiden on the arm.

"Come on, I know exactly where she's gonna be." Mariana takes the lead.

We walked a couple of blocks, and there she was, through the window, looking as beautiful as ever, sitting at a bar with a drink in her hand. As I looked at her somber face, my heart sank, the guilt sinking in for making her run out of the karaoke club.

"How did you know she would be here, of all places?" Reina asks.

"I'm her best friend, I know all. This bar is special to Ramona; it's a safe place for her. Plus, I have her location on my phone."

"Since we're friends now, can I get your location or…" Aiden pushes his phone towards Mariana.

"I would have to be willing to give you my phone number first. Which isn't happening."

"That's not fair. Friends have each other's phone numbers."

"I'll make a deal with you. You can have my number if you use it for friendly communication *only*. I swear if I get a dick pic…."

"You won't, I swear." Aiden gives his pinky to Mariana.

She wraps her pinky around his, "Good. Maybe I'll think about sharing my location later on."

Aiden's face lights up, "Deal."

Poor Mariana, she has no idea what she just did.

"Is no one else concerned that Ravyn's safe space is a bar?" Reina asks.

"I'm not judging, but hearing that is sad, and it also sounds like a cry for an AA meeting," I replied.

"Oh, please. That little drinking contest you two had was cute, but I can out-drink you both. Also, you saying you're not judging doesn't take away the fact that it sounds like you're judging, Amaya." Mariana slaps my arm.

"I'm gonna go say sorry." I start to walk towards the bar entrance when

Mariana's gasp stops me in my tracks.

"Oh. My. God," she whispers.

I whip my head, curious to see what the hell has her awe-struck. Ravyn's embracing some guy at the bar who towers over her. His whole body envelops hers; the only sign she's in his arms is the little piece of silver hair peaking out from the top of his arms. I can't make out his face. That's because it's currently nuzzled into the crook of her neck. They stand there embracing for what feels longer than a normal hug should be.

"Okay, I'm gonna go kick this guy's ass," I mumble.

"Right behind you, sis." Aiden cracks his knuckles

Reina grabs me by the wrist, "I think you've had enough confrontations with giant men for tonight."

"Aiden, no middle name, Acosta. Get your ass back here right now." Mariana scowls.

"I have a middle name."

"I'll learn that later, then. My command still stands: you two will stay right where you are."

Who the hell hugs for that long? I swear it's already been five minutes.

"Who the fuck is that anyway?" I ask.

"Trust me, Amaya, you do not want to get between those two." Mariana's hands are on her chest, covering her heart.

"I have never seen my sister this red before; her skin is about to match her hair," Aiden whispers.

"Shut the fuck up." I snarl.

"His name is Levi," Mariana answers.

"Why does Levi look like he's about to swallow your friend whole?" Reina cringes in disgust.

Reina has never been one for physical affection, and looks like she's about to vomit.

"He's her ex." Mariana looks as though she's on the verge of tears.

"That's one hell of a way to say hi to an ex. If he were any of my exes, I would've run in the other direction." Reina scoffs.

Reina also doesn't do relationships.

"Rightfully so, all your exes were trash. If you could even classify them as exes," I roll my eyes as Reina punches my arm.

"Well, there was —" Reina stomps on my foot to silence me.

"Woman, I need that foot." I hiss.

Mariana's eyes stay on Ravyn. Levi's arms finally release Ravyn, and she's smiling.

She's never smiled at me like that.

"Levi is Ramona's epic love. The one that got away."

Mariana claps her hands like a seal, her face full of glee. Meanwhile, it feels like a rock has been placed on my chest.

15

Ravyn

This has to be a dream. A very vivid dream, but a dream.

Did I fall on the way to the bar and hit my head on the concrete?

"It's good to see you, Ramona," his whispers tickling my ear.

The familiar scent of Levi Miller lingers in my nostrils. A beautiful mixture of sandalwood and musky rose. Memories flood my brain, making my heart flutter and my mouth as dry as the Sahara desert. I'm in such a daze that I didn't realize he released me from his grasp.

"Sorry. Am I still allowed to call you that? Or do I have to go by Ravyn now?" he asks.

The sensation of something wet touching my cheeks snaps me out of my haze.

Fuck. I'm crying.

I wipe away my tears, hoping that Levi didn't notice.

"Ramona, you can always call me Ramona," I whisper.

Just like that, I'm reduced back to a weak-kneed teenager. Levi Miller was *the* popular boy in school. He was the football team's quarterback, valedictorian, hot, extremely hot. So hot to the point that I stood no chance, or so I thought. Nothing has changed in that department; he's still drop-dead gorgeous. I will never forget how quickly my view of Levi completely changed.

One night, my foster parents and I got into a heated fight. I don't even remember what it was about, but it wasn't out of the norm for us to get into fights over any little thing. I stormed out of the house, needing the crisp fall air to hit my face so I could breathe in something other than rage. There was a park around the corner that I visited frequently. I'm a sucker for a good swing. When I arrived, Levi was there in his red varsity jacket, swinging around on the only working swing. We made eye contact, which immediately made me want to shit my pants. I turned around to head where exactly, no clue, but anywhere was better than there with Levi.

"Hey, Ramona, right?" he asked.

I winced, turning back around to face him.

"Yeah, Ramona," I answered.

"Did you want to swing?" he stood up, motioning for me to take his place.

"Oh, it's okay. I don't want to take it from you."

"It's fine. I've been here for a while anyway, and there are plenty of other things around the playground to occupy my time with. Unless you need my help to push you," he smirked.

I walked past him, taking in his scent. He smelled like any other boy his age did, like he bathed himself in Axe body spray.

"I can push myself just fine, thank you." My hair started to move in the wind as I pushed my feet back and forth.

"You're in my chemistry class, right?"

"Yup," I replied. My feet are taking me higher and higher into the air.

The higher I got, the more I felt my rage melt away. I closed my eyes, pretending that Levi wasn't there. Hoping that he would take the hint that I wanted to be alone. He'll realize I'm not a person who fits into his social class soon enough and stop wanting to talk.

"How did you do on the last exam?"

"Pretty good." I kept my replies short, focusing on the brisk air entering my lungs.

"I'm usually great in chem, but this test was ass. I completely tanked it, and Mr. C is letting me retake it in a week. Think you would be down to tutor me?"

My legs stopped pumping, I dug my heels into the mulch below, bringing the swing to a complete stop, and my eyes were now open wide in shock.

"I know this is a lot to ask, we aren't even friends."

"Yeah, we aren't." I blurted out.

"I'm desperate. I need to pass Ramona, name your price, and I'll give it to you."

"The fate of the football team lies in your hands." I mocked.

"The football team? I can give two fucks about the football team. I'm so close to being named valedictorian."

I laughed, "Levi Miller cares more about his grades than football? I'm shocked."

"I don't even like football. I play, so it betters my chances to get a full ride for college." his eyes widened at his admission.

"I have never told anyone that before," he mumbled.

"Welcome to my confessional." I spread my arms wide, making Levi laugh.

"You're funny. So is that a yes?"

"Sure, I have nothing better to do." I shrugged.

"Is there anything I can do for you in return?" he questioned.

"We can keep it as an I.O.U. for now. I'll let you know when I think of something."

"Fair enough. Are you sure you don't need a push?"

"My two feet are still working."

"Yes, but they're shaking from the cold just like the rest of your body." He smirked.

I hadn't noticed how cold it was outside; it's rare that Florida has a cold front.

"Here." Levi took off his jacket, draping it over my shoulders.

"Oh no, I can't take this."

"You're not taking anything. I'm giving it to you to borrow. You can give it back during our first tutoring session."

"Fine, as long as you know I'm not one of those girls who wait their whole life for a football boy to give them his jacket. It's just another piece of clothing."

"Never thought of you as one of those girls," he clarified.

"You've thought of me?" I questioned.

Levi cleared his throat, "Yeah, for tutoring purposes."

I nodded my head. The swing moved back and forth once again.

"Hey!" I whipped my head around, glaring at Levi as he pushed the swing.

"Shh... just let it happen. Turn around and enjoy the ride."

So that's what I did. I enjoyed the ride that was Levi Miller. We met every day after school at that park to review our chemistry notes. The routine stuck even after Levi passed his retake exam. Graduation came, and Levi earned the title of valedictorian. The whole class turned towards me as he thanked me in his speech. Levi claimed he still wanted to study during summer vacation to prepare for college. I happily agreed even though I knew college was never in the cards for me. We had fun together, learned more about each other, and found comfort in one another. I'm not sure when I fell in love with Levi Miller, but I fell hard. Of course, I never made a move. I was lucky that he still wanted me around. I wasn't going to push my luck and ruin everything with something as stupid as unrequited love. It wasn't until the day before Levi left for college that I felt that pit in my stomach. Mariana's voice inside my head the whole time yelling at me to confess my feelings before it's too late.

"Earth to Ramona!" Levi waved his hands in front of my face.

"Sorry, what were you saying?"

"That distraught over me leaving, huh?" he snickered.

"Something like that," I muttered.

Between Levi leaving and Mariana and I's countdown to the big eighteen, meaning that we would officially be out of the foster system, my mind was a pit of never-ending worry.

"Are you going to be okay?" Levi asked.

"I always am." I fiddled with the gold bracelet on my arm that Levi gave me as a thank-you for tutoring him.

It's the kind of bracelet that doesn't demand attention. He used his allowance money to buy it, and I refused it at first. Levi begged me for days before I accepted it. He knew if my foster parents saw me with anything of value, they would steal it and sell it to make a profit. They already hounded me over Levi's varsity jacket I never returned. The bracelet is the nicest thing I've ever owned. Every time I look at it, I can't help but smile, a quiet reminder of Levi. I never take it off, scared that the moment I do, I'll wake up from this dream.

"I'm going to miss you, too, you know." He lifted my chin, forcing me to look into his chocolate-brown eyes.

A sharp pain hit me straight in the heart as I said it first. I said the words that I told myself I would never say to anyone. "I love you."

"I loved you first," he said before his lips brushed mine.

The air became electric as if the world around us slowed down. The kiss was soft at first, unsure, like Levi wanted to test the waters and make sure I was okay with this. I was more than okay. He takes his time, and I can feel the weight of my emotions that were buried for so long My hands make their way into Levi's hair, making him deepen the kiss ever so slightly. After what feels like hours, we break apart, trying to catch our breath.

A mixture of excitement and confusion is on our faces as we stare into each other's eyes.

I couldn't help but laugh nervously before asking him, "Now what?"

Levi and I spoke every day while he was away in college. We spent hours going through our days, how amazing he was doing in his classes, and how I was following my wrestling dreams. Neither of us could afford plane tickets to see each other, so we were grateful for FaceTime. We didn't put a label on anything, not wanting to force a long-distance relationship on each other. As the years passed, the calls became less and less frequent, both of us getting wrapped up in our own lives. That was until my twenty-first birthday, when Mariana took me out for drinks at a bar, and there he was. It was as if time stopped.

"This is your birthday gift, by the way. The one I told you you would love so much." Mariana whispered.

I stood frozen, staring at Levi like he was a ghost.

"Did you do this?" I asked her.

"I might've gotten tipped really well at work, enough for a plane ticket," Mariana shrugged.

"Mariana, you shouldn't have. I'll pay you back, I swear I—"

Mariana placed her hand over my mouth and sighed, "Shut up and go get your man."

She pushed me towards Levi, causing me to stumble right into his arms.

"Still falling for me, I see, Ramona," he snickered.

"Always," I replied.

"Nice jacket."

I couldn't help but blush, utterly embarrassed that I was wearing his varsity jacket all these years later.

"Mariana was pestering me to wear it tonight. I guess I know why. Is that why

you came? To finally get your jacket back." I smirked.

"Nah, it looks better on you anyway. I came for you."

To this day, my heart refuses to acknowledge the aftermath of that night.

"What are you doing here, Levi?" I ask.

"I tried texting and someone else replied, saying I had the wrong number."

I changed my number as soon as he left.

"I tried messaging you on your socials, but I'm sure it got lost in all the fan messages you get."

I'd seen his messages and one hundred percent ignored all of them.

Levi clears his throat before continuing, "So I've come to this bar every night since I've been back, hoping that I would bump into you here."

"Why?" I question.

You're the one who left. You broke our promise.

"New York wasn't what I thought it would be. I tried, and the job was hell, the people there were worse, and the dating scene... I found myself comparing every woman to you. Spoiler alert, none of them were."

"Yeah, well, spoiler alert, there's only one me and you left me, so excuse me." I make sure to hold in my tears until I slam the door to the women's restroom.

Everyone that you love leaves.

Everyone that you love disappoints you.

Everyone that you love chooses you second.

Everyone that you love hurts you.

I try to regulate my breathing, taking deep breaths in and out, squeezing my eyes shut, and forcing myself to concentrate on the air coming in and out of my lungs. My body jumps as cold hands touch my arm.

"Sorry. I shouldn't have just grabbed you." Amaya's green eyes are full of worry.

"How did you know where... Mariana." I sigh.

"Yeah, she's talking to that Levi guy now. Reina is with her, and Aiden was sent on a fool's errand."

"Should I even ask?"

"Mariana is having him prove himself worthy of her friendship."

"Poor guy."

"Don't feel bad for my idiot brother. He asked for it. Did Levi hurt you?"

"Physically, no, never. Emotionally, plenty."

She starts towards the door, her hands balling into fists for the second time tonight. "Good enough reason for me to kick his ass back to whatever hellhole he came from."

"New York, he came from New York."

"I know, my comment still stands."

"Amaya, stop." I grab onto her bicep.

"You've had enough brawling with men for the night." I sneer at her, which makes her smile.

"That's what Reina said, but I didn't get to throw a drink in anyone's face, and I'm getting a severe case of FOMO."

My laugh echoes in the restroom so loudly that I shock myself.

"Feeling better?" Amaya places a strand of my hair behind my ear.

Goosebumps cover my arms at her touch.

"Yeah, how did you know about New York— Mariana, again?" I shake my head.

"Don't be mad at her, she didn't give me the full story, just that he left," Amaya explains.

I stand there quietly, replaying the last time I saw him in my head.

"Wanna get out of here? It smells like ass." Amaya asks.

"Why do we always find ourselves in a dingy bathroom together?"

"I don't know, but let's not make it our thing."

The thought of running into Levi again was too much to handle. "Is he still out there?"

Amaya sticks her head out of the door. "Nope. Mariana and Reina completed their mission."

"Their mission?"

"Operation get the dick head that made Ravyn cry out of here."

Another guttural laugh escapes my mouth.

"Who was the head of this operation?" I question.

"Me, of course."

"My hobby of hating you is in danger." I scold.

"That's what I like to hear."She winked at me before putting her hand on my lower back and guiding me out of the restroom.

16

Amaya

I'm running on zero sleep, wondering how much concealer is too much as I work on covering my under-eye bags for tonight's match. Last night was full of drama and unwanted surprises. I had walked Ravyn back to her place, and we talked the whole time. I apologized for my song choice, and she admitted how clever it was. She claims it was off base since she "didn't like the kiss," but I know that's complete bullshit. I didn't call her out, wanting to keep the peace. Ravyn didn't mention Levi once during the walk back to her place. I was dying to know the story between them. Mariana said that he was the one who got away, an epic love, so what the fuck went wrong, and how does one compete with epic love?

You're not in competition. It was one kiss, a kiss she obviously sees as a mistake.

It's stupid of me to focus on Ravyn when I'm a couple of hours from being in front of thousands of people fighting for my title, but how could I not think about her?

"Hey."

I jump up, completely spooked by the woman whose mere existence is occupying my entire brain.

"What's up?" I continue to work on my makeup, ignoring the butterflies in my stomach.

"Just wanted to check in with you. Did Sid go over the game plan for tonight with you?"

"Yeah, Tashi is going to be close to pinning me, and then you're gonna swoop in and save the day with a DQ. Not a big fan of where the storyline is going, but it's good writing."

EWC writers have Tashi and me fighting for the title tonight, and even though I gave them shit about giving a newcomer the chance of a title match right off the bat, they didn't care. They want to give the viewers what they want, and apparently, they want a blood bath between us. If that's what they want, that's what they'll get. I have a good idea why they want Ravyn to intervene, but I'm crossing my fingers that I'm wrong.

"I'm not saving the day, I'm saving my title from getting into the wrong hands."

"So you agree, the title belongs in my pretty little hands and not Tashi's."

"You know damn well that's not what I meant. See you in the ring, Red."

* * *

The crowd is on the edge of their seats as the lights pulse and the arena vibrates with energy. I'm struggling to keep up with Tashi's never-ending energy. I have to hand it to her; this match has been brutal. My body is completely battered and bruised. I haven't felt this type of exhaustion from a match in a while.

The last time was with Ravyn, the day she almost took your title from you.

Tashi's moves are both powerful and technical. I feel myself moving slowly, and I'm grateful that Ravyn is coming in to end this soon, but until then, I'll dig deep and continue taking hits. My movements are sluggish, and my arms feel heavy, but I'm not a quitter. I narrowly avoid a crushing clothesline from Tashi, but as I stumble backward, my legs give way, giving her an opening. Tashi grabs me, holding me in a front facelock and falls backwards, driving my head right into the mat.

Dammit, that was a perfect DDT.

The arena erupts with gasps along with a mixture of boos and cheers as Tashi goes for the pin.

Fucking finally.

My shoulders are down flat as the referee's hand slaps the mat for the first count.

"One… two…"

Like clockwork, I hear her boots hitting the floor, and the crowd roars. Ravyn rushes into the ring, sliding perfectly under the ropes while her eyes stay locked on Tashi with an intensity that could burn a hole through steel. She doesn't hesitate, grabbing Tashi by the hair and yanking her off me with a violent jerk.

Do not be aroused right now, Amaya, focus. Shit, that was hot.

The arena is in an uproar and is eating this up, going wild as Ravyn begins to rain down a series of vicious blows to Tashi, forcing her to stumble back.

"You thought this belt was going to be yours?" Ravyn yells as she continues to punch Tashi in the head.

The referee immediately calls for the bell, signaling a disqualification of the match. Tashi is furious, scrambling to her feet, but Ravyn isn't done. She shoves Tashi into the corner, slamming her knee into Tashi's midsection.

"You're new meat, you don't get to take what's mine."

I scramble out of the way, putting myself in the opposite corner of the ring as Ravyn drags Tashi to the center. Tashi's eyebrow is smeared with blood. Ravyn sees it, smirks, and there's a gleam in her eye telling me she's gonna finish this.

It's time for her finisher, Ravyn's Rapture.

She grabs hold of her neck and lifts her, spinning Tashi around so fast that she becomes a blur. She ends Tashi's misery by slamming her onto the mat.

The crowd goes wild as they always do when Ravyn does her finisher. The referee passes me my belt as I collect myself. I clutch it tightly as Ravyn stands over me, eyes flashing with smug satisfaction before she fucking winks at me.

Holy hell.

Ravyn waves down someone from the crew to get her a mic. The tension in the arena is thick; everyone is confused as to what they just witnessed.

I know exactly what I'm witnessing: Ravyn becoming a bigger star than she could imagine in this industry.

"I want everyone to remember what they saw here tonight," she speaks into the mic.

Ravyn moves her attention to me, "Don't mistake what I did as an act of kindness to you, Amaya. You're still number one on my hit list. No one will take that title from you. I want every woman on the roster to hear me loud and clear. I will DQ *any* title match because *no one* will have this belt around their waist but me."

Ravyn drops the mic on top of Tashi's limp body as she makes her way out of the ring, and from this day forward, the ECW women's division will never be the same.

17

Ravyn

My body hasn't stopped trembling since I left Tashi a bloody mess in that ring, which was hours ago. I'm sitting in the driver's seat of my car, trying to even out my breathing so I can make it home in one piece. I usually drive myself to and from events when I'm home, but I'm currently regretting that decision. I haven't felt an adrenaline rush like this since my early days at EWC. My ears are still buzzing from the crowd's deafening screams, and I will never forget the look on Amaya's face when I winked at her. I'm unsure what came over me. I just saw Tashi's face, and I swear I blacked out. Deep down, I know that Tashi is just doing her job; she's doing what she's been told to do, but dammit, I'll be lying if it didn't hurt that she got a shot at the title so easily. I have never been the underdog. I came into EWC just as good, if not better, than people who have been in the league for years, yet I hate that Tashi's arrival makes me feel like one. It's not a good enough excuse to go off on her like I did, even if the crowd ate it up. Maybe I should apologize the next time I see her.

A loud knock on my window causes me to jump out of my seat. I guess my moment to apologize is coming sooner rather than later. I roll down my tinted window, and a heavy citrus scent hits me in the face.

"Hey, just the person I was thinking about."

"Oh, yeah? Thinking about how awesome the stitches I got look." Tashi points to her perfectly arched eyebrow.

"I remember my first pair of stitches on the main roster. Wore them like a badge of honor."

"Just like I plan to do. Be careful, I intend to come back just as hard next week."

"I wouldn't expect anything less."

There's an awkward pause between us. Then, at the exact same moment, we both blurt out,

"I'm sorry."

"You did great."

We break into laughter, the tension melts as we each motion for the other to speak first.

"Why are you apologizing?" Tashi asks.

"I went a little too hard in there. It was our first time in the ring together, and I whaled on you like some wild animal." I point to the stitches to prove my point.

"There's no need to apologize, especially when the crowd reacted how they did. You killed it in there, and I can't wait to be in the ring with you again. Hopefully, it'll be a fair fight next time. No sneak attacks."

"Are you trying to say that the only reason I beat your ass is cause it was a sneak attack?"

Tashi parts her lips to speak, but the voice that follows doesn't belong to her.

"That's what it sounds like to me, Silver," Amaya smirks as her duffel bag thuds on the floor beside her.

"Oh no, you don't, Amaya. I want no real-life beef. I'm drama-free outside the ring and prefer to keep the drama between you two." Tashi looks between Amaya and me.

Amaya and I exchange scowls at one another.

"That look right there, that is my cue to head out. See you both next week, have a good weekend."

Tashi pats Amaya's shoulder and whispers something in her ear that makes Amaya's eyebrows shoot up to the top of her forehead and blush.

Amaya never blushes. What the hell did Tashi say to her, and why do I want to

give Tashi a matching gash on the other side of her face for it?

Amaya clears her throat, bringing me back to reality. She's closer now, leaning down, my eyes making direct contact with her cleavage.

"My eyes are up here, Silver."

Yeah, but your boobs are down there, and I can't help but notice how the freckles that frame your face so beautifully also frame your chest perfectly.

"I know that, I'm just tired from saving your ass tonight. Now, if you would get the fuck off my car, I would like to go home."

"You mind giving me a ride? Reina was supposed to pick me up, but something came up, and Uber says it would be an hour wait or more. I live only a couple of blocks from you."

"How do you know where I live?" I arch my brow.

Amaya's stance stiffens. "Glad to know that you forgot about my gift already. Remind me never to buy you anything ever again."

Oh yeah, the photo I never got to read the back of because of Mariana being annoying.

"You did not buy me anything. Knowing you, you probably have a bunch of headshots lying around your house pre-signed, ready to give out to anyone desperate enough to want one. I bet you give it to whatever unlucky bastard sleeps with you after you're done, like it's a reward."

I put my car in reverse, but just as I start to take my foot off the brake and hit the gas, Amaya reaches into the car and shifts it back into park.

"Hey!" I yell out, swatting at her arm.

She doesn't move; she keeps her hand on the shift and is inches away from my face. Amaya is looking from my eyes to my lips, and if I weren't already sitting, I would've collapsed from the way she's watching me. Her scent is intoxicating, warm, and soft, and fills the air inside my car. It's a delicate mix of jasmine and sandalwood, with just a hint of vanilla. Amaya's scent is the kind that stays with you, staining every surface so that you will still feel her presence long after she's gone. She licks her lips before she speaks, and I swear the car vibrates from her words.

"Ramona, I promise you that anyone who sleeps with me doesn't need a headshot as a prize. The orgasm I give them is the prize."

My mouth feels dry, and the English language seems to escape my brain as I try to speak. How does one reply to something like that?

"I told you never to call me that."

Smooth.

Amaya smirks, and before she can reply, my phone goes off. I know who it was without even checking. Mariana had a specific sound assigned to her number on my phone, even though I told her that my phone is on silent ninety-nine percent of the time. I'm not sure why it's not on silent now. *Maybe it's God giving you a way out of this situation, and you'll have to thank him later.*

I clear my throat; thankfully, Amaya takes that as a sign to back away so I can reach my phone.

Mariana: *"Please don't be mad. Ethan's stupid roommates were supposed to go out tonight to give us alone time, but the plans got canceled. The whole frat house is here, so I told Ethan it would be cool to come over to our place. I spaced and forgot you were in town. Say the word, and I can tell him we have to reschedule."*

"Fucking hell." I sigh as I reply to Mariana.

Me: *"It's cool, I made plans with some of the girls anyway. Have fun ;)"*

I know that I can tell Mariana no. She can always see Ethan another time, and I would rather her not see him at all, but I am not the tell-it-how-it-is friend. That's Mariana's role, I'm the supportive-even if you're being stupid-friend.

"You okay?" Amaya asks.

How can someone go from irritating to unbelievably sexy to concerned all under the span of five minutes?

"Yeah, Mariana just needs the house for a couple of hours, so my hopes and dreams of showering and going straight into bed have been shattered."

"Perfect, now you can't say no."

Amaya opens the back door of my car, flinging her duffel bag into the backseat. Before I can stop her, she slams the door and jogs over towards the passenger seat of my car, plopping her perfect little ass on top of my black leather seat and buckling the seatbelt.

"That wasn't an invitation to get into my car."

Great, now her smell is definitely going to get soaked up into this car. Thank God I don't drive it much, or it would drive me insane.

"Oh, come on. You have nothing better to do; might as well be useful." Amaya quickly types her address into the GPS on my dashboard and reclines her seat like it's the most natural thing on earth for her to be in my car.

This time, I know I'm staring, and I'm painfully aware of it. My mouth hangs open in stunned disbelief, growing dry by the second. The audacity of this woman, acting like I'm her chauffeur. I may not be able to go home right now, but what on God's green earth makes her think I want to be anywhere near her or her lair?

Amaya sighs, rubbing her temples in frustration.

How can she be frustrated at me when I'm the one being held hostage? Okay, hostage is a strong word, but I can't think of a more fitting word right now.

"Fine, I'll just ask Tashi."

Like hell you will.

"Amaya—"

She cuts me off before I can finish.

"Listen, Ravyn. It's been a long day, and I just want to go home. Please?"

I would love to blame tequila for the stupid decision I'm about to make, but I haven't touched the stuff since that faithful night. I'm honestly unsure if I made the decision myself; my body just reacted. The look on Amaya's face was one I'd never seen her make before; there was a quiet plea behind her heavy eyes rimmed with exhaustion. There is no obligation to do anything she says; I don't owe her any favors, but something about Amaya's plea wraps around my heart and doesn't let go. I slowly nod before changing the gear in my car to reverse and following the GPS.

⚹ ⚹ ⚹

I've taken these roads plenty of times, like Amaya said, her place is on the way to mine, yet this car ride feels eternal. Every streetlight takes forever to turn green, every second stretching out longer than it should. The engine hums low, the windows are shut, and just the faint whir of the a/c and the occasional click of the turn signal, loud in the quiet. I internally voted against turning on the radio. I can feel the tension vibrating in the space between us, like a string pulled too tight, ready to snap. I don't glance over; I'm sure there's a scowl on her face. Ms. Perfect has probably been judging my driving this whole car ride and is ready to give me an imaginary one-star rating once I drop her off.

When the GPS states that we reached our destination, I pull up to Amaya's driveway.

Of course, she has a ridiculously gorgeous house that is too big just for one person to occupy. I wouldn't expect less.

The car settles into park with a soft thud, but the silence doesn't go anywhere. It thickens. We both sit there, hands still, eyes forward, looking anywhere but each other. Amaya doesn't reach for the door. No one says goodbye. I think we're both waiting for the other to move first. To crack. To say something kind or cruel, just *something*. But we don't.

After what feels like an eternity, Amaya speaks, "Do you want to come inside?"

"You're inviting me into your home. Did you get checked out by medical after the fight tonight?"

"Yes, you asshole. Concussion-free. God forbid a woman decides to give you a place to hang out while your best friend is banging her douche boyfriend."

"How do you know Ethan is a douche? You haven't even met the guy."

"It was a guess, and your reaction just now confirmed it." Amaya raised her eyebrow.

She got me there.

"If I agree to go inside, will you stop trying to trick confessions out of me?"

"Of course. The wine that we'll drink will do that for me. Unless you want tequila instead?"

I gag at the thought of tequila touching my lips, and Amaya winks. I remove the key from the ignition and immediately regret my decision. Amaya unlocks her front door, and holy shit, I know she was well off, but her house is incredible.

The front doors, massive, double mahogany slabs, open to a two-story foyer with beautiful marble floors. The main living room is an open-concept expanse of high ceilings, and in the center is a perfectly white, plush sectional sofa.

Has she ever used this couch before? How has she kept it so white?

There is a fireplace surrounded by vintage wrestling memorabilia, wristbands, ticket stubs, and even a cracked chair from an EWC Dominance Day match in the '90s. Floor-to-ceiling windows give way to a panoramic view of a lagoon-style pool and private dock on the waterway.

This bitch has a boat. I need to have words later this week about my contract with Scarlett.

Amaya dumps her duffel bag in the living room as we move to the kitchen. It gleams like a showroom: quartzite counters, top-of-the-line kitchen appliances that are perfectly clean. I look towards my right, and there's a well-stocked walk-in wine cellar.

"Would you like a tour?" Amaya asks before disappearing inside the cellar.

"You don't have to do that," I say sheepishly

She emerges from the cellar with two bottles in hand.

How long does she expect me to stay here? As soon as Mariana sends me the all clear, I'm heading out.

"The look on your face is priceless, and I haven't even shown you the best part of the house yet."

"So it's not about wanting to give me a tour, you want to brag. Just say that."

"Okay, you caught me, I want to brag. Elevator or stairs?"

I freeze, my mouth gaping at the choices she just threw at me.

Amaya bursts into a fit of laughter, "I'm fucking with you. Come on, Silver."

We make our way up her grand staircase; the walls of her hallway upstairs are covered with framed photos, some of the family in the ring, others with A-list friends from crossover fame: rappers, influencers, movie stars. One picture in particular caught my attention, and my eyes feel like they're about to pop out of their sockets.

"No fucking way! This picture isn't real."

"It is, permission to brag or?" Amaya smirks.

"You have a picture with the cast of fucking *Twilight*. Yeah, you get bragging rights bitch."

"Didn't realize you were a fan."

"Any girl who grew up in the early 2000s is a fan. Let me guess, you're Team Jacob." I scrunch my nose in disgust.

She gasps, "I'm offended. Team Edward all day. Bella was smart and was thinking of the long game. She wanted to live forever, have money, and get cool powers."

Okay, point to Amaya for having good taste in supernatural creatures.

Amaya's master suite occupies nearly half the second floor: burgundy velvet walls with gold molding, a king-sized canopy bed, and right across from it, a huge gold antique mirror.

Ramona, do not go there. The mirror right across from the bed is just to check her outfit before she goes out. Get your head out of the gutter.

Off to the side of the room was a sitting area, a walk-in closet with thousands of designer labels, but my favorite part of her room was her bathroom. Amaya's bathroom rivals a spa, with backlit onyx counters, a rain shower the size of Mariana and I's apartment, and a tub with a retractable TV.

What I wouldn't give to soak in that bathtub right now. I wonder how many people have been in that tub with Amaya. There's room for two, even more.

"The other rooms are guest rooms, and then there's a movie room and a home gym that doubles as a training room, complete with a wrestling ring, cameras, and lighting rigs for when I have to post on my socials."

"You are never invited over to my place." I shake my head.

"Trust me, I know this house is over the top. I didn't pick it out; my parents insisted I take it as a gift."

To think, all I got as a gift from my family was being placed in the foster system.

"It might've been a gift, but you've definitely made it your own. The vibe is *very* Amaya."

"Oh, yeah? Please, describe what the hell that means."

Fuck, what the hell does that mean? The only word coming to mind is that the house is beautiful, and I'm not going to tell Amaya how beautiful she is. No matter how true it is.

Amaya chuckles, "I've known you for years, and you have never been speechless or flustered around me. Are you still worried about what happened at the club?"

"Oh, no. I am not drunk enough to have this conversation." I grab my phone from my back pocket, hoping Mariana messaged me.

"I'm working on it." Amaya pops the cork off the first bottle of red wine and pours it into our glasses.

"Red for Red. Fitting." I smirk as we clink our glasses.

* * *

Mariana messaged me hours ago that it was safe to come home. I could've left the moment the message showed on my screen, yet I didn't. Amaya and I are now three bottles deep in wine, and we haven't fought once. If a stranger saw us, they would think we were old friends catching up. After bottle number two, Amaya suggested we take a dip in her hot tub and handed me one of her suits.

"Amaya, the bathing suit you gave me leaves nothing to the imagination." I came out with a towel wrapped around me.

Don't get me wrong, I would consider myself a confident woman. My body is sculpted by Eddie after all, and Amaya has literally seen my ass before, but something about being in this bathing suit around her is making me feel vulnerable.

"Exactly how I like my bathing suits. Come on, the water feels so nice." Amaya's whole body is covered in bubbles from the jets.

With a deep sigh, I place the towel on the closest chair. I jump as Amaya starts to howl.

"Hot damn," she mutters.

She puckers her lips and lets out a loud, theatrical whistle.

"Awooooo! Somebody call the fire department, 'cause this jacuzzi is about to get so hot my skin's gonna melt right off."

"Can you stop! You're so embarrassing."

Amaya fans herself with her hand like she's about to faint. "I'm sorry, I'll have better manners. Wouldn't want our audience to see your embarrassment." She gestures to her empty backyard.

I roll my eyes, trying to ignore her and bask in the glorious heat of the water. My eyes close as my muscles automatically relax.

"Sorry if I made you uncomfortable just now. I was just having some fun." Amaya whispers.

"Since when do you care about my feelings?" I question.

"Since we're actually having a good time hanging out together. At least I am, anyway."

Crap. Way to be an asshole, Ravyn.

"Sorry. I'm having fun too. You didn't make me feel uncomfortable at all. Mariana has said much worse and in public."

I can't help but chuckle at the memory of her cat calling me in the middle of downtown after a drunken night out, and everyone started to join in. I'm not the biggest fan of being the center of attention, which I know is shocking because of what I do for a living. It's why I have Ravyn; she is my alter ego, and I keep her in the ring as much as I can. I never want my worlds to feel blurred, even if Ramona's backstory is ass.

"You keep saying that you and Mariana are just friends, but she's giving 'I'm secretly in love with my best friend' energy, trust me, I would know."

Amaya rises from the hot tub, steam swirling in the cool night air as she slowly rises from the water. My eyes trail her body from head to toe, and holy shit, she wasn't lying about her bathing suits. Her red hair is damp and clinging to her neck. Beads of moisture cling to her flushed skin, glistening in the soft glow of string lights above. She grabs her glass of wine, taking a long sip that allows me to admire how her bathing suit hugs her form with effortless confidence. The black top's two triangles barely cover her breasts, while the strings of her bottom are loosely tied. One wrong move and the bathing suit would be in jeopardy of becoming completely undone.

She brings both our glasses over to the edge of the hot tub, setting them within easy reach on the ledge. As she slips back into the steaming water, she doesn't return to her original spot across from me. Instead, she settles beside me, her bare shoulder brushing lightly against mine, and her thigh now against mine under the water. Our closeness sends a quiet thrill through my body.

You're just tipsy; your whole body is buzzing because of the alcohol, not because of Amaya.

"Is that how you knew you liked girls? Fell in love with your best friend?" I question in a desperate attempt to push my feelings to the side.

"There wasn't an exact 'aha moment' for me, no fireworks, no sudden epiphany. It was quiet, gradual. Growing up, I found myself attracted to animated women like Meg from *Hercules* or Shego from *Kim Possible,* but I brushed those off cause I also found Scar from *The Lion King* hot, so obviously those feelings aren't valid. Honestly, Disney has some explaining to do, but I digress."

Amaya takes another large gulp of her drink before continuing, "It wasn't until my early twenties that I realized that I'd always noticed women, admired them in ways I brushed off as aesthetic, innocent, 'She's just pretty,' I'd tell myself."

That is a valid reason.

"Did you talk to your parents at all about it?" I ask.

I couldn't imagine Mr.Acosta would take something like this well, but people can surprise you.

"I'm not a real talker when it comes to my parents. Don't get me wrong, I love them and we're a close family, but we've never been a family to really talk about our feelings, let alone our sexuality. We're a Hispanic cliché. My dad is super machismo, and my mom is a firecracker, but talking about sexuality? Never that. Aiden and I never received the sex talk other than the standard 'don't get a girl pregnant' for Aiden and a 'don't get pregnant' for me."

"I mean, you do have a family legacy to think of." I chuckle, and Amaya scoffs.

"It's like you were in the room," she said.

I've given so much shit to Amaya for being a part of the Acosta family dynasty, yet I've never given it much thought on the pressures that would put on her shoulders.

"The first time I kissed a girl, it was odd. Not a bad odd, there was no confusion, no hesitation, just this overwhelming sense of *oh... so this is what it feels like, why was I so scared?* It wasn't about replacing anything I felt for men. It was about expanding, opening myself to receive more love. It's about *wholeness.* About letting myself be fully drawn to an individual, no matter what their gender is. I'm open to *them,* their presence, their voice, their laugh, the way they see the world."

"Was that the best friend?" I ask.

"Oh yeah. Let's just say we both had different experiences of that night, and it ended in us no longer being friends."

"I'm sorry." I apologize.

I'm not sure why I feel like I have to apologize. My brain is replaying losing my childhood friend over our own curiosity.

"No need to be sorry when I'm not. Losing my best friend sucked, sure, but I found myself. It's a unique feeling, a sort of high that you realize you've spent so long denying a part of yourself, and then finally... finally letting it breathe."

Amaya sinks deeper into the water and sighs.

I find myself admiring the woman I swore to hate for the entirety of my life. She speaks with this raw, steady clarity, no shame, no performance. Just her truth. Watching her, I feel something stir in me that's equal parts awe and ache. Amaya is so sure of herself, like finding out who she is was the simplest thing in the world, which makes my chest tighten in a way I don't fully understand, or maybe I don't want to understand it. Ignorance is bliss.

Ravyn isn't a mystery to me. She is strong; she steps into the ring like she owns the damn place, because she does. Ravyn wears her tattoos like war paint, each one earned, not chosen lightly. She is raw power, grit, and has a look that says *try me.*

Ramona, on the other hand. She moves through life like a ghost and lives with an exhaustion that doesn't come from sleepless nights, but from carrying too much, too early. Ramona never stood a chance; she was born into chaos, with a mom who was too busy chasing highs instead of chasing her daughter at a playground. A mom who gave constant hollow apologies until one day she decided that strangers would treat Ramona better than she could. Ramona, raised by strangers who would never love her. She learned not to unpack, still waiting to feel rooted somewhere, to be *wanted* without the need to prove she's worth it. Love felt foreign until Levi and even he left.

"You okay?" Amaya asks.

I smile and nod, but inside… I'm spiraling.

God, how does she do that? How can she be fully herself when I have to split myself in two to keep myself from falling apart?

I look at Amaya again, confident grounded, like she's earned every piece of herself.

"Your silence is killing me. What are you thinking about Silver?"

Ravyn is unafraid, wanting to tell her everything… but Ramona. She's scared, and it takes every ounce of courage she has to whisper, "What if it changes things?"

18

Amaya

Did I hear her right? I can't be sure due to the amount of wine we've both consumed.

We really need to hang out without alcohol being involved.

"What would change?" I ask.

Ravyn scoffs, "Everything would change."

I don't say a word. Ravyn's eyes are distant, her mind is racing, and I can tell she's calculating how much to let me in, if she even wants to at all. Not knowing is killing me. I need to understand what's going on in her head. I *have* to, and I fucking hate how much I've grown to care for a woman who hates my guts. Let me rephrase that: a woman who *claims* to hate my guts.

Ravyn can blame the tequila for her 'mistakes' all she wants, but I'm not convinced that excuse will only go so far with me. I'm surprised by how much of myself I see in her. It's unsettling, honestly, because I don't know anything about her past or what shaped her. I find myself wanting to know, especially about Levi. I hate to admit how much he's been on my mind, the curiosity of him slowly eating at me. Mariana called him Ravyn's epic love, and I want to know what made it so epic.

"Can I be honest with you?" The words escape me before I can stop them, tumbling out in a rush of nerves and impulse.

Ravyn tilts her head, one brow arched in mild amusement. "Have you not been?"

A crooked smile creeps onto my face. "You caught me," I said, my voice laced with mock defeat.

She sighs and rolls her eyes, but with a flick of her hand, she gestures for me to go on.

"It's like... I'm a fish in an aquarium that everyone gets to see because being an Acosta means nothing about me stays private. But you, Silver? You're a complete mystery. It's unfair and cruel how I know nothing about you."

Ravyn's lips twitch into a faint smile. "That's not exactly true. You know my real name is Ramona." She points her finger at me as if she's bursting my bubble.

I lunge forward and playfully snap my teeth near her hand. "Alert the media, breaking news! I know your name," I said, rolling my eyes dramatically.

"You joke, but it actually *is* breaking news. No one else knows that. You won't find it anywhere online."

"Okay... enlighten me. Why is Ramona erased from the world?"

There's that look again, a mixture of pain, uncertainty, and vulnerability. I've seen plenty of versions of Ravyn over the years, a majority of them being the hateful and vengeful version, and yet... right here, right now, she's never looked more beautiful.

Amaya, stop. You cannot fall for this girl. Pretty or not, she's not just your rival, she's your coworker. You've set rules.

After a deep breath, Ravyn closes her eyes. Refusing to look at me as she spoke, "Ramona's story can't exist in the same world as Ravyn's. No one would respect a heel if they found out that her mom was a druggie who lied to her for her entire life and then dumped her onto the streets, forcing her to grow up in the foster system. How could anyone fear a poor little orphan girl?"

And just like that, my heart crumbles into tiny little pieces. A range of emotions flows through me. Rage for her piece of shit mother leaving her. Embarrassment for complaining about my family when hers let her down. Heartbroken for her, feeling like she needs to hide this part of herself to make it in the wrestling world.

Ravyn's hazel eyes flutter open; they shimmer in the moonlight with her unshed tears. She's still refusing to make eye contact, looking up into the night sky. Her full lips begin to tremble as she struggles to keep her emotions from spilling out. I want to tell her she's safe with me, that she can let out her feelings and trust me with the weight of her truth. But then I think about all the times she's likely heard those same promises, spoken with good intentions, yet broken just as easily. Would she believe me? I doubt it, especially since I haven't done anything in these past years to earn her trust. I vow to change that, to be someone she can turn to because this hating each other is bullshit, and let's face it, we can both use a friend. As I open my mouth to tell her, a single tear escapes, slowly trickling down her cheek. My arm flinches, wanting to reach over and wipe it away.

She brushes away her tears, and her eyes finally meet mine. "That look right there," she said quietly. "That's what I have to avoid when I'm in the ring. I'm damn good at playing the villain, I *like* it. But if the EWC crowd ever knew the truth about me, I'll be their poster child for what a kid in the foster system can become."

I can't bring myself to argue with her because she's right. Val loves to take people's backgrounds and use them for their character storylines. She once tried to have me speak Spanish on air, and I had to beg her not to and embarrassingly explain to her what a No Sabo kid is.

"Well, villains usually do have a tragic backstory. You have Magneto, A Holocaust survivor whose trauma and loss led him to believe that mutants must dominate humans to survive. Then there's Killmonger, who grew up fatherless and abandoned by Wakanda, driven by vengeance and a vision for justice through domination."

The side of Ravyn's lips starts to lift, a ghost of a smile starting to appear, and just like that, my new mission of the night is to make her smile.

I continue my list, "I didn't forget about the ladies. In my opinion, women villains are the best. You have Maleficent, betrayed by someone she loved and trusted, which leads her to bitterness and vengeance. Azula, a child prodigy molded by a cruel, power-hungry father and an emotionally neglected mother. Her fear of being unloved and abandoned slowly unravels her mental health. Last but not least, my favorite, Dr. Harleen Quinzel, aka Harley Quinn, a psychiatrist at Arkham Asylum who fell in love with the Joker, a man who manipulated and emotionally abused her so much that she descended into madness and crime, losing her identity in the process."

Ravyn's face is now lit up with a full-blown smile, the shimmer of lingering tears completely gone from her eyes.

Mission accomplished.

"Why is she your favorite?" Ravyn asks.

"Well, she's smart, I mean, she is a doctor after all."

"I think that is should be a *was*. I would think that *Gotham City* would revoke her license after she started to pursue a life of crime."

"Fuck that. If I spent twelve years becoming a psychiatrist, I'm a psychiatrist for life."

A laugh erupts from Ravyn, and it's music to my ears.

"I also love her because even though she's smart and totally should've known better, she still fell for Joker," I said, nudging her knee lightly with mine, a teasing smile tugging at my lips. "It just proves that even the brightest girls can get swept up in the wrong kind of love."

My mind drifts back to her and Levi; they must've been the wrong kind of love if it ended, right?

I let my gaze linger a second longer than necessary. "And come on, she's a total badass in a fight. Plus, major points for finally dumping that clown and hooking up with the hot earth goddess Poison Ivy."

Ravyn tilts her head, a curious glint in her eyes. "I'm not that caught up on my *DC Universe* knowledge. How did that happen?"

"Long story short… they started as friends," I pause for effect, "and then it blossomed into more."

She catches the pun instantly and rolls her eyes with a laugh. "I see what you did there. Amaya Acosta is punny, who would've thought that you would like the lowest form of comedy?"

I pretend to be wounded, placing a hand dramatically over my heart. "I'm deeply offended. Puns are sexy. You just have to say them with confidence."

Ravyn looks me up and down, "You have plenty of that to go around."

I scoff, "Coming from the woman who had enough confidence to kiss me."

Ravyn opens her mouth to speak, but I immediately cut her off, "I don't want to hear that bullshit excuse of yours either. 'That wasn't confidence, that was tequila.' Your deflection won't work here."

My heart pounds in my chest, and I'm not even sure I'm breathing at this point. The air is starting to thicken, and the silence is broken by the sound of Ravyn's heart pulsing louder and her body tensing. I'm doing everything I can to stay patient, silently willing Ravyn to say something, to explain why she kissed me that night. I *need* to hear her say it. That night keeps looping in my mind like a scene I can't escape. Her lips have been haunting me ever since. I've tried to scrub my mind raw, night after night, but the warmth of her kiss and the taste of her still cling to me like a secret I can't wash away, no matter how many times I've tried. Yet, here I am weeks later, and her taste still lingers. Sweet and heady, like wine on the tongue, forbidden fruit. I don't know how to explain it, but that kiss felt different; it didn't feel like it was just a kiss, it was a confession, a revelation.

I jump, becoming startled when Ravyn springs up from the hot tub, water cascading down the curves of her body. Her tan skin flushed from the heat, or maybe from the tension that's been building. She heads towards the stairs, refusing to look back as she reaches for the railing to maintain her balance.

My breathing picks up. I don't want her to leave. How can I stop her? I reached out, fingers wrapping gently but firmly around her arm. Her skin is slick and warm beneath my touch, her muscles tensing like she's ready to run. Ravyn's eyes are fixed on anything but me, the sky, the water.

"Why won't you just talk to me?" I ask, pulling her back just enough so she has to face me.

"I just told you things about me that I haven't told anyone. I think I've spoken enough."

"That's not what I mean, and you know it." My thumb caresses her wrist, and I feel her body begin to relax.

I'm not sure when it happened, but our faces were close now, closer than they'd been all night. As close as they were that night, the night Ravyn refuses to acknowledge, and I can never forget. Drops of water clung to her jaw, sliding down to her collarbone, and I find myself having the sudden urge to follow their path with my mouth. Her eyes flick to mine, then to my lips, and I can feel the air between us shift.

"It's not fair to you," Ravyn whispers.

"What's not fair?" I question.

"What I did to you wasn't fair."

"You didn't do anything to me that I didn't reciprocate. Didn't do anything to me that I don't want to do again."

Did I just say that? Did I just confess to Ravyn that I want to kiss her again?

Ravyn doesn't move. She just stares at me, eyes unreadable, and for the first time in a long time, I have no fucking idea what the hell I'm supposed to do.

You can kiss her. You can grab her from the nape of her neck and let your fingers get tangled in her wet hair and get lost in her lips.

I want to do it, yet I can't. I've always been the one in control of the situation, of my feelings, of the outcome. Whether it was a random dating app hookup or the start of something deeper, I played the game on my terms. I made the first move, the second, and usually the last.

But this? This doesn't feel like a game, at least not one that I've played before.

With Ravyn, the rules don't seem to apply. She's not just a random person I swiped right on an app. I'm standing here, exposed and waiting, but I refuse to pressure her.

Ravyn cleared her throat, "I've never…"

A strand of her hair covers her face, and I don't hesitate this time. I reach over to tuck it behind her ear, my eyes flicking between her lips and her eyes. Ravyn smiles, soft, nervous, like maybe she's thinking the same thing I am, and I'm hoping I'm right because that smile feels like permission, and so I go for it. Unlike our kiss in the club, I lean in, slow, hesitant, giving her an out if she wanted one, but she doesn't move. Finally, her lips met mine, the kiss so light it barely touched skin. This girl is barely touching me, and yet I'm the most aroused I've ever been.

Her hands tremble as they hover, unsure of where to go, of what to do next. I have an internal battle on whether I should take the lead, but I decide against it, not wanting to push her into anything she doesn't want to do. Ravyn deepens the kiss, still gentle, still tender, and it seems as though she's forgotten about her nerves. It becomes clear that her nerves are something of the past when her hands make their way to the small of my back and gently grip my hips. Heat begins to build at the bottom of my stomach as Ravyn's right hand palms my ass cheek. The restraint that I was practicing snaps, and my body takes over. I guide Ravyn to sit back down in the water, our lips never breaking contact as I straddle her. Our breathing becomes heavy as I slowly grind on her, and soft moans come out of both of our lips. Her hands travel up my back, fingers lingering on the strings of my bathing suit top. I can feel her hesitation. I bite on her lower lip before breaking our kiss, loving how swollen her lips look.

"It's okay," I whisper as I grab her hands, instructing her to untie my top.

We undo the bottom ties together, but my hands don't follow hers as she reaches for the top strings and pulls. Our eyes follow my top as it floats away with the bubbles. Ravyn's eyes explore my chest in a way that makes me feel like a work of art, and I so desperately want to tell her it's okay to touch. She grabs my chin and lunges forward, attacking my mouth with a ravenous hunger; the nervous woman who previously stood before me is now gone. Ravyn answers my mental pleas and palms my breast, pinching my nipples in an intoxicating way, and I swear they've never been this hard before in my life. She surprises me by removing her lips from mine and placing them on my neck. Ravyn licks, bites, and sucks on my neck so beautifully that I feel like I'm on ecstasy, and when I think it couldn't get any better, her mouth explores my chest. My hands find their way to her hair, gently tugging to let her know what she's doing feels amazing. Her teeth graze my nipple, and I can't help but curse.

"Fuck, Silver." I moan.

She lifts her head, a worried expression on her face, "Did I hurt you?"

"No, God no. Keep going." I beg.

Ravyn smirks and gets back to work. I close my eyes, tilting my head back to give her better access. She takes her time, giving each tit the attention it deserves. I'm honestly surprised she's never done this before; she's a natural. I make a mental note to tell her that when we're finished.

I don't know where this is going, but I'm more than happy to go along for the ride. Right now, I'm lost in the moment, fully aware I'm being a selfish lover, but damn, it feels too good to stop. Still, the craving is growing, and it's time I return the favor. Ravyn deserves to feel just as good as she's making me feel.

I gently pull on Ravyn's hair, directing her away from my chest. My lips envelop hers before she could dare ask if she was doing anything wrong, and my hand slowly made its way down her body. My fingertips brushed the top of her swimsuit bottoms, waiting for any sign that she might change her mind, that this might be going too far for her, but instead, I was met with a moan from Ravyn, and so I slipped my fingers under her bathing suit bottoms.

I'll be honest, lately, I've found myself thinking about Ravyn's body more than I expected, but I didn't anticipate her being the kind of girl with a landing strip. It's a pleasant surprise, and I follow it straight to where my fingers want to be. Ravyn gasps as I place my thumb on her clit, making circular motions that are causing her thighs to shake. I take my time, teasing her, and while my finger works her clit I use my other hand to play with her nipples, which to my amazement were pierced.

It's moments like these that make me really appreciate being a woman. If I were a man, I'd have finished before I even made it inside of her.

"More," Ravyn whimpers, and I am happy to oblige.

I keep my thumb circling her clit as my middle finger makes its way between her folds. Ravyn's head rolls back, her eyes closing as she moans. I use this opportunity to finally use my mouth to kiss away those drops of water from earlier. One of Ravyn's hands is on my waist while the other is gripping my thigh as I insert another finger.

"Oh my God, Amaya," Ravyn whispers.

I want to tell her it's alright to let go, to scream if she needs to, she can be as loud as she wants. Part of me wants to hear her shout my name, not murmur it, and part of me senses she's holding back, wanting to release but unsure. I want her to know she can lose herself in this, that it's safe to be with me this way. I can feel she's on the edge with every shift of our bodies pressed together.

My lips trailed up her neck. I nipped her earlobe before whispering, "Let go," and just like that, Ravyn trembles in my hands. She's coming apart, and I've never seen anything more beautiful.

We sit in silence, breathless, the moment hanging heavy between us.

Did that really just happen?

"Amaya, there you are," Reina's voice calls from inside the house.

I instantly regret ever giving her a key.

Before I can gather myself, Ravyn shoves me off her lap, hard. I would've moved if she'd just given me a second, but the sudden force catches me off guard. I plunge beneath the water, and the warmth of it suddenly feels ice cold as my heart fills with rejection.

I try to retrieve whatever is left of my dignity from the bottom of the hot tub before resurfacing. Reina stands nearby, casually chatting with Ravyn, who's currently pretending I don't exist.

I just had my fingers inside you and gave you an earth-shattering orgasm. Don't I deserve some eye contact after that?

Reina, on the other hand, throws me a quick side-eye and a smirk, barely missing a beat in her conversation about who knows what.

My ears ring with humiliation, loud enough to drown out their voices. That mortification only deepens when I realize why Reina is smirking: I'm still topless. Hastily, I snatch up my bikini top and fumble to retie it.

Just as I'm securing the last knot, Ravyn steps out of the water.

"Thanks for having me over, Amaya. I'm heading out. Mariana just texted the all-clear. See you soon, Reina."

She wraps herself in a towel and disappears into the house without so much as a glance in my direction.

"Bitch." Reina's eyes widen as she looks at me.

"I don't want to talk about it." I sink back into the water, wishing that I could just drown in it.

"Oh, come on. You're no fun." Reina pouts.

"Why are you here, Reina? That key is for emergencies only. Is someone dying?"

Other than me, of humiliation and rejection.

"Oh, shit. Yeah, it's your dad. He's in the hospital. We tried calling you, but you weren't answering."

I jolt out of the water and sprint towards my phone, my pruney fingers making it impossible to tap the screen. Missed calls from Mom, Reina, Aiden… even Sid. Guilt hits fast and hard, burning at my chest. I didn't answer. I'd been too caught up, too distracted by a woman who can't stand to be seen with me the moment someone else is around.

"What happened?"

"I don't know much," Reina shrugs. "Your mom's a wreck. She just told me to get you there as fast as I could."

My stomach drops. I know I give Dad a lot of crap for being overbearing, for the constant pressure he puts on Aiden and me, but the thought of him lying motionless in a hospital bed, surrounded by machines… I've never seen him vulnerable. Never seen him anything less than invincible, and poor mom.

"I'm going to change." I scramble towards the door.

"I brought the motorcycle," Reina shouts.

That's when I finally notice Reina's helmet in her hands.

"You know I can't ride that death trap. My keys are on the counter, go start my car."

Ever since one of Dad's best friends and tag team partners, Max Havoc, died in a motorcycle accident, I promised him that I would never sit my ass in one. He keeps trying to tell Reina to sell hers, but she never listens.

"I don't know why you even own a car if you refuse to drive it."

"Reina, just shut up, I don't have time for this shit right now."

She's right, though. I never drive. Passenger princess for life.

I throw on a pair of leggings and a graphic tee, trying to make my hair look like a woman's fingers haven't just gone through it in the throes of passion, and rush to the garage.

Whatever mess I've got going on with Ravyn has to wait. Dad's in the hospital, broken, maybe worse. And no matter what I'm feeling, I have to lock it down, bury it deep. Right now, I have to show up. Because before anything else, I'm an Acosta.

19

Ravyn

It's been a week since I lost myself in Amaya's hot tub, and I still don't know how we ended up there, wrapped in silence, in heat, in each other. Maybe it started with the way our glances lingered too long. Maybe it was the way the silence between us carried more weight than words ever could. But there *were* words. I told Amaya things I hadn't told anyone, and I'm still unsure why. Maybe because she told me things too, unfiltered, honest, she showed me her whole self, and for once, I wanted to show mine.

Not the version I offer the outside world, but the real me that only Mariana and Levi have seen.

And Levi, he won't stop messaging me. I keep hovering over his name, tempted to answer. Maybe he's what I need. But how do I go back to him after what happened with Amaya? After that night, that felt like an out-of-body experience in the best way possible.

There are too many questions crowding my mind:

Is this *safe*?

Is this *real*?

Can I *want* this out loud?

I keep replaying the way Amaya's curves felt in my hands, the dip of her hips, the soft give of her skin, the fullness of her breasts. Our bodies just *fit*, like instinct took over. She let me lead, and I did, gladly. I welcomed the heat rising in my chest, the sensation of her fingers threading through my hair, the soft, involuntary sound she made when my lips grazed her neck. In that hot tub, the world narrowed. All my fears, the noise, and the versions of myself I've worn for everyone else melted away, completely dissolved into the water.

With Amaya, it wasn't just skin against skin. It was heartbeat syncing with heartbeat, and the quiet awe of realizing I didn't have to pretend.

I text Eddie, telling him it's urgent. He replies instantly, he'll be at my hotel room in twenty minutes, and I breathe a sigh of relief. I believe what I told him, that I've gone through my "figure-it-out" phase when it comes to my sexuality. But after Amaya, I'm not so sure.

Why is this coming back now? Is it just her? Amaya, with her unapologetic presence and confidence. I've always been intimidated by her. Jealous of her, even. Of her ease, her family, her freedom. So why *now*, why *her*? Why am I feeling this magnetic pull?

I haven't said anything to Mariana. She'll go full therapist on me, and I can't handle that. But she knows something's off; she always does. That night I came home, I ran straight to my room, mumbling about a stomach ache. Since then, I've been traveling for work, keeping our calls short. She's already threatening to book a flight.

Every night, I wake up in a sweat. My dreams are filled with Amaya or Levi. Once, it was the three of us, and I'm not proud of it, but let's just say my battery-operated companion saw a lot of action.

A soft knock saves me from going down that rabbit hole again. I swing open the door, and I'm greeted by a wet mop of blond hair and Eddie's hands full of every type of junk food imaginable.

"I expected a healthier choice from a trainer," I said, clicking my teeth in disapproval.

"Did I misread the situation? I figured chocolate was essential for this conversation," Eddie said, gesturing to the pile of snacks. "I can head back down to the lobby and return everything, though you'd be shocked at how much this costs."

He turns as if to leave, but I stop him.

"Get inside and hand me a damn chocolate bar." I roll my eyes, tearing open the wrapper.

I spill everything to Eddie, every last detail. The poor guy's inhaling sweets as he listens, and I can already tell he'll be hitting the gym hard tomorrow to make up for it.

Once I finish my whole story, Eddie lets out a long sigh. "Shit, Ravyn."

I groan, tossing myself face-first into the pillow. "So, you get why I'm stuck here, right?"

"You're not seriously thinking of replying to Levi, are you?" Eddie questions.

"You said this was a judgment-free zone, but your face and tone right now are screaming judgment."

"I'm sorry, but I really think it's a mistake if you do," Eddie said, his voice tight with concern, his brow furrowing.

"I have to hear him out." I shift, avoiding his gaze as I play with the ends of my pillow cover, feeling the cool cotton beneath my fingertips.

"Why? For closure?" Eddie's words hit hard, his eyes narrowing like he's searching for some truth I'm not ready to give.

"Exactly." I let out a shaky breath, my words feeling too small in the heavy air between us. Closure, that's the excuse, the justification. But I know deep down that excuse is bullshit, Eddie knows it too.

"Closure? Ravyn, it's been years since he just left you hanging." Eddie's voice cracks slightly as he leans forward, frustration creeping into his tone. "You're running to Levi because he's *familiar,* he's *safe.* What you're feeling for Amaya is new and confusing, but I can tell it's real by how you talk about it, Ravyn. You can't keep pretending they don't exist."

"I'm acknowledging them; if I weren't, you wouldn't be here right now. I just don't think that it's worth the risk to explore those feelings."

"Oh, so instead, you're just going to retreat into Levi. Levi, who thinks he can just come back into town like nothing ever happened. He's done playing 'city boy' and now he's back, expecting you to pretend like you weren't left behind, like he didn't walk away and leave you *shattered.*"

His words hang in the air, harsh and raw. My throat tightens, and I look away, the weight of his truth pressing against my chest.

"He left Ramona shattered, not Ravyn." I correct.

"Stop pretending you're two separate people to protect yourself. You are Ramona, and Ravyn is just an extension of you."

"The point is, I'm a different person now, stronger. I'm not going to jump into a relationship with the man. I just—"

I met Eddie's gaze; his eyes are full of concern, and I can't help but feel an overwhelming sense of gratitude. I think back to the days when I had no one in my corner, when it felt like I was alone in this world. Now, I have Eddie and Mariana by my side. Sure, my family isn't what you'd call "conventional," but it's mine—and the best part? I got to choose them, and they chose me right back.

"Eddie, there's something I need to tell you. It's part of the reason why it's hard to let Levi go."

My fingers fidget with the hem of my sleeve, and it feels like the words might burn my tongue.

"I grew up in foster care. I've never talked about it because I didn't want anyone to look at me like I was… different. Or broken."

I tell Eddie my truth, Ramona's story, and just like that, he's added to the list of people who know my secret.

I never thought Amaya would be on that list.

"So you see why I need to hear him out? Levi was once a constant, woven into my life; I couldn't imagine living without him. We were entwined in everything: the inside jokes, the late-night conversations that stretched into the early hours, the way his voice could calm me with just a few words. Levi and Mariana were the two people in my life I could turn to when I needed comfort, the ones who knew me better than I knew myself, and the people who felt like the home I never had."

I try to catch my breath, stopping myself from the tears that are threatening to come out. "When he walked away… No explanation, no closure, just gone. He chose a job over me, but now he's back, and I know I sound so weak, but he's knocking at the door of my life, and I need to answer."

Levi's face flashes through my mind, that night in the bar still vivid. His smile, the same one that used to light up everything around us, and his eyes, those eyes that still hold the warmth that used to make me feel like I mattered, like I was seen.

"I understand that, Ravyn, but the person who was standing in front of you is now a stranger. Just like you've changed, so has he. He once held your heart, and he decided to walk away with it. You're a sister to me, so I will always look out for *you.* Men have a way of coming into your life when it's going well and fucking shit up. Trust me, I know. I just don't want you to give in to the temptation to let him back in, and then he breaks you all over again."

I can't help but feel the pull Eddie is talking about, the temptation to let Levi back in. Part of me wants to believe that time has healed the wounds, that he and I can be fixed with a few conversations, a few apologies. Levi was my friend long before we ever fell in love, and right now, it's not about rekindling that spark; it's about getting my friend back. Eddie is right, I have to be cautious. Just because Levi's back doesn't mean he's staying. He changed his mind once before, so what's to say he won't walk away again, this time for good?

* * *

"Has anyone seen Amaya?" I ask, stopping the hundredth person I've passed backstage.

Same answer every time, a shake of the head, a shrug, no one has seen her today.

I knew I'd have to talk to her eventually. We haven't spoken since the jacuzzi incident, and since then, she's gone off the grid. I've tried reaching out. After that night, I finally checked behind the picture she'd nagged me about. It was her number with a note: *Text me when you're tired of pretending to hate me.*

I stared at it for a long time before texting her. I kept it short. *Don't hold your breath.*

No reply.

So I did what any self-respecting, spiraling idiot would do: I double-texted. Let her know it was me, just in case she thought some rando had gotten her number.

Still nothing.

I've already scoured catering. She wasn't there. The production team is still locked in their meeting, meaning I can't check the run sheet to see if she's scheduled today.

And yet, despite all of this, I can't shake the restlessness crawling under my skin. I don't know why it matters so much, why *she* matters so much. I should feel a sense of relief. No, Amaya means no awkward confrontation. No emotionally messy back-and-forth. I've dealt with enough emotions this past week to last me a lifetime.

But instead, I feel this gnawing anxiety. Is she avoiding me?

I push open the locker room door, telling myself not to get my hopes up. She's not here.

Just Tashi. She's lacing up one of her boots; her gear gleams under the fluorescent lights. Tight black spandex shorts with crimson trim hug her powerful legs, and a matching sports bra-style top shows off the defined cut of her shoulders and abs.

Her curly hair is slicked back into a high ponytail, and the eyeliner on her lids is so sharp and dramatic, just how I like to wear mine.

She looks up when I enter. "Hey," she greets me as she laces her other boot.

"Hey, have you seen Amaya?" I ask, trying to sound casual, like I haven't been searching for her all day.

"No. And even if I had, I wouldn't send you her way. Keep the brawling in the ring, you two."

If only she knew.

"We're good now," I said. "Well… amicable, at least. I just need to talk to her."

Tashi looks at me with one of her perfectly sculpted brows raised. "Maybe she's still in the hospital."

I blink. "Sorry, what? Hospital?"

The word hits like a punch to the chest. My heart drops straight into my stomach. Hospital? Something happened to Amaya? My mind instantly shifts into panic mode, thinking of ways to get out of today's match, if I have one, I need to get to her, make sure she's okay. All this time, I thought she was just ghosting me. Now it looks like she might be lying in a hospital bed.

"Oh, shit," Tashi said, eyes widening. "That came out wrong. Amaya is fine. It's her dad. He was admitted on the day of our match. Nobody knows what happened."

Fuck, is that why Reina showed up?

Relief floods through me, sharp and immediate. Amaya's okay, physically, at least. Just because she's safe doesn't mean she's not hurting. Her dad's in the hospital.

I know that pain of having a parent in the hospital all too well. Though... I have a feeling his reason for being there isn't the same as my mother's used to be.

"Run Sheet is out," someone screams from the hallway.

Please, please, please don't have me wrestling today so I can fly back and check on Amaya.

Tashi trails behind me, her footsteps light but steady, while mine are quick, trying to get to the sheet as fast as possible.

Shit.

Tashi's laugh sends a shiver of anticipation down my spine. "Oh, you're in trouble now, Ravyn," she smirks, her lips curling into a knowing grin.

I shoot her a glance, but I don't smile back. There's no way I can get out of this fight tonight. Not only am I fighting, but we're the main event. The crowd's going to be buzzing with excitement, ready to see us in the ring. Tashi is getting her revenge after I beat her to a pulp.

Of course, the one night I don't want to fight is the night I'm losing.

I let out a frustrated sigh. Tashi claps a hand on my back.

"I'll take it easy on you, chill."

"It's not that," I mutter. "I'm just worried about Amaya. I'm going to try calling her again."

"Hey, before you do. I've been meaning to ask. Would you wanna go out for drinks tonight? I feel like we got off on the wrong foot."

I don't have time for this, and I don't want to come off as rude. Been there, done that.

"Yeah, Tashi, I'll meet you at the hotel bar later tonight."

The phone is already pressed to my ear, ringing before I even finish my sentence. Amaya's voice filters through the speaker, but it's just her voicemail. Again.

I don't want to do this. Mostly because I don't want anyone to know how worried I really am, *especially* him. But I'm out of options.

The phone rings again. Once, twice… long enough that I brace for another voicemail.

Then, finally, "Hey, Ravyn. It's not really a good time right now."

I can hear the beeping of the hospital's machines on the other side of the phone. "I know Aiden, but I've been trying to get a hold of Amaya, and she hasn't responded to any of my texts or calls."

"Since when do you and my sister have any sort of contact outside the ring?" Aiden sounds as confused as I feel.

"Can I speak to her?"

There's no response as I hear whispers on the phone. Then the sound of a door opening and closing, some shuffling of feet, and then, finally, I get to hear her voice.

"Ravyn, what are you doing calling me?"

Amaya's voice trembles. I can feel her heavy exhaustion through the phone.

"I just wanted to check on you. You weren't answering any of my texts or calls."

"Did you ever stop to think that maybe it's for a reason? I don't want to talk to you."

Each word comes slowly, like it has to fight its way out, yet it feels like a punch to my gut. I've been worried sick about her, wondering how she's holding up with her dad in the hospital. And yet, she sounds like she gives two shits about me reaching out.

Then came a long silence. I didn't know what to say.

I'm in my head, rationalizing.

She's in distress. She doesn't mean it. She hasn't slept. She's overwhelmed.

But why am I working so hard to excuse her? Why can't I just believe what she's saying? She doesn't want to talk to me.

I was going to tell her we should take some space anyway. This, her pushing me away, should feel like a relief. It's what I told myself I wanted.

So why the hell does it feel like everything's falling apart just because she doesn't want to speak to me?

"I just—"

"Just what? Suddenly give a fuck about my family? Cut the bullshit, Silver. You hate me and my family. None of that has changed just because I made you come in a hot tub."

I flinch at her words. She's not wrong. The Acosta family has been nothing but a thorn in my side, especially Amaya. She's been in my way since day one, but that doesn't mean I want anything bad to happen to them. I'm not heartless. Yeah, I can be a bitch, but there's a line, and I know damn well I haven't crossed it.

"Whatever, Amaya. I hope your dad gets better. See you in the ring."

Moments like this make me wish flip phones were still around, because damn, I just wanna snap this thing shut. Slamming a smartphone just isn't the same, and all I'd get is a cracked screen. Instead, I just make my way over to my locker to toss the damn thing in there and try to focus on the match I have tonight with Tashi, but before I slam my locker shut, my phone screen lights up with a message.

Levi: *"I'm not sure if you'll see this message, but I'm here to watch you wrestle. I just want to talk to you, Ramona, please."*

Levi is here? He flew six hours to come see me. Where was that energy when I needed him to stay? I'm not sure if it's the anger I'm feeling towards Amaya or if the anger is bubbling up from our past, but I'm not impressed by him coming all this way. If anything, I'm pissed he's here and is going to see me lose in person.

Things with Amaya went to shit, but I did just tell Eddie how I wanted to talk to Levi. I swallow my anger and send a message back, just one word.

Me: *"Tomorrow."*

20

Ravyn

Tashi beat my ass. She chewed me up and spit me out, and the worst part? I didn't even care. A part of me was relieved to lose last night; my head wasn't in the game. I was too distracted, caught between the icy phone call with Amaya and the text from Levi. I was so out of it, I botched a move that could've easily earned me a hospital bracelet of my own.

The moment I got back to the hotel, I cranked the shower to its hottest setting and stood under the water, letting it burn away whatever was left of the hellish night I was having. Amaya never messaged me. The silence was so complete, it was like she'd never given me her number in the first place.

* * *

"Thanks for grabbing a drink with me. Honestly, I was terrified to ask."

Tashi sips on her martini, and it feels odd to see her in regular clothes. I'm so used to seeing her in wrestling gear or workout clothes that watching her now in a pair of jeans and a crop top feels like I'm in an alternate universe. Yeah, she's the enemy, but right now I find myself just looking at a girl who has the same dreams as the rest of us in the EWC, to make an impact on the wrestling world.

"I promise I'm not that scary outside of the ring. Even though I can be a little intense."

"A little?" Tashi arches her brow, and both of us laugh.

"I'm glad you asked me out for a drink. With the night I just had, this is hitting the spot."

"Oh, come on. I didn't beat you that badly. Only a little bruising." Tashi grabs my chin as she inspects the bruises on my face.

Well, she's touchy, isn't she?

"It's not the outside that hurts." I sigh, taking another sip and enjoying the burn of the liquor as it goes down my throat.

"Do you wanna talk about it?"

"Why is it that when it comes to wrestling, I find everything so simple? Yet, when it comes to relationships, I'm clueless."

"Ahhh, love. You know what Joan Crawford said." Tashi finishes her drink and asks for another.

"No, I don't. Please enlighten me."

"'Love is a fire. But whether it is going to warm your hearth or burn down your house, you can never tell.'"

* * *

I'm proud of myself for not waking up with a hangover. Instead, I woke up terrified about my meeting today with Levi. He hasn't stopped texting me since I agreed to meet. Even now, as I sit at a nearby coffee shop waiting for him, he's sending updates on his ETA like he's afraid I'll get mad and leave.

Maybe you should.

I start wondering if I'm even in the right headspace for this. I've had four years to think about what I'd say to him, to scream, to curse, to finally let out all of this pent-up rage. But the second I saw him at the bar, I folded. I hugged him as if his betrayal didn't happen, like I was still that same fragile girl he used to know. I keep telling myself that if I hadn't just come from a karaoke brawl, it would've gone differently. But deep down, I'm not so sure.

My tongue burns from the latte I'm sipping on, and I welcome the pain, wanting to feel anything but the anxiety currently flowing through my body. Amaya might be giving me the silent treatment, but Scarlett and Val sure aren't. As soon as I land back in Florida, I'm to report to Val's office. I know I was off my game yesterday, but I didn't think it was bad enough to get called into the principal's office. I'm staring at the meeting reminder on my phone when the chair across from me scrapes gently across the floor. I look up directly into the beautiful whisky brown eyes that I've loved since I was a teen.

Levi is wearing dark jeans and a fitted white T-shirt under a denim jacket. I'm aware that I'm staring, but it's because something about that jacket is familiar. It reminds me of the same one I used to steal from him because I loved how oversized it looked on me. His sneakers, naturally, are spotless; he's always been meticulous about keeping them pristine.

His raspy morning voice hits me like a tidal wave.

"You look good."

I made sure to wear makeup for this outing, due to the black eye on my face, thanks to Tashi. It's barely covered, but that's the risk of the job. I gave no second thought to my outfit; Levi has seen me at my worst, with clothes that barely fit because my foster family refused to use the money they received from the state for its actual purpose: taking care of me and my needs. I nervously play with the sleeves of my oversized black knit sweater.

"Why are you here, Levi?"

He sighs, rubbing his palms. "Going straight to the point, I see."

"You know me. I like to cut out the bullshit."

"I needed to see you. I haven't been able to stop thinking about you since that day at the bar. Mariana warned me not to, actually, it was more of a threat."

That sounds like Mariana.

"I fucked up," Levi mutters, his voice barely above a whisper.

"That's quite the understatement." My fingers are tightly gripping the edge of my cup, nails digging into the ceramic, wanting it to shatter.

Levi's shoulders are slumping, and he exhales a shaky breath. "Ramona, stop. I'm here trying to fix my fuck-up, if you're just going to sit there and—"

"Sit here and what? Be hurt?" I can't help but laugh.

I'm trying to stay composed, but all I can see is red, and this is the feeling I should've had the first night I saw him. "Excuse me for being a fucking mess after the shit you pulled."

I need to breathe, try to regain some semblance of control. "You *knew* what you meant to me. You *knew* what our relationship meant to me. Levi, you threw it all away. For a job opportunity."

The words taste like venom, each one landing with more force than the last. "Do you have any idea how that made me feel?"

"I can imagine." He mumbles

"No, Levi, you can't. You cannot *fathom* how that feels because you have parents who love you, who took care of you. You've never been abandoned by someone who *claimed* to love you."

"That's not fair, Ramona. I *do* love you."

I scoff, "You don't leave the people you love. Especially the way you did."

Levi flinches at my words.

"I've had to fight for every scrap of love I've ever gotten. And I thought…" My voice cracks. I look away, blinking hard to keep my tears from breaking through. "I thought you were different."

"I told you everything, Levi. Everything," I whisper, the hurt turning into something colder, sharper. "And you didn't even have the decency to tell me you weren't going to follow through with our plans. You were going to come back after college, get a job, and I was going to start my wrestling career with the EWC. Instead, you come down on my twenty-first birthday to surprise me. Well, it was one hell of a surprise when I woke up to an empty bed the next day and a note from you. A *fucking* note, Levi."

"No amount of apologizing will fix the past. We were kids. I was a stupid kid who thought leaving the note was a good idea."

"Any idiot would know that you don't fuck a girl on the night of her birthday and then leave a note. Was I in the wrong to think we had a future? Did I make it all up in my head?" This time, there's no holding back the tears. My emotions are swallowing me whole.

Levi reaches across the table, offering me a tissue to wipe away my tears.

His fingers brush against mine before gently wrapping around my hand, his thumb running in slow circles across my skin. I should pull away, reject the warmth of his touch, but the truth is… I don't want to. He's always grounded me, and after all these years, that hasn't changed. Truthfully, I'm not sure if it ever will.

"You didn't make anything up. We did have a future, and that scared the shit out of me. It's hard to be so young and see your life has already been planned out for you. I ran like a fucking coward, Ramona. This was all me, and you did nothing wrong. I wasn't lying when I told you I looked for you in everything. For four years, I've been searching for what I stupidly left."

Our fingers are now intertwined our bodies recognizing the familiarity with one another.

"I'm not asking for another chance at this, Rami," Levi said, his grip tightening around my hand.

My heart aches at hearing his nickname for me after all these years.

"I know I don't deserve it," he continued, his voice quieter now, almost vulnerable. "I just… I miss my friend. And if you don't feel the same, that's okay. I get it. I'll just go back to my lonely apartment in Florida and cry about it some more."

I try to hold back a smile, but I can't help myself. "Oh, please don't cry. You're such an ugly crier."

We both explode into a fit of laughter, "We can't all cry like a model, Rami." Levi nudges me, and just like that, it feels like we are back to our old selves.

"Apartment in Florida?" I question.

Levi rubs the back of his neck, blushing. "Yeah, I moved about six months ago. I've been going to that bar for the last couple of months to see if I would run into you there."

"What a stalker." I scoff.

"Mariana thought it was romantic."

I roll my eyes, "Of course she did. Those movies she loves so much are rotting her brain."

"I did what I had to do since *someone* refused to reply to any of my messages. I even tried messaging Mariana, and she would just reply with the middle finger emoji every time."

"Sounds about right." I chuckle.

She's going to freak the fuck out once I catch her up on everything. I just don't want to get her hopes up about Levi and me getting back together. She took our breakup just as hard as I did; you would've thought her parents got divorced.

"So, friends?" Levi asked.

I never thought that I would be sitting across from him again. The smile on my face is genuine, but there's an uneasy feeling in the pit of my stomach. I can forgive Levi. He was right, we were just kids, and maybe there was just too much pressure around securing a future at such a young age. I can't deny that I miss him, too, but how does one navigate the delicate line between the past and the present? My eyes drift to his face, catching glimpses of the man I once knew so intimately. I have to remind myself that I've grown, and so has he; we're not those people anymore.

My right leg starts to shake as I struggle to find the right words. He's asking to be friends, but I'm not crazy; there's an undeniable attraction in the way he looks at me. I can *feel* it, like an electric charge between us.

Can we just be friends? Can two people who once loved each other ever truly be just friends?

"Yeah, friends," I replied.

I guess I'm about to find out.

21

Amaya

Val's office is dead quiet, but the sound of the hospital monitors still echoes in my mind. My dad went his entire career in EWC without having a major injury that required surgery, and then he gets taken down by a wobbly ladder while trying to help the neighbor's kid get a frisbee off the roof. You honestly can't make this stuff up. The whole time he's been at the hospital, he's been cracking jokes and chatting with the nurses and doctors, while the rest of us are freaking out over the fact that he just went through surgery for his shattered legs. This man breaks both his legs and is out here signing autographs for the hospital staff.

You would think a father would be grateful that his children dropped everything to be there for him. Not Andres Acosta. He chewed us out for missing out on screen time. Reina had to pull me out of the room more than once to stop me from going off.

"Cálmate, Amaya," was Reina's catchphrase for the week.

Today is my first day back, and Sid made sure Val's office was my first stop. He's sitting next to me and looking incredibly nervous.

"What is this meeting about?" I ask.

"Val has sworn me to secrecy," Sid replies without even glancing in my direction.

Whatever's going on with his phone is clearly distracting him. I lean in, trying to sneak a peek over his shoulder, but he shifts away quickly.

"When did she swear you to secrecy? Was it over text, in her office, in your bed…"

That quickly caught his attention, "Amaya," he whispers sharply.

"You said you would not mention that ever again," he hisses.

"Oops." I shrug my shoulders.

The office door swings open just as Sid is about to curse me out. My mouth is suddenly bone dry. I'm not an idiot; I knew I would have to see her eventually, but I didn't think it would be the first thing I would have to confront today. I'm keeping my eyes glued to Val's desk, cursing her for being late to her own meeting. I don't need to look at Ravyn to know she looks amazing; my peripheral vision doesn't do her justice.

"Hey, Sid. Hey, Amaya." Scarlett greets us both before taking a seat next to Ravyn.

I know I was tough on Ravyn, but I did what I thought I had to do at the moment. You don't get to straight-up reject me and then blow up my phone, acting concerned when I don't reply to your calls or texts. I will never forget the look on her face when she saw Reina at my house. It's engraved in my mind how quickly she tossed me right into that water. I'm trying to cut her some slack because I remember what it felt like to be so fucking confused and lost in your own skin. I know she's scared, and I'm probably the last person she ever imagined opening up to. Hell, I didn't see this coming either. But that doesn't mean I have to sacrifice my feelings just because she's discovering what she wants. I refused to be her little plaything that she experiments with in secret. I won't do it. If I hadn't gotten caught up with her in the first place, I'd have been able to get to my dad a lot sooner. At least his accident wasn't as bad as it could've been.

I let out a sigh of relief as the door finally swung open. Val's here, but my body goes rigid the moment I see she's not alone. Tashi's right behind her.

Tashi waves hello to me, but when she says hi to Ravyn, she hugs her.

What the hell is going on? Did I miss something? I wasn't gone for that long.

I shoot Sid a glare, but he's pretending like he didn't notice.

"My lovely ladies are here. Oh, and Sid." Val grimaces.

She looks hot as always, wearing a black blazer that was tailored to fit her body perfectly. Underneath a white silk blouse peaks out and her deep charcoal pants, and black heels make her peach ass stand out. Should I be checking out my boss? Probably not, but I'm not any better than the next guy. Honestly, good for Sid for landing someone like her, even if it was just 'that one time'. Her brown hair is in a perfectly sleek ponytail, and her expensive ass silver watch could blind me right now if it wanted to; maybe that's why she's still wearing her sunglasses indoors.

"Let's cut straight to the chase, shall we?"

Don't we always?

"You three are my brightest stars right now. The amount of traction we're getting from that DQ match is *insane.* I hate that you missed last week, Amaya, but I get it, family comes first. How's your dad?"

In a wheelchair but still finding a way to be a pain in my ass.

"He's good," I replied.

"Good to hear. There are some goodies on their way to the hospital room from me and my mom."

"Thanks."

"No problem. Now, Tashi and Ravyn."

Val turns towards them, and it's my first time looking at Ravyn. As soon as her hazel eyes met mine, I forgot how to breathe. There's nothing new about how she's looking at me; the icy glare that I've grown accustomed to all these years is there. That glare never bothered me before, but now, I feel ashamed that she's looking at me that way, especially now that I know she can lovingly look at me. Now that I know how she looks when she orgasms, and I'm the one giving her the pleasure of doing so.

"Your match was good, but it could've been better. Ravyn, you were sloppy in there, and fans noticed. Hashtags are circling the internet. #RavynxAmaya, #GirlFightEWC, #TashiToTakeGold is an interesting one. Viewers love it when you three are together on the screen."

Oh, no. I can see where this is going, and I feel like I'm going to throw up.

"Tashi, you're killing it, and I have no notes."

I see Ravyn flinch at Val's statement.

"All of that to say, I obviously need to find a way to make sure you all are together in the ring as much as possible. The best way to do that is to have Amaya and Ravyn attached at the hip."

Yup, I'm going to throw up.

"You want us to be a tag team?" I question.

"I was thinking more like Ravyn would be your valet."

This is not good.

"A fucking valet," Ravyn growls.

"I don't need a valet, Val." I roll my eyes, the words dripping with annoyance, hoping to end this conversation before it goes any further, but knowing Val, this conversation is just getting started.

Val removes her sunglasses and doesn't even blink. She leans back in her chair, her nails tapping rhythmically on the sleek surface of her desk, her gaze locking on me with a kind of sharp amusement. "No one *needs* a valet. I need to give the people what they want, and what they want is you and Ravyn together. They're going to eat this up. You'll have your own scary dog with you, making sure no one pins you and takes your title. Think of it like what happened during the DQ match, but every night."

Her eyes are practically glowing with excitement, and I want nothing more than to shut this down.

"I don't need Ravyn to help me defend my title. I've been doing a great job all on my own." I shot back, keeping my voice steady, but the tension in the air was thick.

Val smirks, leaning forward. "Yeah, well, that was before Tashi came into the picture." Her words hang in the air, sharp and final.

I can see Ravyn flinching at those words, her jaw tightening, her usual cocky swagger now replaced with annoyance. "So you're demoting me?" she snaps, her voice laced with a cold bite.

Val's eyes narrow, unbothered. "Stop with the dramatics, Ravyn. You're still going to be on screen every night."

Ravyn scoffs, crossing her arms, clearly irritated. "Valets barely fucking wrestle. They play a supporting role to the *real* wrestlers, essentially glorified cheerleaders. That's some shit you would give a rookie," she scowls.

"You'll get to wrestle, Ravyn, when you're helping Amaya retain her title."

"And what about *my* title, Val?" Ravyn shoots back, her voice rising, the defiance clear in her tone. "When is it my turn to get what I've been busting my ass for?"

The room goes dead silent. No one in EWC *ever* dares to speak to Val that way, not without consequences.

Val rises from her chair, refusing to break eye contact with Ravyn. Both her and Ravyn's eyes are narrowing into slits.

"Everyone out," Val's voice is a low command.

Ravyn doesn't move; she knows what Val means. Everyone needs to leave *but* her.

I guess we aren't moving quickly enough for her liking because Val's voice goes up a few notches, "Now," she shouts.

Without another word, we all exit her office, leaving the two of them to duke it out, but we all know who's winning this fight.

* * *

"Well, that's not going to end well." Tashi grimaces as Val's screams hit our ears.

"It doesn't take a rocket scientist to figure that one out." I flinch as a loud bang hits Val's door.

Did she just throw something?

"Want to go to Crafty and get something to eat?"

"Sure. I'd rather stuff my face than listen to the tornado that's happening in there."

Tashi and I sit in silence for a while, eating and scrolling on our phones. I'm staring at the time, watching the hours pass, and wondering if I should text Ravyn. I know I told her I didn't want to speak to her, but it's killing me knowing that she's getting chewed out by Val.

"What's the deal with you and Ravyn?" Tashi questions.

"We're coworkers," I explain plainly.

"No shit, but I mean, what's the lore? Why do you guys hate each other so much? It's one thing in front of the cameras, but why is that shit bleeding into real life?"

"I'm an Acosta. It comes with the territory."

"Do you see her stealing your title in the future?"

I scoff, "I don't see anyone stealing my title. No need to manifest."

"Interesting. Say you did have to lose your title. Do you think Val would ask your input on who it should be to take it?"

"Val doesn't ask anyone's opinion for anything. What Val wants, she gets."

Tashi gets up from her seat, collecting her trash. She bends down to whisper in my ear before leaving, "Well, I hope if she ever did, you would put in a good word for me. I would be a great ally to have, both in and out of the ring."

22

Ravyn

So this is what my life has come to: playing glorified bodyguard to my biggest rival. Seriously, what the hell did I do to deserve this? I had a bad ass match and yet I'm getting the shit end of the stick for it. How does that make sense? That's exactly what I told Val, and she did not like that.

Val tore into me the moment we were alone in her office. I knew it was a dumb move to talk back, especially in front of everyone, but I couldn't stop myself. I lost it.

Yeah, I care about the EWC. They gave me my start, I want what's best for them, but does anyone in the company give a shit about what's best for *me*? My career is finally heading in the direction I want it to. Now? It feels like I just got dragged ten steps backward.

Tonight, the producers are laying the groundwork for my valet stint. I'm helping to disqualify another one of Amaya's title matches. It's ridiculous how many title matches EWC is producing, but I'm not going to tell Val how to run her company. Once that's done, Tashi's going to storm out with her big, dramatic entrance, deliver her speech about how much she despises me, and whine about how Amaya should fight her own battles, blah, blah, blah. I get to wrestle tonight, so I'm going to show Val how fucking wrong she is for pushing me to the sidelines.

I grab another water bottle from the fridge in craft services, wishing it were a beer instead, cause Lord knows I need it. A pair of hands covers my eyes, and she doesn't need to speak for me to know exactly who it is.

"I would say, guess who, but if someone else is doing this to you, I will murder them. I don't care how many belts they've had."

"If you mess up my lashes, Mariana, I will be the one murdering people around here, and by people, I mean you. It took me forever to put these damn things on today."

"Rough day already, huh?" Mariana wraps her arms around my midsection.

"You *already* know. The second my eyeliner or lashes start acting up, it's a sign from the universe that everything else is about to fall apart." I squeeze Mariana hard, not realizing how much I need a hug from her. "I shouldn't even be hugging you right now," Mariana huffs, pulling back with a glare. "I'm mad at you. The audacity you have. Who do you think you are, ignoring my calls and texts? If I didn't have a comp ticket with my name on it, I was about to raise absolute hell."

She crosses her arms tightly across her chest, a pint-sized storm of attitude.

"I know, I'm sorry," I said, rubbing the back of my neck. "A lot of stuff's been going on."

Right then, my phone buzzed in my pocket. I glanced at the screen and couldn't help the grin that crept across my face.

Mariana notices. Of course, she does; she doesn't miss anything, and before I can even react, she snatches the phone out of my hand.

Her jaw drops as her eyes scan the screen. "No. *Fucking.* Way."

Levi: *"Good luck tonight. Can't be there in person, but I'll be watching. Are you free tonight?"*

"I can explain, Mariana."

"Damn right you're gonna explain," she said, already pulling up a chair. "What is Levi Miller doing on your phone? Are we forgiving him? I sent that man a lot of middle finger emojis."

"So I've heard," I said, trying and failing not to smirk.

Mariana throws her hands in the air, "For the *love of God*, if you don't tell me what happened soon, I am going to combust. Like, full spontaneous human combustion. I'm pretty sure I read in a textbook somewhere that could actually happen to a person."

I bend down, giving her a quick peck on her forehead. "I love you. And I *promise* I will spill every single detail *after* work."

She lets out a loud groan that makes everyone turn their heads in our direction. "Ugh, *fine*. Go be a badass wrestler or whatever. But drinks after, or I swear I will track you down, and I know where you live."

"After hearing that delicious noise come out of your mouth, I want to know where you live, Mi Amor."

Mariana and I already know who's speaking before we even look in his direction. We exchange a look, bracing ourselves. Sure enough, Aiden leans casually against the doorframe, a crooked smile playing on his lips and mischief dancing in his eyes. He locks entirely too pleased with himself.

Mariana sighs, pinching the bridge of her nose, as if the sound of his voice is giving her an instant headache. "Aiden, we've had this conversation. You *cannot* call me Mi Amor. We're friends."

He pushes off the frame and strolls closer, that infuriating grin never faltering. "Friends love each other, don't they? Don't *you* love Ravyn?"

Mariana scoffs and folds her arms. "It's not the same, and you know it."

Aiden looks at me. "Ravyn, come on, back me up here."

I raise both hands in surrender. "Oh no. I am *not* getting caught in the middle of whatever *this* is." I gesture between them, eyebrows raised. "Sort it out yourselves."

* * *

I'm backstage, my eyes glued to the TV screen that's on the wall and waiting for my cue to run down the ramp and interfere with Amaya's match against Savannah Steel. I've called Amaya a lot of things in the years I've known her, but I could never bring myself to call her a bad wrestler because that would be a flat-out lie. I'm finding myself entranced with the match just as much as the audience currently is.

Amaya is wearing electric blue gear, which is fitting since she is moving like lightning. She knocks the wind out of Savannah, who's now flat on her back on the mat. Amaya is scaling the top turnbuckle, her back facing the ring. With a deep breath and the audience on edge, she launches into a flawless moonsault. The impact of it is a devastating hit full of brutal precision. The ring shakes under the force, and the crowd explodes in cheers.

Savannah is trying to catch her breath as Amaya works the crowd.

"Come on," she yells to the crowd so they can get louder.

Her back is towards Savannah, and that's when Savannah makes her move. She slowly rises to her feet, the adrenaline driving her on. Savannah grabs Amaya by her hair and, with a fistful of hair, she drags her to the middle of the ring and gives Amaya blow after blow to her midsection with her right fist. Savannah doesn't let go of Amaya's hair; if anything, her grip tightens, as she drags her to the top rope. The two of them balance on the turnbuckle, the stands shaking with excitement as Savannah executes a thunderous superplex. Both women soar and slam into the mat with a bone-rattling crash, echoing through the arena.

Both Amaya and Savannah are now lying on the mat when a producer taps me on the shoulder.

"Ravyn, Savannah is about to try and pin Amaya, so as soon as you see that run, okay?"

I nod my head in agreement.

Amaya is struggling to get up; she's clutching her ribs. Savannah takes advantage and climbs on top of Amaya, delivering multiple blows to her head, and that's when I make my move, because when you've been in the business long enough, you know when someone is about to try and pin their opponent.

I run down the entrance ramp like my life depends on it, and before the referee can say the number two, I grab Savannah by the ankles and pull her off of Amaya. With fluid precision, I hook Savannah's body over my knee, delivering a brutal backbreaker. There's a mixture of boos and gasps in the crowd.

A sharp, piercing clang echoes through the arena as the bell rings and the ring announcer announces the disqualification of the match. Just like clockwork, Tashi's entrance music starts blaring throughout the arena, and the crowd is going wild.

"Ravyn, Ravyn, Ravyn. When did you become Amaya's little bitch." Tashi speaks into her mic.

Bitch wasn't in the script, but I'll let that go.

Savannah moves herself to the corner of the ring to allow me and Amaya to stand in the center. Amaya isn't making eye contact with me as she adjusts her championship belt.

"For someone who claims to hate Amaya's guts, you sure have been coming to the rescue when she's getting her ass handed to her." Tashi is continuing her speech as she slowly makes her way towards us.

"I'm disappointed, honestly. I thought you would be better than that. I guess you're just like everyone else in the EWC, kissing the ass of the Acosta family."

Tashi is making her way into the ring now, and it's taking everything in me not to grab the mic out of her hand. I have no script, I'm not supposed to be giving any speeches tonight, but I want so badly to tell her off. It's not personal, none of this is, but the crowd is eating up her words like it's the truth, and it's getting under my skin.

"How much did your new guard dog cost, Amaya?" Tashi asks as she gets in Amaya's face.

In a twist of fate, it's not me who goes off script. Amaya takes her title belt off her shoulder and slams it into Tashi's face. The mic crashes into the mat with a heavy thump and a sharp screech of feedback that pierces the arena air.

Holy shit.

Apparently, I'm not the only one thinking that; the crowd erupts into a deafening chant:

"Holy shit! Holy shit! Holy shit!"

Should I be breaking this up?

Amaya's not stopping. She's going off on Tashi, fists flying, fury in full force.

Tashi isn't fighting back, and now I'm wondering if this was supposed to happen, and I just wasn't in on the plan.

Amaya is giving blow after blow to Tashi, fast and merciless. She's using her whole body to attack Tashi, fists, forearms, and boots landing in rapid-fire succession. There was no rhythm, no pause, just raw aggression.

Every time Tashi tries to roll away or lift her head, she gets hit again by Amaya.

I swear the shit Acostas can get away with.

It wasn't until I saw a swarm of refs coming down the ramp that I realized how real this is.

"Enough, Amaya," I yell, grabbing her by the midsection and pulling her off of Tashi, who's gasping for air.

Amaya kicks and flails in my grasp until I whisper harshly in her ear:

"What the actual fuck, Amaya? Calm down."

The refs grab Tashi, knowing I have a solid grip on Amaya.

She stops struggling. Her eyes flick to the mic on the mat next to us. She lunges for it and snatches it up. "Let's get something straight here, Tashi," she growls into the mic, voice slicing through the chaos. "You're new, so let me teach you how things work in the EWC. Amaya Acosta doesn't *need* a guard dog. I *am* the guard dog. I fight my own battles."

The crowd is losing it. I'm trying to save face, but inside? I'm freaking the fuck out.

"Ravyn's been trying to rip this belt from my hands for years and failed. You think you'll do better? You're delusional. Ravyn's smart enough to learn the lesson: if you can't beat me, join me."

Amaya turns to me. Her eyes lock onto mine, "Ravyn's with me now. Let's see if you've got what it takes to handle both of us."

She drops the mic in front of Tashi and reaches for my hand. Fingers laced together, we disappear backstage, leaving the chaos of the ring behind us. The whole thing feels unreal, like I'm watching it happen from outside my own body. It's official, I'm Amaya's valet.

The question now is, did Amaya just turn heel?

23

Amaya

The door slams shut behind me, and I barely have time to blink before Val explodes.

"What the hell were you three thinking?" Her voice thunders through the room, sharp and cutting. Both Tashi and Ravyn sit quietly in the office with me. We're all still in our gear because Val pulled all three of us into the office as soon as we left the ring.

"They had nothing to do with what happened tonight. That was all me." I confess.

It's true, for the first time in my career, I went off script, but I didn't plan to. Tashi's speech just hit a chord, and I saw red.

"Oh, I'm well aware since they're the only two that stuck to the fucking script, Acosta." Val's rubbing at her temple as she pulls out two ibuprofen from her desk drawer and swallows them dry.

I knew there would be hell to pay for not following what Val wanted to be done, but I think she's overreacting. Ravyn's still going to be my valet.

"May I say something?" Tashi asks sheepishly.

Val waves her hand, telling her to proceed.

"I think what Amaya did was kind of genius."

Val stays silent, waiting for Tashi to elaborate.

"I mean, I didn't particularly enjoy getting the shit kicked out of me, but it makes for an interesting dynamic. Rivals turned allies to take down the newbie who hasn't paid their dues."

Tashi is saving my ass right now, and I'm going to let her.

"Yeah, that's what I was going for, Val, at least someone noticed my vision." I cross my legs, relaxing in my chair.

Let them think what they want, as long as they don't figure out the real reason for my blackout was because I hated how she was talking about Ravyn. I know this whole storyline is hurting her. She's an amazing wrestler who is being downgraded to a valet. If I had known this was where her storyline was heading, I wouldn't have been so cold to her over the phone. Poor girl is going through it, and I feel like shit for being a part of it.

"Regardless of the *vision*, we now have a heel title holder, and if that was something that we wanted, we would've given Ravyn the belt by now."

Ravyn shudders at that statement.

"There's no way to spin this into you being the good guy still, not the way that you beat Tashi."

"I mean, is me being a heel *that* bad?" I ask, already knowing the answer.

"In all the years the Acostas have been a part of the EWC, they've been baby-faced. *Always*, it's a part of their clause."

I slowly blink, eyebrows lifting as the words settle in. "I'm sorry… run that by me one more time?" I ask, my voice calm.

Ravyn breaks out into a fit of laughter. "I'm sorry, you're telling me that it's written on paper that any Acosta that wrestles with the EWC cannot be a heel?"

Val sighs, "I'm not supposed to be discussing the logistics of other wrestlers' contracts, but yes, and your father is going to fucking have my head for this. He's called me ten times already, and I've been sending him directly to voicemail. No offense, but thank God he can't drive over here right now."

Fuck my life. If my dad is blowing up Val's phone, I don't even want to *look* at my phone. I'm turning it off as *soon* as I get my hands on it.

"You didn't know?" Ravyn asks.

"Does this look like the face of the person of someone who fucking knew?" I snap.

"I guess being an Acosta means you don't have to read your contracts before signing them," Ravyn mumbles.

"What's done is done. I'm going to meet with the producers to figure out how—" Val's sentence is sliced in half by the sudden, shrill ringing of her phone.

She looks down at the screen and groans, "Oh God."

"My dad again?" I ask, already bracing myself.

"Worse." She winces. "My mother."

Without missing a beat, she waves a hand toward the door. "Everyone out. Get some rest. I'll see you next week."

As we head out, she finally answers the call. Even with the door still swinging shut behind us, we can hear the unmistakable fury of Melanie Archer's voice.

* * *

"Chica, you killed it tonight." Reina gives me a playful punch to the arm before pulling me into a hug.

Val told us to rest up for the week ahead, but honestly? I'm already on a streak of ignoring her orders. So when Reina invited me out for drinks, I figured, fuck it. Why stop now?

Reina picks a bar that reeks of stale beer and sweat. My shoes are sticking to the beer-stained floor with each step I take. We each pop a squat at the bar, smiling at the grizzly bartender with a permanent scowl. There's a jukebox in the corner that's blaring an old rock anthem. We get our drinks, and I tell Reina everything. Explain how Ravyn ended up at my place, what we did in the hot tub, and why I snapped in the ring. I tell her everything except what Ravyn told me about her past; it's no one's business, and it's not my story to tell.

"¡Diablo!" Reina lets out a low whistle, eyebrows lifting as she takes a long gulp of her beer. The glass clinks softly when she sets it back down.

"Yup," I mutter, dragging a hand down my face.

"Okay, that phone call with Ravyn wasn't your finest moment. But I get it.

You're trying to keep your distance."

"Exactly," I said, exhaling hard. "And now we're joined at the hip at work. I have no clue how to handle it."

She smirks, lifting her bottle in mock sympathy.

"Well, if you came to me for relationship advice, you're going to be highly disappointed."

I give her a look. "Oh, please. I know better than to ask someone with a severe case of philophobia."

Her head jerks slightly. "I'm sorry—what did you just call me?"

"Philophobia," I said with a grin. "An intense fear of falling in love or being in love."

Reina leans back in her chair, "Whatever. I've been in love, and trust me, it's not all it's cracked up to be."

"Don't you think it's time to forgive and forget? I would love for you to come to one of my matches in person instead of just sitting at home alone to watch them."

"I'm not alone," she said, lifting her chin stubbornly. "I have Mochi."

I snort. "Your dog doesn't count. He wouldn't even notice if you left the room."

"That's insulting. I'd have you know that my sweet little angel boy is a velcro baby. Where I go, he goes. I'm telling Mochi you said that."

"I stand by what I said. Come to a match already, he won't even notice that you're there." I roll my eyes.

"I'd rather not take the chance. My ass will be staying on my couch."

"It's like you don't love me." I pout my lip.

Reina's eyes widen, her face drains of color, and her posture shifts.

"I was just joking, Reina."

"Oh, I know." Reina's eyes drift past me.

What the fuck is she looking at?

I try to turn around, and she stops me.

"You know how you were just talking about Ravyn and how you want to keep your distance?"

"Yeah?"

"Well, don't turn around."

No fucking way.

I whip my head around, and my stomach drops. There she is, sitting across from Mariana, laughing, drink in hand, completely at ease. She's wearing a sleek black crop top under a leather jacket that hugs her figure just right and high-waisted jeans. A silver chain glints at her collarbone, catching the bar's dim light as she moves.

Of all the places. Of all the nights.

"Are you kidding me?" I shout right as the jukebox decides to stop playing music.

All eyes are on me, including Ravyn's.

"Nena, I told you not to turn around." Reina slaps my shoulder.

The bar suddenly feels smaller, louder, and too crowded. I consider slipping out the front door, but I know that would be too obvious.

"This is your fault. You just had to choose this bar," I hiss at Reina.

"How the hell was I supposed to know she would be here. Do I look like Walter Mercado to you?"

"No, he's better looking. Can we just go?" I start to gather my things and place some cash on the counter to cover our drinks and tip.

"We could… if Mariana wasn't texting me to come over." Reina shoves her phone in my face.

"Just text her an excuse, tell her one of us doesn't feel good."

Reina's phone vibrates with another text,

Mariana: *"Don't you dare try to text some b.s. excuse to leave. Get your asses over here. Or would you prefer I come to you?"*

For some reason, the idea of Mariana coming to us is way more unsettling than if we went to her.

"Fine. Hi, and bye, Reina." I warn.

Each step towards the table feels heavier than the last.

Just play nice, Amaya.

Ravyn's eyes have a sheen to them that tells me she's had more than one drink, but she's smiling in my direction, and I can't help but smile back.

Maybe this won't be so bad. I can do this.

And that's when I see *him*. Ravyn shifts in her seat to grab her drink, and there he is, sitting beside her.

I only saw him that one time, but that was enough for my liking. My spine straightens instinctively, giving Reina a look.

"Holy, shit, what is he doing here?" she mumbles under her breath.

I don't like how relaxed Levi is. He's looking a little too much like he belongs.

Maybe he does.

Levi is laughing at something, his arm slung casually along the back of Ravyn's chair.

Mariana greets us, pulling out the two extra chairs at the table for us to sit.

"Oh, that's not necessary, we just wanted to say hi before heading out." Reina politely tells Mariana.

"Oh, boo. We just ordered another round."

I have to stop myself from rolling my eyes as he stands up to introduce himself, "Hey, I'm Levi."

He looks toward Reina, "You're Reina, right? I remember you from our run-in at the other bar."

"Yeah, this is my cousin Amaya."

"Oh, I know. I'm a fan."

Ravyn scoffs, grabbing Levi's attention.

"Of course, I'm not as big a fan as I am of Rami. She's my favorite wrestler."

He winks, *fucking* winks, at Ravyn, and what the *fuck* did he just call her?

"Yeah, well, Silver deserves all the praise. She's been killing it in the ring."

Levi smirks, "Huh, Silver. I like that."

He grabs a piece of Ravyn's silver hair and tucks it behind her ear. I want to rip his fucking hand off, and I'll be damned if he starts using *my* nickname for Ravyn.

"Don't get any ideas, only Amaya is allowed to call me that."

Damn right.

I tilt my head, lips tugging into a crooked grin, and then it clicks for Ravyn. The mistake she just made.

"No. I didn't mean that. Amaya, I didn't mean that." She groans and places her forehead on the table.

"Sure you didn't, Silver."

Right then, the server arrives with a metal bucket full of ice-cold beer.

"Are you sure you two don't want to stay?" Mariana asks, waving the bucket in my and Reina's faces.

No, I don't want to stay. Every part of me is ready to bolt, but if I leave, who's going to keep an eye on Levi? Who's going to make sure he doesn't cross a line with Ravyn? And why the hell is Mariana acting like this is all perfectly normal?

"We really should—" Reina starts, but I cut her off.

"Actually, yeah. One drink won't kill us."

I grab a beer from the bucket, twisting the cap off, taking a long swig as I pull out a chair and swing a leg over to straddle it. If Levi's going to play games, fine. I'll be right here to watch.

"I guess we're having a drink." Reina pinches the side of my stomach before sitting down.

"So, Levi. What's your story?" I ask.

Know thy enemy.

"Oh, you don't want to hear about me. I'm so boring." Levi shrugs off my question.

"No, please. I wanna hear more about how you left Ravyn and went to The Big Apple. More importantly, I wanna know when you're going back."

Reina kicks me under the table.

"Actually, I'm not. I have an apartment here and I'm planning on sticking around for a while."

His words hit like a slap in the face. I blink, trying to process what I just heard, pretending it doesn't bother me in the slightest.

"That's amazing." A tight smile creeps onto my face. Automatic. Hollow. The kind you put on when you're about three seconds from losing your shit.

I need to get away from this man before I do something stupid.

"Excuse me for a sec," I said, standing so fast my chair scrapes the floor.

I make my way to the restroom, and the second the door shuts behind me, the noises of the bar are dulled. I lean against the sink, gripping the edge like it can anchor me to the floor. This asshole is going to waltz back into Ravyn's life like nothing happened? He's gonna fuck with her head and her heart, and then it's going to affect her career.

Or maybe he's what she needs, and they'll live happily ever after like they were supposed to. Ravyn is not your responsibility; her heart is not yours to take care of.

My reflection in the mirror looks just as rattled as I feel. I turn on the faucet and let the cold water run over my hands before splashing some on my face.

The bathroom smells like cheap soap and whatever perfume the last person sprayed to cover up the stench of shit.

"What the hell was that?" Ravyn growls.

I look at her through the mirror as I wash my hands. "It's a valid question."

"That was a fucking interrogation," she snaps.

I lean back against the sink, arms crossed, "You're so dramatic, Silver."

"Don't call me that." Ravyn steps forward, and the space between us disappears as she towers over me.

My lips curve into a smirk. "Would you prefer *valet?*"

Ravyn's hands clench at her sides. "I swear to God, Amaya, if you weren't the one thing standing between me and getting into that ring, I'd beat your ass right here, right now."

I arch my brow, unmoved. "Don't be mad at me just because I had the nerve to ask the question you didn't have the guts to."

"You really think I'm that naïve?" she spits, her voice tight. "That Levi just got a free pass to come back into my life without me chewing him the fuck out for what he did? We're just friends. That's all."

"Does *he* know that?"

Ravyn's jaw clenches. "Oh my God, why do you even care?" The words come out in a rush. "Is this about the hot tub? Because if it is, let me make something perfectly clear: you don't own me. I am not yours to piss on like a dog," she snaps.

"I care because we are now a unit in that ring, no matter how much we hate it, and if you go down, I go down with you. I could give two fucks about what happened in that hot tub. But since *you're* the one bringing it up, maybe it's still rattling around *your* head."

Her eyes flick downward, and when her gaze settles on my mouth, a devilish glint is in her eyes. The same one I'd seen the night her hand slid under the water, bold and reckless.

She's been thinking about it. Just as much as I have.

"I haven't given it a second thought."

Liar.

I can't help but laugh, "Sure you haven't, *Silver*. What about that first night, then? I'm getting a little deja vu myself, seeing as we've found ourselves once again in a bathroom alone together."

I turn to walk away, but I don't get the chance. Her hand closes around my bicep, strong and sure. She yanks me back around, spinning me with enough force to press my back against the bathroom door.

The slam echoes through the grimy space, and suddenly she's inches away. Her hazel eyes are burning into mine.

Her voice drops to a whisper, "I said, don't call me that... *Red*."

The air between us thickens, and it's charged with a tension so heavy I can almost taste it. The temptation to close the distance and kiss her is nearly unbearable.

You can't, Amaya. This can't happen.

But the words slip out; I know they'll provoke her, and I don't care. I keep eye contact with her, steady and daring. "Make me."

Ravyn doesn't hesitate. Her lips crash against mine, a kiss so hot that it makes me forget we're in this dingy, grimy dive bar bathroom.

It's the kind of kiss we both know comes with consequences, and I'm ready to say fuck it all. Her tongue traces along my bottom lip, seeking permission, which I give without hesitation. It's then that the sharp burn hits me, a whiskey tang clings to my mouth.

She only wants you when she's drunk. You're just her drunken experiment.

"No." I shove her away, breaking the spell.

Ravyn blinks, completely startled. "I'm sorry, I don't know what happened—"

"You're drunk. That's what happened." My voice is cold, cutting through my lust-filled haze. "You only come to me when you have alcohol as an excuse for your actions. Why don't you ever make a move when you're sober?"

Silence. She doesn't say a word.

"I'm not your damn test dummy, Ravyn. I'm not here for you to figure out what you want or don't want."

"That's not what I think," she murmurs, voice barely audible.

"Then what do you think? You can't even admit to yourself that you're attracted to women, and I'm not going to be the one to force you to see it. If you want to fool around with random women after a few drinks, go ahead; that's your choice. Don't expect me to be part of your drunken experiments. Have a great night with Levi. You two seem made for each other. You both don't know what the fuck you want."

I yank the bathroom door open and step out without so much as a glance over my shoulder. The cool, stale air of the bar hits me as I make my way through the haze of drunk people.

"I'm gonna head out. It's been a long night," I said, my voice barely above a whisper.

"I'll go with you," Reina offers, concern flickering in her eyes.

"No, you don't have to. Stay, enjoy the rest of the night," I insist, forcing a tight smile that Reina knows is fake.

The noise of the bar fades behind me as I push through the door into the quiet night. It's outside of this grimy bar that I vow that tonight will be the last time that Ravyn's drunken lips touch mine.

24

Ravyn

"I'm not your damn test dummy, Ravyn. I'm not here for you to figure out what you want or don't want."

Amaya's words replay in my head. It's been hours since she left the bar, and her words are all I can think about. Why the fuck did I kiss her? Why did I put myself in this position again when I already told myself that I was going to stay away? The universe keeps playing dirty tricks on me, and I don't appreciate it one bit. I came out to drink with Mariana, and she just had to show up. Mariana listened intently to everything I had to catch her up on the mess that was my life, and just as I knew she would, she supported my decision to forgive Levi and step away from Amaya.

"As long as that's what you want, sweetie," Mariana assured me.

"Is it what you think I *should* do?" I questioned.

"I can't tell you what to do when it comes to affairs of the heart."

There's psychology major, Mariana, showing up at the most inopportune times.

It wasn't my intention to invite Levi out tonight, but after a couple of drinks, I found myself wanting to text Amaya and invite her out. Instead, I sent a location pin to Levi, in hopes that he would help me forget about craving Amaya's presence.

"You're running to Levi because he's familiar, he's safe."

Eddie's words pop into my head, and I push them away. He's going to have a field day with this. Mariana, Reina, and Levi are talking and laughing at the table, and I have no clue about what. I've just been nodding my head in agreement and pretending to engage in their conversation.

I'm not your damn test dummy, Ravyn. I'm not here for you to figure out what you want or don't want.

"Earth to Ramona." Mariana snaps her fingers in my face.

"I'm sorry, what?"

Mariana rolls her eyes in annoyance, "I said that Reina and I are going to head out to grab a bite to eat. Do you wanna join? Levi is gonna stay here for another round."

Levi has that easy, half-cocked grin on his face. "You can go with them if you want. I'll be fine here alone." His eyes roam around the bar, catching the eyes of a perky blonde across the room.

Oh, hell no.

"I'll stay with Levi. Text me when you're home. It was nice to see you, Reina."

Mariana's phone screen lights up, and she glances at her phone. She immediately rolls her eyes, but there's a hint of blush on her cheeks.

I don't get to sneak a peek at the name on the screen, but Reina does, and her eyes widen.

"Excuse me, why is my cousin texting you heart eye emojis?" Reina questions.

"Because your cousin has yet to learn a thing called boundaries. No worries, I will break Aiden Acosta."

"Are you a masochist?" Reina asks before linking arms with Mariana and walking out of the bar.

"Well, Rami, what do you wanna talk about?" Levi grins.

* * *

I couldn't tell you how it happened, because I honestly have no idea. Yet here I am, wide awake, completely naked, and in Levi's bed. He's knocked out and has been snoring his head off.

Ah, just like old times.

Carefully, I wrap a blanket around my naked body, tiptoeing around his room and collecting pieces of clothing from the floor as I go. I quickly get dressed in the living room, without my underwear because they've disappeared, and it's the first time I truly look around.

Levi's place looks more like a showroom than somewhere someone actually lives. A black leather couch sits perfectly centered in front of a mounted TV. The walls are bare except for one framed photo, a faded snapshot of him and his parents at one of his football games. The kitchen's sleek but suspiciously untouched, aside from a fridge stocked with beer, takeout containers, and exactly one condiment: hot sauce.

Still on his college diet, I see.

I dig into the couch, hoping to find my phone somewhere in the cracks. Mariana is going to kill me for not checking in with her. I find a dust-covered chip and some change, which I tuck into my back pocket.

I don't care how much money I have. You find a penny, you keep a penny.

"Where the hell are you?" I hiss.

A silent vibration shakes the couch cushions, directing me to my phone's exact location. I pull it out to find Mariana's face on the screen.

Shit.

"I know, I know. Please don't give me a speech right now." I whisper.

"I'm looking at your location, and it's showing an apartment complex that's thirty minutes away, but I bet I could make it there in fifteen if you need me to." I can hear the start of a car engine in the background, telling me that Mariana is already heating up her engine.

"Yes, please. A ride would be nice."

"So, do you want to tell me about it now or during the car ride?"

"Seeing as I'm having to whisper to you right now to not wake up Levi, this is a car ride conversation."

"Are you going to leave a note or?" Mariana winces once she realizes her poor choice of words.

"No note. Ironic though if I did, huh."

"See you in ten." Mariana hangs up, leaving me alone in the dark with my thoughts.

I exhale in frustration. How did I go from being satisfied with my toy drawer to hooking up with two different people in the span of a few weeks? One of them is my coworker, and the other is my ex-boyfriend.

Why must everything in my life be complicated?

Eddie warned me. Amaya sees right through me. It seems like everyone around me knows me better than I know myself. Am I that sad and desperate for someone to love me, for them to feel like home, that I'm willing to give myself to anyone willing to take me, even someone who's let me down in the past, or someone I've hated for years?

My memory of tonight is a blur, but I remember that one word, clear as day. That's all it took for me to fall back into him. Now I'm slouching on the sofa, head dangling over the armrest, spiraling as I replay every moment with Levi on an endless loop.

"I can't believe you're here in my apartment." Levi's words sounded velvety in my ear as we sat close to one another on his couch.

"Be careful, you're sounding like one of those fanboys," I giggled.

Levi shrugged, "Well, I am. I'm so proud of you. You actually did it, Rami, your dream came true." He squeezed my hand.

"Yeah, part of it did, anyway." I drew back, pulling my hand out of his.

"I've missed this."

"What?"

"This. Us."

His statement pulled at my heart because I missed it too, but I don't want to admit that to him or myself.

"This apartment is nice," I say, only pretending to pay attention to my surroundings.

"I guess. It's just an apartment to me; it doesn't feel like home."

I scoffed, remembering his childhood home and how envious I was that he had a place he could truly call home, feel comfortable enough to decorate, and not be afraid that he would be kicked out. "Your parents' house will be hard to beat, it's huge."

"That's not my home, you are."

Without a second thought, I reached over to Levi, grabbing onto the collar of his shirt and tugging him close. In an instant, our lips collided, hungry to taste one another, to have the familiarity of one another envelop us.

I tried to focus, to stay in the present, but each press of lips seemed to blur the lines. Levi has always been an amazing kisser; these years apart haven't changed that. Yet, as his lips touch mine, they crave hers. As Levi's hand grabbed my waist, placing me on top of his lap, images of her hands flooded my head, the way they held me so carefully. I felt the ghost of her lips against mine. Levi nipped at my neck, in the exact spot that he knows I like, and I can't help but moan. I tug at the hair on the base of his neck, my fingers looking for longer hair that I know won't be there, red hair that I know is out of my grasp. Without warning, Levi picks me up, carrying me to his room and throwing me onto his bed. He grabs the collar of his shirt and yanks it over his head in one swift motion.

God, he must be working out overtime, and even though I find myself admiring his chiseled chest and abs, I want more. I want it to be Amaya in her barely there bathing suit, looking at me like she is about to devour me whole.

In one easy tug, Levi removes my jeans and thong. As he climbs on top of me, the weight of his body feels so good, and the warmth is welcoming. We go back to stealing kisses as we remove the rest of each other's clothing. A small gasp escapes my lips as one of Levi's fingers makes its way inside me.

Another finger joins, and fuck does it feel good. My body is responding the way it always does to Levi, short of breath and shuddering at his touch. It's just not Amaya's touch. I know it's not fair to compare, but my mind can't help but go there. Her touch was fire, my skin tingled, and I felt weightless. My body remembered how to feel around Levi, but my heart had let him go a long time ago.

I kept waiting for something to spark, but it never came, and I never came. Levi's touch was right, the rhythm was there. But the fire, the need, the way I used to melt without even thinking around him was missing. I'm not proud of it, but I faked it. I had never faked it with Levi, so he'll never suspect it, and honestly, I hope he just doesn't remember this night at all.

Just as the memory started to replay from the beginning in my head, my phone buzzed against the couch cushion.

Mariana: *"Come down, you whore❤"*

25

Ravyn

Another day, another city. Mariana dropped me off at the airport, reminding me to play nice with Amaya before I left on my flight. I've barely slept, and it doesn't help that I've been trying to avoid Levi like the plague. I made sure to text him after our drunken night together, because I'm not a complete monster. Mariana helped me construct the perfect text, not too flirty, not too cold, we came up with:

"Nice catching up, see you around."

It was perfect at first; his response was just a heart reaction and a

Levi: *"Me too. Good luck this week at work."*

Days pass without me responding and so the double texts begin to flood my inbox.

Levi: *"Hey, how's your day going?"*

Levi: *"Guess you're busy."*

Levi: *"When do you leave?"*

Levi: *"If you have time before you go, I would love to see you."*

I'm starting to wonder if he was always this suffocating or if I'm just noticing this trait now.

Amaya, on the other hand, has been completely absent. It'll be a couple of months before we have another show back home, which means there will be little to no space between her and me. I stayed true to my word and gave Mariana a detailed account of the night I had with Levi, but I don't share what's happening in my mind at that moment. I might not have a college degree, but I don't need one to know what she would say about me fantasizing about Amaya while being with Levi, and I don't want to hear it.

Since the next city is so close, EWC has us flying commercially; they reserve the use of the private jet for when we go overseas. I love it when we get to fly commercially because there's a lower chance of running into anyone from work, including Amaya. It usually means there's more fan interaction, but I enjoy those. Every time I see a little girl in my merch, it makes me feel like all the hard work was worth it. I'm going to get on this plane and not think about Amaya Acosta. My carry-on is where it's supposed to be, my backpack is under the seat in front of me, headphones are playing lo-fi so I can finally get some sleep, and my pillow is snug around my neck, but before I can close my eyes to relax, I spot a head of red hair walking down the aisle.

No fucking way.

Amaya is getting closer and closer to me. I turn my attention out the window, pretending that the right wing of the plane is suddenly interesting to me. I'm praying that she won't notice me or worse...

"No fucking way." Amaya scoffs as she stops in front of me.

It's official. Whatever higher power is in charge hates me.

"I guess Val meant it literally when she said we had to be joined at the hip." Amaya scowls as she struggles to fit her carry-on inside the overhead compartment.

I don't reply, I just watch as she fights with her suitcase.

"Seriously. Must we do this dance every time? You fit in there." Amaya is now punching her bag, and I can't help but chuckle.

Her green eyes narrow in on me, and her face is as red as her hair. If we were in a cartoon, smoke could be coming out of her ears.

"Move over," I sigh.

It takes me one push to get her bag in and close the door. I sit back down and watch as Amaya's mouth is gaping open.

"Yeah, well, I did most of the work," she mumbles.

We go through all of the flight safety procedures in silence, eyes facing front and paying attention idly to the flight attendants, even though we both have spent most of our wrestling years on planes that we can recite their script word for word.

"Thank you for helping me," Amaya whispers while still refusing eye contact.

I could never forget how beautiful Amaya is, but how is it that even under these horrible airplane lights, she's still breathtakingly perfect? The curve of a cheekbone, the slope of her shoulder.

Snap out of it, woman.

"You don't have to thank me. I was getting second-hand embarrassment, so I helped more for my benefits than for yours."

Amaya rolls her eyes, and that's the extent of our conversation. I wake up to the soft hum of the plane; my eyes feel heavy, but I'm grateful I was able to get some sort of rest. I try to adjust myself in my seat, and that's when I feel it: the gentle weight on my shoulder. I turn my head just enough to see Amaya fast asleep. Her breathing is slow and steady. The sight stops me in my tracks, and I stay frozen in my seat, barely breathing, afraid to shift and ruin it.

Amaya's hair brushes my cheek, and I close my eyes, inhaling the scent of her shampoo. It's different from her usual lavender. Her hair is a mixture of coconut and vanilla that lulls me back to sleep.

⁕ ⁕ ⁕

It turns out that not only did EWC book us plane tickets right next to one another, they also booked us into the same hotel. I'm busy fighting the front desk agent when I spot her.

"I'm starting to think you're stalking me." I mock.

"You wish." Amaya rolls her eyes.

The front desk agent looks between us in confusion.

"Are you Ms. Acosta?" she asks Amaya.

"Yes, I am." She said in her sweetest demeanor.

"Perfect. I was explaining to Ms. Ramirez that we received a rooming list from EWC, and you two will be sharing a room."

"Ramirez?" Amaya's eyebrow lifts.

"That's what you got from this? She's saying that we have to share a room and is refusing to give me my own."

Amaya looks at the front desk agent's name badge before leaning over the desk, giving her a view straight down her shirt. "Allison, I know you're just doing your job, and I respect that. However, I would also like not to share a room with Ms. Ramirez. So you would be doing us both a huge favor by giving us our own rooms." Amaya bats her eyes at Allison, and I almost throw up at her attempt at seduction.

"I apologize for the inconvenience, Ms. Acosta, and I would love to assist, but we are fully committed for tonight."

Amaya sighs, returning to her upright position, "Even the presidential?"

I don't want to sleep in the same room as Amaya either, but I'm not going to shell out a shit ton of money for the presidential.

"Yes, even the presidential." Allison smiles as though the information she's giving us wasn't annoying.

"You can just take the room, Amaya. I'll find another hotel close by."

I gather my belongings from on top of the counter, ready to start searching online for another place to stay, when Allison's lovely and *not at all* annoying voice delivers some more amazing news.

"I'm sorry, Ms.Ramirez, but all of the hotels in the area are sold out due to the show."

God is really testing my patience today.

"It's fine, Allison, we'll take our keys now, please." Amaya grabs the keys, her smile never faltering.

"Move it or lose it, Silver."

I reluctantly followed my new roommate into the elevator. The elevator doors slide shut with a soft thud, and neither of us says a word. It's just us two in the elevator, yet we're standing a little too close and a little too far apart all at once.

My eyes flick to the red glowing floor numbers, watching them change far too slowly. My hands are clasping around my luggage handle, anchoring me in place, trying to ground me and keep my thoughts from slipping out of my mouth.

The tension between us is killing me. Sharing a room is an issue, yes. It'll be easier if it were just for one night, but it isn't. We're in this city for three whole nights. Tonight is our travel day, tomorrow is for press and filming of EWC, and the last night is the Hall of Fame award show. How am I supposed to spend these nights with her in a single hotel room?

Surprisingly, she is the first to break the silence; she shifts slightly, clearing her throat. "This elevator's slow, huh?" she said with a faint smile, her voice softer than usual.

Could she be nervous, too?

"Yeah," I reply, voice tight. "Almost like it knows we shouldn't be in a room alone together."

Her eyebrows lift just a fraction, and she lets out a quiet laugh. It dies too quickly.

Ding. The elevator doors finally open, and we step out, side by side, not looking at each other.

Again, Amaya breaks the silence.

"Just so you know, I'm able to be in a room alone with you. Plus, it's not like we have to cuddle."

Amaya slides the keycard, and with a quiet beep, the door clicks open. She pushes it gently, stepping inside first. I follow behind and bump into her because she's frozen in place.

"You've *got* to be kidding me," Amaya whispers.

I scan the room. It's the standard layout, minibar, TV, a window with the curtains already drawn, and then I see it.

One bed.

Not two queens, not a king and a pull-out, not even a hopeful couch tucked in the corner.

Just one bed. Large. Centered.

"Okay, now I'm convinced that Allison is fucking with us," I growl.

"I'm going to call the front desk," she offers.

I glare at the bed again. "To curse out Allison, please let me have the pleasure."

"No, to ask for a rollaway bed." Amaya starts to dial.

I know this isn't Amaya's fault, but once I'm in a rampage type of mood, anyone who is around is subject to my wrath. "Who is going to sleep on that?" I question, knowing how uncomfortable those damn beds are.

"I will, you drama queen." Amaya rolls her eyes, and before I can reassure her I'm not being dramatic, the front desk answers her call.

I sit on the bed, watching Amaya's facial expression change from hopeful to annoyed in the blink of an eye.

"Let me guess, no rollaway beds available," I mumble, and Amaya puts her hand up, gesturing for me to shut up.

"I know this is a shot in the dark, but have there been any cancellations in the past five minutes since we last asked?" Amaya sighs and then hangs up the phone.

She looks towards me, irritation painted on her face, "Cuddling it is."

"I'll sleep on the floor before I share a bed with you," my voice comes out sharp.

The floor isn't going to be more comfortable than a rollaway bed, but it feels safer than the idea of lying inches away from her all night, pretending my heart isn't about to beat out of my chest, and my hands wanting to drift to touch her.

Just then, my phone buzzes on the bed, and Amaya's eyes land on the screen.

I didn't make a move to answer it as I saw the name and photo that appeared on the screen.

"...Your *friend* is calling." Her voice is quiet but sharp at the edges.

The ringtone keeps going. A few more seconds, then it stops.

"I've had a long day. I'm going to shower, give you some privacy to call *him* back," she said.

Amaya disappears into the bathroom, the door clicking shut behind her.

I stare at my phone, the screen showing a missed call notification and a new text.

Levi: *"Hope you landed safely. I miss you, call me back."*

Getting back to Levi is the last thing on my mind. What I'm trying to do is survive sharing this room with Amaya. I've been trying to keep my distance, and now I'm stuck in this room with everything I've been trying not to feel.

26

Amaya

I didn't lie to Ravyn when I told her I could be in a room alone with her. I'm perfectly capable of sharing a room and not acting on my feelings. Did things get more complicated when we walked into a room with one bed? Yes, but again, I have self-control. Seeing Levi's stupid face light up her phone felt like a bucket of ice water was thrown on top of me; it brought me back to reality that she does not want me, at least when she's sober.

I find Ravyn making a bed on the floor when I come out of the bathroom. I guess she's dead set on not sharing a braed with me.

Fine, more room for me.

"The hotel might not have enough rooms or rollaway beds, but they did have extra blankets and pillows." Ravyn tosses them onto the floor with a dramatic flair and a mutter, "So take that, Allison."

I can't help the laugh that slips out. "Are you seriously waging a one-sided war against the pretty front desk assistant?"

Her head snaps toward me, eyebrows raised. "You thought she was *pretty?*"

Was that a hint of jealousy?

I smirk. "Did you *not?*"

She scoffs, crossing her arms. "Didn't really get a good look. I was too busy being pissed off about our sleeping arrangements."

I lean back against the bed, stretching out a little. "Hmm. Well, if you must know… yes, I found her attractive."

Ravyn's eyes narrow. "Is that why you were doing that *thing* with your boobs?"

I choke on a laugh.

Yup. Jealousy confirmed.

"I'm not against using what I've got to get what I want," I said with a shrug, then added with a wink, "Besides, you never know what team someone plays for."

Ravyn stands quietly before grabbing her toiletry bag. "I'm going to get ready for bed," she said, heading toward the bathroom without looking back.

The bathroom door closes with a soft click behind her. The sound of running water follows soon after. Time passes slowly, and the sound of rustling sheets and the occasional creak of the old hotel bed frame joins the sound of the water as I shift to get comfortable. I scroll on my phone to pass the time. Texting my mother to let her know that I'm safe, because if I forget, she'll think I was murdered, even though she has my location. The water finally shuts off, and anticipation buzzes in the space between the ticking clock and my thoughts.

A few more minutes pass before the bathroom door opens, the steam from the shower slowly making its way into the bedroom. She steps out, hair damp, tucked behind her ears, and wearing an oversized EWC t-shirt that falls to her mid-thigh, legs bare, skin still flushed from the heat of the shower.

How is it possible for someone to look that seductive in nothing but an oversized T-shirt?

It's not tight. It doesn't cling. It's not short enough to show if she's wearing shorts or not underneath, and maybe that's what makes it worse, because somehow, the casual softness of it, the way it slips off one shoulder and hints at the shape beneath without revealing anything, was infinitely more distracting than any lingerie I've ever seen.

Effortless. Unbothered. Unfair. She doesn't have to try, and still, my thoughts are already off the rails. Her eyes met mine, just for a second. She hesitates at the doorway, taking in the sight of me already tucked beneath the covers, relaxing, trying not to look like I've been waiting for her. I offer a small smile, and without a word, she turns off the bathroom light and pads softly into the room.

She makes her way to her makeshift bed on the floor. She grabs a kit from her suitcase before she sits down on the sheets. Curiosity gets the best of me, and I shimmy my way closer to her.

"Watcha doing?" I ask.

"What does it look like I'm doing? I'm doing some last-minute touches on my gear."

"I didn't know you knew how to sew."

"Yeah, well, I had to teach myself because not everyone can afford a seamstress."

I know a dig when I hear one. "I'm sure you could afford one now."

"I could, but I got so used to doing everything myself that I don't trust anyone else to do it the right way."

"Hmm, cute glasses," my index finger flicks Ravyn's frames, making them uneven.

She sighs heavily before adjusting them, "My eyesight has always been shit, I'm as blind as a bat without contacts or glasses."

"What about—"

"And before you say, 'Ravyn, just get LASIK,' have you seen videos of that surgery? Terrifying. Hell no."

"I'm sure it's not that bad." I grab my phone to look up a video, and omg she's right.

Ravyn laughs as she studies my face, "I told you. Gross."

"That settles it, I'm going to have nightmares tonight. Thanks for that, Silver."

"You're welcome. I'm all done." She lifts her gear to admire her work before putting it away. "Goodnight, Amaya,".

"Goodnight, Ravyn," I turned off the bedside lamp.

The exhaustion I felt all day has disappeared, and I am completely wired. Knowing that Ravyn is so close yet so far. I find myself asking questions I never thought of before.

Does she snore?

Does she like it being completely dark when she sleeps?

Is she a light sleeper?

The sounds of soft, restless rustling of blankets fill the room. A sigh, followed by the squeak of the thin hotel pillow being punched into a new shape. Fabric shifting and then another sigh, this one heavier.

Ravyn's trying to get comfortable, but it clearly isn't working.

Another long pause is broken by the quiet thump of her arm hitting the floor as she flops onto her back with a dramatic groan.

I stare at the ceiling, biting back a smile. Listening to her struggle down there, half annoyed, half stubborn, is endearing in a way that makes it impossible to keep pretending I'm asleep.

"You don't have to sleep down there. This is a king bed, for God's sake, there's enough room for both of us."

"Nope, I'm good."

The carpet softens the sound, but I can still hear it all. The faint creak of the floor beneath her, the constant shifting as she readjusted over and over.

Before I can stop myself, the thought slips out, unfiltered, unplanned.

"I guess Levi wouldn't be too thrilled about you sharing a bed with me, huh?"

The words hang in the air, heavier than I expect. I swear the room is quieter, like even the walls are waiting to see how she'll respond. Ravyn gets up; the moonlight is the only thing lighting the room, slipping in through the thin hotel curtains, catching the edges of her face, her hair, the outline of her body.

"Fine, you win. I'll sleep in the bed, but we're sleeping head to toe.

She places her pillows on the end of the bed and slides into her side of the bed, careful not to brush against me, though the mattress dips slightly under her weight. Her head rests where my feet are, and I've never been so happy to have a fresh pedicure.

The room settles back into silence, and still, sleep isn't coming. The only noise is the slow, steady rhythm of our breathing and the faint hum of the city beyond the curtains.

"So, Ramirez?"

She sighed, "You caught that, huh?"

"Oh yeah, the minute I heard it, I stashed that away for safekeeping in my brain."

"It was my mom's last name. She didn't know who my father was, so I got the pleasure of inheriting her surname."

"Ah, gotcha. So did she speak Spanish at home?"

"When she was home, she could barely string together a single sentence. Mariana and I had a lot of time on our hands when we were in the system, and so we learned different languages. She's fluent in Spanish, but I picked it up easily, so I decided why not try other languages too. It comes in handy."

"Not Mariana knowing Spanish, too. Aiden is going to have my head when he finds out," I groan.

"Oh, he already knows. Mariana said he's waiting for the right moment to rub it in your face," she laughs.

Silence fills the room once again, and without warning, she speaks, "I slept with Levi." Ravyn whispers.

The words hit like a sudden chill.

You knew this was going to happen. She's not yours, she's never been yours.

I'm trying to control my thoughts, find the right response.

Sometimes the hardest thing isn't losing someone who was never fully yours, but watching them choose someone else. "I get it. Some things don't just fade away."

"It felt... different."

I'm trying to be strong, but hearing her sexual escapades with Levi will be the death of me. "No offense, but I do not want to hear about sex with Levi."

"I faked it."

Well, now I'm intrigued.

"Why?" I ask.

She hesitates, "I didn't want to hurt his feelings. Honestly, I'm not even sure why I slept with him in the first place."

That was a lie. I knew exactly why, but I wasn't about to be the one to say it.

"With him, intimacy was effortless. Physically, it was incredible; I never faked it once. But now..."

She trails off, and I hold my breath, waiting for her to say it.

To say he isn't *you*, Amaya. That she wants *me*.

Instead, she whispers, "It's like there's a barrier I can't break through, no matter how much I want to."

"It felt like a random hookup, not someone who truly knows you."

"Exactly," she tapped me with her foot.

I know that feeling all too well. It's all I've ever had, except that night with Ravyn. That night was different.

"You know, that night at the bar? He said, 'It's insane how seriously the crowd takes the matches. They do know wrestling's fake, right?"

I shoot up from the bed. "He did *not*."

"Amaya, it took everything in me not to slap that man across his face."

"Yet you still slept with him." The words come out sharper than I mean them to.

"Yeah, well… shit happens."

Is that what she told people about us? Shit happens.

"Is it safe to assume you haven't told Levi any of this? Since he's still calling you."

She groans, running a hand through her hair. "I'm a shitty person, I know."

"You're not," I said, surprising even myself.

Ravyn shifts, sitting cross-legged on the bed. "Wait. Was that a compliment?"

I ignore the bait. "I'm just saying you tried. You tried to go back to what you had with Levi, but you couldn't, because you're not the same person anymore. He knew you as that broken girl looking for somewhere to belong. Now? You're a grown woman who knows exactly where she's meant to be. You grew apart. It's okay to admit that."

She stays quiet, her leg jittering.

"But eventually, you're going to have to talk to him. Ghosting him *would* make you a shitty person."

Her voice comes quickly, almost defensively. "I would never."

I nod my head in agreement, readjusting myself on the bed, finally feeling my eyelids get heavy.

"I used to think Levi and I were endgame," she said softly. "That's why I never really looked anywhere else for something real. Some part of me always held onto the hope that he'd come back." She lets out a dry laugh. "And now that he finally has… I don't even want him anymore. Funny how that works."

"You want my advice?" I ask.

Ravyn stays quiet, and I don't wait for a response to continue.

"It's not stupid to give people second chances. I've been trying to tell Reina this for years. You gave Levi a second chance, but it didn't work. That's life. One day, you're going to find someone special. You're going to care so much that it's gonna be terrifying, but if you care about someone, really care… don't hold back just because it's scary. Say it first. People think that timing matters more than truth, but it doesn't. You can miss something real waiting for the 'right' moment."

"That's pretty solid advice."

"Thank you. I'm not completely hopeless in the relationship department."

"I've never seen you with anyone."

"That's because I haven't found someone special. It's hard to find a person who can understand what it means to be an Acosta without wanting to date me for being an Acosta. Or finding a person who isn't threatened by the fact that I'm bi and I'm constantly surrounded by hot men and women for work. I understand that I'm a nepo baby, but it doesn't mean that it's all sunshine and rainbows."

I feel the bed shift as Ravyn moves, bringing her pillow with her to rest her head next to mine. We lay there in the peaceful quiet, looking into each other's eyes.

"I'm sorry for all the shit I gave you in the past for being an Acosta. I never thought about the pressure you would be under. I promise you won't hear the word nepo baby come out of my lips ever again."

I look down at her lips, wanting to feel their softness against mine, to use a kiss to seal in her promise. Instead, I shake my head, a silent thank you.

My eyes begin to flutter shut, fighting sleep so I can look at Ravyn a little longer. I know when we wake up tomorrow, she'll be guarded again.

"Can I ask you a question?" Ravyn whispers.

"That's a question," I replied.

"Why did you *really* go off script that night with Tashi?"

I can tell Ravyn is just as sleepy as I am; it creeps in like a slow tide. She's curling up beside me, blanket pulled to her chin, blinking slowly and lazily.

"I shouldn't say this," I murmured, voice barely above a whisper.

She glances over. "Then don't. It's okay, I don't have to know."

I smile faintly. "Who am I kidding? I'm too tired to care."

Her eyes close, then open again halfway, like she's teetering on the edge of sleep.

"I didn't like the way she was talking about you. She called you my little bitch, and you're not that. You're so much more than what people think, Ramona." I confess, so softly it almost blends into the silence. "You mean so much more to me... I'm just scared to admit it."

She's silent, breathing slowly, eyes shut, completely still.

Did she hear me?

I can't tell. Maybe she did, maybe she didn't. But the words are out there, finally. Still, I know how tomorrow will go. I'll wake up and pretend it never slipped out, because I can't give my heart to her. Not when she's still pretending she doesn't know what *this* is. I can't be the one who falls first just to prove it's safe.

I've been down this road, falling for the ones who kiss me in the dark and call it a mistake in the morning. I won't do it again, not even for her.

She's beautiful and brave, but if she's not ready to be brave about this... about *me*... then I have to protect my heart, even if it means breaking it a little in the process.

27

Ravyn

Today has been a blur of lights, cameras, and the same ten questions asked a dozen different ways. It's been go, go, go since Amaya and I woke up this morning.

Thankfully, she's a heavy sleeper because I had to roll out of her arms. I woke up to her warmth, steady breathing, and arm slung across my waist. Her legs were tangled with mine, our bodies pressed close like puzzle pieces that had quietly found their fit sometime in the night. I was wrapped around the one person I'd promised myself I'd keep at arm's length. For a second, I let myself stay there. Let myself feel what it was like to belong in someone's arms, even by accident.

The reality of what she said last night hit me, *"You mean so much more to me... I'm just scared to admit it."*

We both got ready for our day in silence and stayed that way the entire car ride to the studio. From the moment we walked in, it was go-time, smiling widely, answering each question like it was the first time. Then there were the photo shoots in between. A few solo and a few with Amaya, the photographer directing our poses, each one getting closer and closer to one another. Quick wardrobe changes.

Days like these usually don't bug me, but the thought of this being the most action I'll be getting tonight is getting to me. Amaya isn't going to need my help tonight; she's set to win this fight on her own to prove a point.

So I will just be sitting on the sidelines, cheering her on. I hate that I'm not wrestling, but I must admit I love that I get to be ringside to see Amaya fight. I've always had to watch from inside the ring or backstage.

By the end of the day, my cheeks ached from holding the same expression, my back hurt from standing in the same three poses, and I could barely remember who I'd told what. It's all a part of the job. Sell the story. Build the moment. Make them believe even when people know it's scripted.

* * *

"Are you ready for tonight?" Amaya asks as we make our way towards the arena, the low rumble of the crowd already buzzing in the distance.

"I should be asking you that," I shoot back. "You're the one actually stepping into the ring."

She glances at me, her expression softening. "I know that this sucks, and I wish you didn't have to do this, but we'll find a way to get you out of this storyline as quickly as possible. Trust me, I hate seeing you play valet just as much as you hate doing it."

Her words from last night echoed in my head: *You're so much more than what people think, Ramona.*

"Yeah, well, whatever your game plan is, just make sure Val thinks it's her idea or she'll never go for it."

Amaya smirks, that familiar fire in her eyes. "Oh, I know how to handle Valerie Archer."

I arch a brow, fighting a smile. "Whatever you say, Red."

The arena lights dim, and the crowd's energy shifts instantly, buzzing with anticipation. Then Amaya's music hits. I'm not sure why it didn't dawn on me that becoming Amaya's valet would mean I'll be walking down to her music instead of mine, and I'm not going to lie, it stings a little. The bass drops, lights pulse to the rhythm, and the screen lit up with her name in bold, electric letters. Another blow to my ego. My ears adjust to the loudness of the crowd, and I notice it then the crowd is booing.

I look over to Amaya, and she's looking around the arena in disbelief. This is the first time in history that an Acosta is making their entrance, and the crowd is booing. I want to ask her how she's feeling and know if she's handling this okay, but I can't. This is live TV, and we can't break character.

So why is it that I do exactly that? Our hands brush. Just a graze at first. It can easily pass as an accident. That is, until I reach for her. Deliberate. Slow. Fingers barely grazing hers before curling between them. Her eyes flick down to our hands, then up to meet my eyes, wide, uncertain, but she doesn't pull away.

This is too intimate. What are we doing? Everything's being filmed, analyzed, and replayed. But at that moment, none of it matters, and I don't let go. Amaya gives me a small nod, cool, composed. The boos are pouring in from every side, but she doesn't flinch. She steps into it, owns it. She raises our hands high, fingers still laced, the championship belt gleaming on her shoulder. A signal to the crowd, we're a unit, valet and champion, standing tall in the face of their hatred, daring them to do something about it.

Just like that, the story shifts. We aren't caught doing something intimate; we were in control, and I can't thank Amaya enough for saving my ass. We kept our hands interlocked, and every movement down the ramp is a statement; this isn't just a match, it's a moment in EWC history.

We lock our eyes on the ring ahead, ignoring the hands, the flashy signs, the noise. Tashi is already waiting in the ring for Amaya, jaw tight, shoulders squared.

"Give her hell. Show them a real reason to boo you." I whisper in Amaya's ear.

She nods and pulls me into a hug. This shouldn't catch me off guard, not after everything we've done, but somehow, it does. My whole body locks up. We've made out, hooked up in a hot tub, and whispered things in the dark. All of that, yet we've never hugged, and weirdly, this feels more intimate than all of it.

I'm standing there, stunned and looking like a complete idiot, when she pulls back and smirks slightly. "Hold this for me, will you?"

She hands me the championship belt. It's heavy in my hands, and part of me wants to run with it, just bolt out of the arena and not look back. But there's this other part, quieter and unfamiliar, that just wants to protect it for her. To keep it safe until she needs it again.

Because she *earned* it. She *deserves* it.

I head over to the announcer table, lowering into my seat, the championship on my lap. I slide on the headset and adjust the mic, eyes flicking back to the ring where she stands, calm, collected, already owning the moment.

Yeah, she's about to put on a show, and I've got the best seat in the house.

28

Amaya

The boos hit me loud; the entire crowd decided, in one breath, to reject my existence.

Oh my God, I *love* it.

Yeah, there's a part of me that hears it differently. Beneath the thunder of boos, there's a voice in my head I can't shut out. It remembers what it feels like to be cheered, but that's not my role anymore. I bury those feelings and bury them deep, because the truth is, it's intoxicating being the villain. I used to think being the good guy was the best; it's what I watched my family do, night after night, arena after arena. I was raised on it.

They don't *have* to love me.

They just have to *remember* me.

And judging by the volume right now? Mission accomplished.

I glance over at Ravyn, and for a second, I almost break character.

She's sitting there at the announcer's table, championship belt resting across her lap like it belongs there, and there's no doubt in my mind that one day it'll be hers. The sight of her in that moment just *fits*, in a way that catches me off guard.

I've never been the type to rewatch my matches unless my dad's breathing down my neck about it for training purposes. Today's match, I'll make sure to watch, because seeing her laugh and lean in toward the commentators, headset on, completely at ease, is something I want to rewatch. The curiosity of what she is saying is also killing me.

I'll rewatch not to study my technique.

Not to watch my win.

Just to hear what *she* has to say.

The fight starts, and it's time for me to shut out the rest of the world. Here's the thing about professional wrestling: Just because you know who's going to win the match, it doesn't mean that you know how the match is going to play out. Things can change in the blink of an eye, a move can go completely wrong, a miscommunication can happen. So much is on the line when you're in this ring.

Tashi and I clash hard in the center of the ring. The match starts hot, stiff, and fast-paced.

She catches me coming off the ropes and hits me with a thunderous spinebuster. The ring shakes under the impact. She hooks my leg, looking for the pin, but I kick out just in time.

I roll to my knees, barely catching my breath, when Tashi wraps a hand around my throat.

The crowd rises. Thinking that this will be what gets me, but today will not be the day I lose my title, especially to Tashi.

She lifts me, trying to get her chokeslam to land, but I escape mid-air, landing behind her. I spin Tashi around and give her a swift knee to the gut.

We play this back and forth for what feels like ages, each of us taking hits.

Finally, it's time to end this. I hook both arms under Tashi's legs and lift her into my finisher, *The Final Flame.*

I slam her with all my power, her back hitting the mat. The ring explodes with sound, and the crowd boos as I go for the pin.

"One. Two —"

Tashi kicks out, and I'm losing it. That should've taken her out, but if she wants to keep on fighting, we can keep going.

We're exchanging slaps and strikes. Tashi screams, and she grabs me by the throat again, and this time her hold is too strong to get out of. She lifts and slams me, knocking the air out of my lungs as she tries again for the pin.

"One. Two—"

I kick out, barely.

Tashi backs into the corner, her frustration growing by the second. I stumble to my feet, and that's when she charges. I dodge her, and as she bounces off the ropes, I superkick her, making her fall on the mat.

I pull Tashi back to her feet. Setting her up for what I hope is the final time. I deliver *The Final Flame* again, and I can tell this time she's out for the count. I drag Tashi into the center of the ring.

"One. Two. Three."

The bell rings and the announcer yells into the mic, "You're winner and still EWC Women's champion, Amaya Acosta."

I roll off of Tashi and raise my arms in victory as the referee checks on her.

Suddenly, my feet lift off the mat, and I'm being swung around like a rag doll by Ravyn before she sets me down and hands me my title belt.

"That's right, all on her own. She doesn't need anyone's help," she yells to make sure everyone in the arena can hear.

My music is playing, and we're celebrating as we walk out of the ring. The crowd is booing us, and we don't care.

"Hey, Ravyn, Amaya."

The music stops as we both turn around. Tashi is standing up, her arm around her stomach, and a mic in the other hand.

"This isn't over. You won the battle, but you haven't won the war."

We both shrug her off, but the crowd is cheering her on, and so she continues.

"I want a rematch, but not just any rematch, no, I want to make things interesting. A triple threat match."

Amaya and I look at one another in disbelief.

There was no talk with Val about a triple threat match. Is the newbie going off script?

The crowd erupts, cheering us on to do it, to accept the challenge.

Ravyn and I have already pissed off Val multiple times. What's one more?

I run towards the ring, sliding under the ropes, and grab the mic from Tashi.

"You love to push your luck, don't you, Tashi. I do love to gamble, so we accept your triple threat match. Matter of fact, where's a better place to gamble than in Vegas?"

The crowd is going wild because they know where this is going. It's the most anticipated night of the year, and I'm just about to make myself the main event fight.

"Ravyn and I will see you on Dominance Day."

29

Amaya

In all the years I've been with the EWC, I could count the time I've been called into Val's office on one hand. Yet, since I've been working with Ravyn, it feels like it's every other day that I'm here.

"I didn't realize we had a bunch of writers out in the ring wrestling. If you were looking for another position in the company, all you had to do was ask." Val snaps.

She stands before us with her arms crossed; the tension in the air is thick enough to choke on.

"Val, you're missing the point," I said, trying to keep my tone even, but my heart is racing in my chest.

She glares at me, and I about shitted myself. "Amaya, tread lightly," she warns, her voice low and dangerous.

I take a careful breath, trying to stand my ground even as my insides squirm. "The whole reason you have Ravyn and me out there together is because of the crowd's reaction. Have you seen the buzz Dominance Day is getting after tonight's announcement?"

"Of course I saw it," she said, her tone clipped. "I'm not blind."

"Then you know your plan worked. Ravyn and I stuck together, going after Tashi, and it lit a fire. People are talking. Hyped. I really think this could be the most-watched Dominance Day in history."

Val doesn't move, doesn't blink. My heart's still pounding hard in my chest, and I'm worried she can hear it.

"We might have deviated from the script a *little*," I add, choosing my words carefully, "but it's because your foundation for the story was so strong that it led us in this direction."

I hold my breath, hoping my flattery will soften Val just enough so she won't kill me.

"Get out of my office, Amaya."

I swallow hard, nod once, and turn on my heels. A small smile tugs at the corner of my lips.

Victory.

* * *

I woke up feeling like a truck had run over me. My body's sore from the fight last night, and my brain is reeling from how amazing Ravyn was. As she sleeps beside me, I put on my headphones and silently watch my match with Tashi. I find myself fully entranced by every word Ravyn said throughout this match.

My favorite line of the night, *"I used to talk a lot of crap about Amaya being where she is because of who her dad is, but I have to admit that I was wrong. She works hard, I mean, look how she easily reversed that choke slam from Tashi. Amaya deserves this belt, but that doesn't mean I'm going to stop trying to take it from her."*

I look over at her, the only light in the room coming from my cellphone screen. Her lips parting slightly, her breathing slow and even. She looks beautiful like this, a softness to her face. Unguarded. Peaceful. I was hoping to see her this morning with her usual bed head, but she was gone by the time I woke up. I look at the clock and shoot out of bed. I'm late for my meeting with Dad, and he's going to kill me.

My phone begins to ring, and I don't want to answer it, but I know I have to. I haven't talked to him since I turned heel. I've been avoiding him like the plague, asking Mom or Reira for updates about his legs, but I can't do that anymore, especially not tonight, since he's being inducted into the EWC Hall of Fame.

"I know, I know. I'll be there in ten minutes, I swear," I said breathlessly, juggling my phone between my shoulder and cheek as I put on a pair of leggings.

"You know how long it takes me to get anywhere these days with this damn wheelchair," my dad snapped, his voice rough with frustration.

"I'm sorry, Dad, I just— I got my period and—"

"Amaya, por favor. Enough." His voice cut through mine, sharp and uncomfortable. "I don't want to hear that. Just… hurry and get here."

After all these years, the period line still works to get my dad to shut down and leave me be.

We met up at a brunch spot a couple of blocks down the road from the hotel. My heart sinks when I see him in his wheelchair. I've never seen my father as frail before, and I don't like it; it's a reminder that he's getting older.

"Hey, Dad." I bend down and press a kiss to his cheek, catching the faint scent of his aftershave—familiar, grounding.

"Hi, *mi hija.*" His voice is even, but there's something tight beneath it. "Thank you for finally joining me."

There it is.

"Sorry." I can't help but look down like I'm a little kid again, getting a stern talking to. "Why didn't you let Mom come? She could've helped you. Or Aiden."

"I don't need anyone's help to get around. I can do it just fine."

Stubborn old man.

"So…" I trail off, still avoiding his eyes.

"I'm glad to see you still have your title," he said. "Even though you went against everything the Acostas have built for generations."

I flinched, his words hitting harder than I expected. I want to push back, explain, but I know better. You don't talk back to Andres Acosta. He doesn't believe in discussions, only declarations. If something isn't done his way, the way he taught you, then it's wrong. No exceptions.

"You never told me there was a clause in our contracts to never become heel," I said quietly.

"I didn't think I had to explain what the family brand is to you. Have you not seen it with your own eyes your entire life?"

"I did what I felt needed to be done."

"You tainted your image and the Acosta name for what? For *Ravyn?*" His voice sharpens. "You *hate* each other."

I open my mouth, then close it. I'm not sure that's true anymore. At least… not for me, I used to think I did. Ravyn's everything I'm not supposed to be in the ring: reckless, unpredictable, raw in a way that couldn't be polished or packaged like the Acosta brand. She doesn't have to worry about legacy or image. Somewhere in between the matches and the forced alliance, the lines blurred and something shifted.

I saw her.

Not the heel.

Not the chaos.

Her.

She's smarter than people give her credit for. Fiercer, too. And real. Unapologetically, maddeningly real. When the cameras stop rolling and the audience fades, she's still the same. Even though it's hard, she owns every part of herself, even the messy, jagged ones that she doesn't let anyone see.

Ravyn challenges me in ways no one else has ever dared. Not because she hates me, but because she sees the parts of me I keep buried under legacy and expectation. She calls them out. Sometimes, I think she knows me better than I know myself.

So no… I don't think I hate her.

I think I'm terrified of what I *do* feel.

"I wanted your alliance to be with Tashi. She's the star. *Not* Ravyn."

"You underestimate her." The words fly out before I can stop them, defensive, instinctive.

His eyes roam, looking me up and down, assessing me. "Then I guess I underestimated *you*, too." A pause. "Val and I have had an interesting conversation about how we can fix this."

"There's nothing to fix," I said, rising to my feet, my voice steady now.

"The crowd's eating this up. They *like* that I turned heel. And honestly... so do I."

He opens his mouth, but I don't let him interrupt.

"I have a main event match on Dominance Day, I still hold the championship, and I'm thriving. Just because it's not happening under *your* terms doesn't mean I'm failing. I wish you could see that your way isn't the *only* way."

I turn before he can respond. My legs move faster than my heart can keep up.

"I'll see you at the ceremony," I call over my shoulder, and I don't stop walking until I'm out of sight.

Only then do I let the tears fall, silent and burning.

30

Ravyn

I'm thankful for the empty agenda before today's Hall of Fame. I woke up early and headed to the hotel's gym. Amaya's sleeping like the dead, doesn't stir at all while I'm getting ready this morning. She lies on her side, one arm tucked beneath the pillow, her red hair a tousled halo around her face. Her brow, always furrowed in the ring, is smooth now. I want to reach out and trace the curve of her cheek, kiss her lips goodbye. Instead, I leave the room, memorizing how beautiful she looks. We'd both go back to playing our roles when she opens her eyes.

I hoped we'd be getting ready for the event together, maybe even make our entrance side by side. Silly, right? Who was I kidding? It's an event to spotlight the best of the best. The spotlight's burning hot, the air thick with ego and legacy. It's the night of the who's who of EWC, and Amaya Acosta? She's very much a *somebody*. And me? I'm just the girl watching from the shadows, pretending it doesn't sting that I'm not standing beside her.

I do one final check in the mirror before heading downstairs. My black, floor-length gown shimmers with every subtle movement, thousands of tiny sequins catching the light in the room, and I know they'll sparkle more under the photographers' flashes. The dress hugs my figure with effortless elegance, the neckline showing just enough cleavage. I've never been a fan of heels, so under my gown is my favorite pair of combat boots.

My makeup makes my skin warm and bronzed. The smoky eye shadow is making my hazel eyes pop. My hair is in loose Hollywood waves, freshly dyed this morning after my workout, making the silver streaks in the front stand out even more as they frame my face like deliberate lightning bolts. I apply the final touches of gloss, adjusting the diamond clasp on my wrist, and exhale slowly before walking out to EWC's most glamorous night of the year.

* * *

The red carpet is lined with flashing cameras and eager reporters. Spotlights beaming from every corner, making everything shimmer: gowns, jewels, and smiles. A dozen voices call my name, microphones extending as I stop at each news outlet in attendance to give them their insider scoop. I keep my stride steady, my practiced smile is in place, pausing just long enough for the photos. The gold of the EWC Hall of Fame backdrop gleams behind me. All around, familiar faces pose and mingle, air-kissing and laughing.

All of this commotion around me, yet my eyes are searching for the only person I care to see at this event.

Of all the faces here... why does yours always feel like the one I'm searching for?

The photographers start to yell her last name, and I follow their direction. First, I see her father getting rolled onto the carpet by her mother. Aiden follows close behind, and then I see *her*. The crowd blurs. Time slows, just for a second. She's glowing.

Her dress is a deep emerald color that hugs her petite frame like it's made just for her; it probably was, I doubt an Acosta wears anything off the rack. The satin fabric catches the light with a soft sheen, the rich green a perfect contrast to her sun-warmed skin and fiery red hair. A delicate off-the-shoulder neckline showcases her collarbones and the freckles that are painted there. The bodice is structured with intricate embroidery that shimmers with subtle gold thread, just enough to catch the eye without stealing the moment. The dress flares gently at the waist into a flowing skirt that sweeps just above the floor, revealing a glimpse of gold-strapped heels with every step. Her hair is swept up in soft curls, the rest cascading down her back, a few strands framing her face and drawing attention to the green eyes that haunt my dreams.

She turns, scanning the crowd casually, until her eyes meet mine, and at that moment, she freezes. Just for a second. Like the air caught in her lungs. Her posture doesn't change, still graceful, still confident. I catch a flicker of warmth behind her green eyes, the slight curve at the corner of her mouth that isn't quite a smile, but close, and it's just for me.

I want to go up to her, but it'll be social suicide to go up to the Acosta family while they're getting their photos taken on the carpet. I'm sure I'll get to see her at the after-party. For now, I'll admire from a distance as she single-handedly outshines everyone on the carpet.

"The royal family of the EWC has arrived." A voice behind me whispers.

I turn around to find Tashi, and per usual, she looks breathtaking. Her gown, a deep, jewel-toned sapphire, perfectly complements her beautiful, deep skin tone. The dress has a high slit that reveals her perfectly toned legs, and is cinched at the waist with a velvet sash that adds just a touch of drama. Her big, voluminous curls are worn proudly, wild and soft all at once, framing her face. Tashi's eyes, those warm, chocolate brown eyes, are lined with a subtle shimmer, their depth drawing every glance in the room. She isn't just wearing the dress; she *owns* it.

"You look great, Tashi," I said, offering a sincere smile.

"I know." She shrugs, a sly smirk tugging at her lips.

I turn back around, watching as Amaya and her family make their way down the carpet. Then, without warning, Tashi asks, "Do you ever get tired of living in the Acostas' shadow?"

The question lands like a slap. "Whoa," I blink, caught off guard. "Where did that come from?" I ask without turning around.

She doesn't miss a beat. "I've only been with EWC a few months, and I'm already exhausted by how everything seems to revolve around them. I can't imagine how it feels for you, years in the company, and still no championship. And now, look." She gestures with her hand toward Amaya, who's smiling effortlessly beside her father as the cameras flash. "Still the center of attention."

"You just have to trust the process," I replied, trying to keep my voice even.

Tashi raises an eyebrow. "Is that what you've been doing?" Her tone dripped with sarcasm. "Because from where I'm standing, 'trusting the process' has turned you into a valet."

I stay in place, refusing to turn towards her. She wants a reaction. She wants to rattle me. But not tonight.

She leans in slightly, lowering her voice just enough to make it sting. "All I'm saying is, you're better than this. EWC should be talking about *you* just as much as they talk about the Acostas. I bet Val's already got it scripted for Amaya to win the triple threat, and when she does, guess who'll be standing at ringside again like a well-dressed prop?"

With that, Tashi turns on her heels, walking away, and I can't help but think there might be some truth to her words.

31

Ravyn

The arena has been transformed. Spotlights sweep across the crowd, wrestlers are seated in rows of velvet-covered chairs on the arena floor, their formal attire a striking contrast to the usual sea of wrestling merch-wearing fans that love a good roaring chant. Banners of legendary matches and iconic moments hang high above the stage. The ring's gone, and in its place is a sleek stage with a podium flanked by giant LED screens looping highlights of the people whose careers we're celebrating tonight.

A reverent hush settles as the ceremony begins. Both Val and her mother, Melanie, walk out, and every wrestler in attendance stands on their feet and cheers them on. The booming voice of the announcer echoes with their introduction, as though they need one.

"Hello there. Haven't seen this bunch in a while." Melanie speaks into the microphone.

"I promise I've been taking good care of them, Mom," Val jokes, and the crowd cheers.

I have to fight off an eye roll, knowing that cameras are on me.

"Tonight we celebrate wrestling and the people that help make so many iconic moments happen on the screen," Melanie said.

Val announces the wrestlers one by one. A wave of applause sweeps through the crowd. Families rise to their feet, fellow wrestlers clap with pride, and in the soft stage lights, more than a few eyes are brimming with tears.

The air is full of nostalgia, memories of blood, sweat, sacrifice, and triumph. These aren't just athletes; they're storytellers, warriors, and icons. They're everything I'm striving to be and more. Each wrestler has chosen someone close to them to speak on their behalf. Friends, mentors, sons, and daughters.

One by one, the speeches unfold. Some are funny, others gut-wrenchingly honest. All are moving, and with each tribute, I feel tears well in my eyes.

Someday, I want this to be a part of my story. I want to walk across that stage not just as a wrestler, but as someone who's made it, someone remembered, someone loved by their family, and honored by their peers. I want my legacy to matter.

Amaya rises slowly from her seat, smoothing the front of her dress with trembling hands. I've never seen Amaya nervous in her life, and I can't help but worry. Besides her, Aiden stands tall, offering a steady hand and a quiet nod. Together, they begin the walk towards the stage as their father's entrance music fills the area. The giant screen behind the podium flickers with images of their father in his prime, arms raised in victory, eyes wild with the same fire I see in Amaya's when she's in the ring.

As they reach the podium, Amaya pauses for the briefest moment, and she draws a deep breath. Then, with her brother at her side, she adjusts the mic, ready to honor the man who has shaped not only wrestling history but their very lives.

"When anyone hears the name Andres Acosta, the first thing that comes to mind is his bad ass German Suplex. That move came to be known as the Acosta Collision, and man, did a lot of wrestlers crash headfirst into it."

The crowd laughs, including me. To anyone else, Amaya looks happy to be here. Yet… there's a flicker, subtle but unmistakable, the way her eyes dart away when her brother starts to talk about what their father has taught them about wrestling and family values.

Most people wouldn't notice.

Most people don't know her like I do.

She's on. Performing. I sit still, heart heavy.

What happened between last night and this morning?

Amaya laughs at a joke Aiden tells before continuing, "We've seen the ice packs, the bruises, the late-night flights, and the early-morning gym sessions. You showed us that hard work matters. That getting knocked down doesn't mean you stay down. Tonight, the world is giving you the recognition you've earned, but we want you to know, you've been our Hall of Famer since the day we were born. We're so proud of you, Dad. We love you, and we'll be cheering you on forever."

"Without further introduction. The man, the myth, the legend, Andres Acosta." Aiden announces into the mic.

Andres is getting pushed down the ramp by his wife, the audience rising to their feet in a wave of thunderous applause. A roar of appreciation fills the arena, echoing off every corner as he makes his way towards the stage. Amaya stands just beside her mother, subtly positioning herself behind her, as though using her as a shield. When Andres reaches the side of the podium, his wife passes him the mic as he looks out at the crowd with a quiet smile.

"Wow," he said, pausing. "Just… wow. I wish I could give you all a standing ovation… but maybe next time."

The audience chuckles warmly.

"Looking out at this crowd, I don't see colleagues, I see family. My brothers and sisters in this business. For years, I flew across the world, laced up my boots, walked down arena ramps, and gave everything I had in that ring. I fought for the titles, for the roar of the crowd, for the moments that live forever. They say wrestling isn't just a job, it's a lifestyle. And they're right. But I'd do it all again, because wrestling didn't just give me a career… it gave me joy, and more than that, it gave me *her,* the ultimate joy in my life."

He reaches for his wife's hand and kisses it gently, his voice softens.

"My wife, who gave up her career as a ring announcer when we started a family. You held it all together when I was chasing this dream across the country. You're the real champ."

Her face becomes flushed as she squeezes his hand.

"I want to thank the fans; without you, we'd be nothing. To EWC, thank you for being the kind of company that lets me and my family thrive in this business we love. To my tag partners, my opponents, my rivals, you'll always have a special place in my heart. Every bump, every promo, every match… it was all part of the story. To the boys and girls in the locker room: keep pushing, keep fighting, keep respecting the craft. And if any of you think you can beat my kids… think again. Thank you."

Another round of laughter rolls through the crowd before they start their applause, and that's when I catch it. Mr. Acosta is looking straight at me. There's a flicker in his eyes. A warning. A quiet message wrapped inside a smile. He turns his gaze back to the audience, raising his hand in appreciation, but I can't shake the chill that runs through me.

32

Amaya

I should be getting an award tonight for the amount of concentration that's needed to not eye fuck Ravyn. Holy shit, she looks amazing. She's moving like she owns the space, like she doesn't need anyone's permission to shine. That *dress.* Her curves are being hugged just right. That *hair.* Those silver streaks that I love so much are on full display. Those *lips.* I stop my train of thought because I can't go there. Especially tonight, with the number of eyes watching me.

Her elegance is effortless, and as she walks, I catch her footwear peeking out from under her dress. A smirk on my lips, combat boots. Of course. Ravyn's skin is glowing, almost like she's lighting up from within. Her smoky eye is drawing me in. *Christ*, those eyes will be my undoing. The way they shift in the light.

The after-party is pulsing with raw, electric energy. Held in the rooftop lounge of our hotel, the city skyline casts a glow over the crowd. The bass from the DJ booth is thumping as wrestlers and their families mingle in tailored suits and glittering gowns, championship belts slung over shoulders like status symbols. I motion with my glass to the bartender, letting him know I'm ready for another round. They have custom cocktails named after finishing moves: The Suplex Sour, The Heel Turn, The Sharpshooter, and, of course, the Acosta Collision. Plates of gourmet finger food make their rounds, and photos are being snapped by both the professionals hired and the partygoers. The bartender hands me my drink, and I thank him before taking a sip and continuing to people-watch.

"You know, you could go socialize instead of being the creep in the corner watching everyone else have fun."

Ravyn's voice is velvet in my ear and immediately sends goosebumps down my arm.

"I could, but I like people-watching. I find it more entertaining than pretending to be interested in a conversation about how *amazing my father is* and *how he changed the industry.*"

"Fair enough. I get tired of hearing about how great the Acostas are, too." Ravyn shrugs as she takes a sip of her drink.

I look at her nervously. Knowing that a drinking Ravyn is a dangerous Ravyn, and we're sharing a room.

"Is that so? Interesting, since one of those people singing me praises is you. I watched your commentary last night." I confess, and Ravyn blushes.

"I was playing my role of dotting valet."

I shake my head, pretending that I believe the words coming out of her mouth.

"Well, if what you said *was* true, you're claiming it *wasn't.*" I pause to take another sip of my drink. "I *would* tell you, what you said was the nicest thing that anyone who has 'hating me' on their favorite hobbies list has ever said to me."

Ravyn bursts into a fit of laughter. "Oh, wow. That feels like ages ago. Funny enough, I can't seem to find that list."

"Looks like it's time to make a new one then," I smirk.

The DJ changes the fast pace of the current song, blending it into a slow tempo. I can't help but smile when I see my parents on the dance floor. Even with my dad in a wheelchair, he asks my mom to dance. He places her on his lap and starts doing wheelies in the middle of the dance floor.

I know he means well; he isn't a bad person, but the conversation from earlier keeps replaying in my head, and as I gave my speech tonight, I felt like a fraud.

"Are you okay?" Ravyn asks, taking me out of my head.

"Is it that obvious?"

"To the trained eye, it is."

"Are you saying that you're trained in all things Amaya?" I arch my eyebrow.

"Not all things," Ravyn replies, licking her lips and looking down at mine.

The shift is subtle but unmistakable. I feel it instantly. I try to break eye contact, but I can't. Instead, I try to change the subject and stupidly stick my foot in my mouth, "I love this song."

Dammit, she's going to think I want to dance.

Of course, I would love to dance with her, but I stay frozen. One foot forward neglects *everything* I've been trying to avoid. A held-out hand will bring us closer and betray *everything* I've been doing to keep us apart.

Ravyn doesn't move either, but she doesn't look away. The question is in her eyes, on the tip of her lips. Yet, neither of us dares cross the line. Not here. Not in front of everyone. Too many eyes. Too much risk. Too many questions that'll arise that Ravyn will brush off as a friendly dance when we both know it's more than that.

"May I have this dance?" A voice I know all too well asks me.

I roll my eyes as I turn around to my brother, bowing with his hand held out.

"If it gets you to stop bowing, then yes."

"Weird, I would think you would be happy to see me bowing down to you since you're the Drama Queen after all."

I smack him on his chest.

"Hey, Ravyn." He moves to hug Ravyn, and I watch, making sure his hands don't linger.

"Hey, Aiden."

"Is Mariana around? If so, I'd rather dance with her; you can have Amaya."

Before Ravyn has a chance to answer, I pull Aiden by the back of his jacket collar, "Let's go, Romeo."

We make it to the dance floor, and I make sure to avoid where our parents are dancing, not wanting my dad to try and cut in. My hands are on Aiden's shoulders, his on my waist, both of us swaying to the song. Not the person I want to dance with, but even when he doesn't know it, Aiden saves my ass. I'm laughing at the thought, shaking my head at the situation.

"You clean up nicely, Acosta. I like the hair." I nod towards Aiden's freshly dyed locks.

"Tonight felt like a blue hair type of occasion," he shrugs.

He spins me around, looking me up and down while he does. "You don't look so bad yourself, Acosta. Though I think your hair could use a bit more color."

I slap him on the chest before pulling him close again, my eyes pulling away towards her, always to her. She's still at the bar, asking the bartender for another drink.

"So, how long have you guys been a thing?" Aiden whispers.

"I'm sorry, what?"

Of all people, I didn't think Aiden would notice *anything* beyond the orbit of his own ego and his infatuation with Mariana. He's watching me, too closely, and I know exactly who he means. I catch her eye again, just for a second, and she doesn't look away.

"I'm not an idiot," his tone is annoyingly casual. "I see the way you look at each other."

"Oh yeah? And how's that, exactly?" I raise my eyebrow.

"Like that." He nods subtly towards the dance floor, towards our parents.

No. Absolutely not. Mom and Dad are *obnoxiously* in love with each other, the kind of nauseating affection that makes Aiden and me always text or call before coming over to the house, afraid of what we would walk into if we didn't. Ravyn and I? We're not that. We're… something. But we're not *in love*.

I try to deflect. "Did you hit your head today?"

Aiden just lifts an eyebrow. One thing about Aiden Acosta: he's as stubborn as our father. Once he smells a secret, he doesn't stop until he's torn it wide open.

"Come on, Amaya," he said, softer now. "You can talk to me. Or did you forget I'm the first person you came out to?"

"Only because you *caught* me making out with our tutor."

"Who was also *my* crush, let's not forget. Still haven't forgiven you for that."

"Don't worry," I say dryly. "Won't happen again. Mariana's all yours."

"Amaya, don't mock me. She's still with that stupid boyfriend of hers."

"My condolences."

He spins me once again on the beat, gracefully despite the bickering. I follow his lead, but my eyes slip again, back to the bar. Ravyn blinks, looks down, and takes a slow sip of her fresh drink. Even from across the room, I can feel it, that electricity between us. It terrifies me.

"She doesn't know what she wants, Aiden. I can't live like that. I can't wait for her to realize that I'm not here to scratch her itch."

Aiden stays quiet, but I can see the wheels turning behind his eyes, his jaw tightening just slightly, the way it always does when he's debating something he probably *shouldn't* say.

"What are you thinking?" I ask, impatience creeping into my voice.

He sighs, "How much trouble I'd be in if I told you what Ravyn told Mariana about you."

I pull him closer as we continue to sway to the music, "Oh, Aiden. *So* much trouble. But spill."

He groans. "Mariana is going to *kill* me."

"She won't know. I pinky promise."

That gets his attention. He glances down at my extended hand, pink standing tall, then rolls his eyes like he's too old for this, but hooks his pinky around mine anyway. If there's one thing that hasn't changed in all our years of sibling chaos, it's that we've *never* broken a pinky promise.

"Okay, but when Mariana makes me mysteriously disappear, I'm haunting you."

"I wouldn't want it any other way. Now talk."

33

Amaya

"Hey, do you want to get out of here?" I ask Ravyn.

After what Aiden told me, I need to get us out of here. I need to talk to her, I need to hear it from her own mouth.

"I thought you would never ask." Ravyn finishes her drink and follows me down to our hotel room.

I'll get shit from my parents tomorrow for not properly saying goodbye, but I don't care right now. All that matters is getting Ravyn in our room so she can tell me the truth, where there are no prying eyes, and she can let her guard down. I want to question her as soon as our hotel door clicks shut behind us, but I don't. Watching her as she removes her boots, jewelry, and bobby pins from her hair. She reaches the back of her dress, struggling with the zipper.

She looks over her shoulder at me, "Are you going to just stand there and watch me, or are you gonna be a kind samaritan and help me?"

My mouth goes dry. I've been thinking about taking this dress off of Ravyn all night. I make my way towards her, my heels still giving me the perfect height to reach the top of the zipper without having to get on my tiptoes. She sweeps her hair to the side, and I slowly tug at the zipper, but it's not budging.

"It's stuck, Silver."

"Of course it is," she sighs

"I'll try to unzip it without breaking it. Hold on."

I wiggle her zipper, hoping that whatever is making it stuck is getting loose. Her perfume invades my senses, soft and warm, unmistakably *her*. I grab her tightly by the waist, trying to anchor myself for a big pull. The zipper isn't budging.

"How did you get this thing on in the first place?" I question.

"I saw this hack online with a paperclip and a string." She points to her tools on the bedside table.

I tug again at the zipper; this time it lowers halfway. I lean in slightly, without meaning to, my breath brushing the nape of her neck. I notice the goosebumps that form on her arm.

She turns her head, our faces now inches apart. I can feel the pull between us; it's magnetic, unbearable, and I don't move.

"I'm going to try one more time."

I hold the fabric near the zipper with one hand, steadying it, the other tugging again, and this time my knuckles graze Ravyn's spine. She sucks in a breath. The heat of her skin under my hand, the way her body reacts, it's reminding me too much of that night in the hot tub.

"I think we're going to have to cut you out of this damn dress," I said in frustration.

"Come on, this is brand new. I want to get at least one more use out of it." Ravyn pouts, and dammit, it's adorable.

"Fine, but this is the last time."

My fingers are brushing just beneath the edge of the dress now, trying to find where the fabric's caught.

"I think I got it…"

One final tug and the zipper gives, sliding smoothly down the rest of the way. Ravyn's hands instinctively move to her chest, holding the fabric in place before it can slip. She turns to face me, and everything goes still.

"Thank you," she said softly.

"No problem," I reply, voice more sheepish than I intended.

We just… stand there. Silent as we stare at each other.

Ravyn breaks the silence, "You never told me why you were upset tonight."

I glance away. "Oh, you don't want to hear about that."

"You're wrong."

There's an authority in her voice and God help me… It's turning me on.

Okay, so we're doing this.

"I had a pretty bad fight with my dad before the show."

Her brow furrows. "About what?"

I forced a smile that I know didn't quite reach my eyes. "Oh, you know. The usual Acosta stuff. How I disgraced the Acosta wrestling legacy by turning heel. How he can't fathom how I still have the title belt."

Her hazel eyes darken, her voice is low and fierce. "What is his problem?"

"His problem is that he's a control freak. Everything has to be done his way or the highway."

Ravyn steps closer, the fabric of her dress rustling as she moves. "I know he's your dad, but *fuck that.* You're killing it right now."

I huff a laugh, "There are no cameras in here, Silver. You don't have to play my hypeman."

"I'm not playing." Her voice is steady, sure. "You're not a joke."

That hits me harder than any bump I've ever taken. For years, Ravyn has told me I'm a joke, both in and out of the ring. I'm breathing like the room's run out of oxygen. Her eyes don't peel away from mine.

"I've told you over the years that you're only in the position that you're in because you're an Acosta. I was wrong. You're *rightfully* where you belong, last name not needed."

I never realized how much I needed to hear that, especially from her. Hearing her do the commentary last night was nice, but this. Guard down, no lights or cameras.

This isn't Ravyn.

This isn't Silver.

This is *Ramona.*

So I take my chance. The moment's already fragile, already cracked open. I might as well push it a little further, risk breaking it all the way. I look at her, really *look* at her, and ask the question that's been eating at me since the second I heard it come from Aiden's lips.

"Were you thinking of me when you hooked up with Levi?"

Ravyn freezes, her eyes widening. "How did you—"

"Answer the question, Ramona."

She catches her breath, "Yes."

Just one word.

Bare. Honest.

"Why?"

"I don't know, Amaya."

"Yes, you do."

She goes quiet, chewing on the bottom of her lip. I watch as she internally struggles with wanting to tell me and the impulse to protect herself. I'm done playing games. I want all of her, or none of her. If I have to be emotionally open, so does she.

"Just forget it," I mutter, shaking my head as I reach down and peel off my heels.

"I'm sorry," she said, stepping closer. "I just—"

"Just what?"

"God," she mutters, dragging her hands through her hair, "I wish I had a drink right now. Doing this sober is too *fucking* hard."

That catches me off guard. "You're sober?"

"Yes. I've been drinking cranberry juice all night because I didn't want to use alcohol as an excuse anymore."

My chest tightens. "An excuse for what?"

She looks right at me then.

No mask.

Just raw, unguarded truth.

What I've been needing from her from the very beginning.

"You're not a drunken experiment, Amaya. The whole time I was with Levi, I couldn't get you out of my *fucking* head."

My breath catches as she continues.

"I didn't drink tonight to prove how much I respect you. I want to tell you this completely sober, so there is no question in your mind of it not being true," she said. "I want you. I've been scared my whole life to want something, to want someone. It's time to be unafraid and go after what I want. Hell, I've been wanting to do this all fucking night."

Her hands drop to her sides. Her dress slips down her body, pooling at her feet, and she doesn't move. It's like she doesn't care that I'm able to see all of her, and what a glorious sight it is. I don't get to admire it for long. She closes the distance between us in two steps, her hands on my face, her mouth crashing into mine with a hunger that silences every question I had left.

34

Ravyn

The first time I ever kissed Amaya, I blamed it on tequila. The second time, I blamed it on wine. The third time, I blamed it on beer. This time, I am completely sober, no alcohol to blame, and yet my lips on hers are intoxicating me.

My mind isn't a mess; it isn't confused. I've never felt more certain of anything in my life. Kissing Amaya Acosta feels right. She is right for me, and I'll happily spend the rest of my life showing her how perfect she is.

The kiss is messy, frantic, but hell, it's everything that I've been craving, and by the sounds coming from Amaya, it's what she's been needing too.

Because it's *real*.

Her lips move against mine like she's been waiting for this, and maybe she has. There's nothing hesitant about the way she's kissing me. It's urgent, breathless, like she's trying to make up for every second I spent pretending we were a drunken mistake. My hands find her waist, and her skin is warm beneath my fingers. She exhales into my mouth, and I feel her press closer, her body flush against mine, nothing between us but the heat we've both been denying. I gasp softly as she pushes me back, walking me toward the bed without breaking the kiss. Her hands are in my hair, her lips at my jaw, roaming like she's memorizing me. Like I might change my mind, and this moment will slip away if she doesn't hold it tight enough.

"Hey," I whisper.

She tenses beneath my touch, and I know her well enough to understand that if I had one flicker of doubt, she'd pull back. No questions asked. No pressure. I don't want her to.

"I want this," I say softly, my hand brushing her cheek. "I'm not going to change my mind."

Her eyes meet mine, searching, still afraid of me regretting my decision once the night fades. I refuse to look away. I let her see the certainty, the pull, the want I've been carrying for too long. Slowly, she relaxes. Amaya turns her back to me, fingers reaching for the side of her dress. With one fluid motion, her zipper glides down effortlessly. I let out a soft laugh as she looks over her shoulder at me, smirking.

"Always get a dress that unzips from the side," she winks.

"I like my way better," I murmured, biting my lower lip.

She rolls her eyes, but there's a spark in them as she steps out of the fabric. There's no barrier between my eyes and her naked body.

No bra. No panties. Just her.

"Panty lines," she shrugs, like it's the most obvious explanation in the world.

God help me.

Amaya straddles my lap, her fingers unclasping my bra like she can't bear the barrier anymore. It hits the floor without a sound. She looks at me, and I feel exposed in the best way. Amaya has seen me topless, but this time it feels different, and we both know it.

"Still sober?" she murmurs, voice thick.

"Yes, but I think I'm getting a contact high from kissing you."

Amaya laughs, and it's not the bold, sharp laugh I usually hear from her in the locker room or ringside. This laugh is soft, and it unravels me completely.

"I don't think that's a thing, Silver."

"You sure? Because I think you should be studied."

I kiss her softly, and I can feel her smile on my lips.

She looks at me then, head tilted, like she knows exactly what it does to me.

I reach out, brushing a piece of hair from her face, my fingers lingering just a second longer than they need to.

"You're dangerous when you smile like that," I murmur.

She raises a brow in amusement, "You gonna tap out already?"

I shake my head slowly. "Not a chance, Red."

Her lips find my neck, trailing slow, burning kisses along my skin, and I can't help the sound that escapes me. My hands move along the curve of her back, pulling her closer, needing to feel all of her. She kisses me again, deeper, slower this time. Amaya reaches for my underwear, and I lift my hips to help her slide them off. Her fingers slid down my slit, sinking inside. My back arches as her fingers crook forward. Just like she did in the hot tub, her thumb circles my clit, and my legs immediately start to tremble. A whimper escapes my throat, and Amaya laughs against the crook of my neck.

"You like that, Silver?" she whispers.

Before I can answer, she replaces her thumb with the heel of her palm, and I grab the sheets of the bed, biting my bottom lip.

"Don't be quiet, I want to hear how much you like this."

Amaya's words open a floodgate, and I give her exactly what she wants.

"Fuck, that feels so fucking good, Amaya." I moan.

She hums, "I love how you moan my name."

Amaya sucks and bites my nipples. I feel my orgasm building, and apparently so does she, because she stops.

"No. Why?" I ask in between heavy breaths.

"Because I want to know what you taste like. I want to feel you come on my tongue. Is that okay with you, Ravyn?"

Her words both turn me on and scare the shit out of me. Men have eaten me out before, but it never feels enjoyable, and they never seem to enjoy it while they do it. It's more like they do it out of obligation.

Amaya senses my hesitation. "I have toys if you want to play with those instead."

"Of course you do."

"I didn't think we would be sharing a room, and a woman has needs."

We both erupt into a burst of laughter. I love how there is no pressure to be sexy, that we can laugh in the middle of sex, and it feels normal.

"I just, I've never finished while getting head," I confess.

A devilish grin is on her face, "Well, there's a first time for everything, isn't there?"

She kisses her way down my body, propping my legs up and getting comfortable between them. Her green eyes meet mine, and she gives me that devilish grin one more time before her tongue dips into me.

"Oh, my God." I whimper.

Amaya's mouth switches between licking and sucking. Her fingers join in, and it feels like I'm about to explode from the pleasure. She lifts her head, her fingers still at work, "Come for me, baby."

The mixture of Amaya's skillful as sin fingers and mouth, and her calling me baby for the first time, causes me to erupt.

That's what I've been missing out on this whole time. Never again will I go without Amaya's touch.

"Good Girl," she whispers as she places soft kisses on my inner thigh.

I reach for Amaya, pulling her up from between my legs, pressing my lips into hers, and tasting myself on her lips.

The high of my orgasm is now getting overtaken by the feeling of nerves. I flip her gently onto her back, pinning her hands above her head. She squeals, laughter bubbling in her throat, eyes locked on mine.

I plant slow, deliberate kisses along her throat, tracing the same path she used on me, until she stops me with a gentle hand.

"You don't have to," she whispers.

"I want to," I say, my voice quieter now. "But you'll have to guide me a little. I've never…"

I trail off, the words hanging in the air. I haven't felt this vulnerable, this exposed, in so long.

"I know you haven't," she said softly. "We don't have to rush into this if you're not ready."

"Red, I appreciate your concern," I say, managing a grin. "But the orgasm score is Ravyn: two, Amaya: zero. I am not a selfish lover; I *must* return the favor. So, like I said… I want to do this. I just want to make sure I can make you feel as good as you make me feel."

She pauses for a heartbeat, then nods, her voice a whisper. "Okay."

I keep going, propping her legs up just like she did mine. I move slowly, placing kisses on her inner thigh, loving how it makes her hips move involuntarily, making it known where she wants my lips.

Her breath catches as I move lower, hesitating just slightly. She can feel the pause and brings her hand to my cheek.

"Hey," she whispers, thumb brushing my skin. "Look at me."

I do. And everything else goes quiet.

"You're going to do fine. I'll talk you through it."

I nod my head and go for it. *Fuck*, she tastes amazing.

"Right there," she said softly. "Just a little slower."

Her voice is like silk. She's not instructing me to correct, but to make sure I know what she likes.

"Kiss right here," she murmurs, guiding me with the gentlest pressure, her fingers slipping into my hair. "Yes. *Fuck*, yes, Ramona."

The sound of my real name on her lips sounds just as sweet as her pussy tastes, and I swear I could come again from that sound alone.

"You can add some fingers."

I adjust, following exactly what she's telling me, watching her face, the way her lips part, how her body reacts.

A quiet moan follows. "Yes. Just like that."

She's showing me what she loves, not just so I'll get it right, but so I'll *know* her and *only* her. So I do, I study her and revel in the feeling of having her tremble in my hands. Every moan, every shift of her hips becomes a memory in my head that I never want to forget. I want to remember this moment forever. I memorize every sound she makes, every place that makes her breathe deeper, every whispered *yes.*

"Don't stop, fuck don't you dare stop."

I do exactly as she asks, savoring every inch of her. Slow, deliberate, hungry. If she were my last meal, I'd be completely fine with that.

Her walls pulse around my fingers, her nails digging into the sheets as her breathing becomes sporadic. I make my way up towards her, lying side by side, coming down from our highs.

"You're a quick learner."

"Well, you're a great teacher."

We both burst into laughter, easy, natural, like we've done this a thousand times before. There's no awkwardness between us, only the kind of comfort that makes everything feel right.

"You *can't* tell Mariana I found out about the Levi thing."

Hearing his name ruins the moment, reminding me I still have to find the courage to let him down gently.

"How did you find out?" I ask.

"Mariana told Aiden, and Aiden told me."

"That bitch," I mutter. "She pinky promised."

"I pinky promised Aiden she wouldn't find out, so please don't tell her."

I scoff in disbelief, "Are pinky promises not sacred anymore?"

We laugh again and settle into each other's arms. Wrapped up together, we both fall into a deep sleep, and it's the best sleep I've had in a very long time.

35

Ravyn

The next few weeks pass in a whirlwind. We check out of our hotel, bidding a final goodbye to the ever-charming Allison. It turns out our next flight also has us sitting side by side again, not that either of us is complaining. A blur of airports, hotels, and inside jokes. We hop from city to city without a single hotel hiccup; every room came equipped with two beds, but we only used one. Our nights are spent talking until way too late into the night, laughing at everything and nothing, and *lots* and *lots* and *lots* of sex.

We make sure to keep our distance in public, not wanting anyone from the EWC to pop our bubble. Everything with Amaya is new to me; we haven't discussed what this is. I'm not sure what it is exactly we're doing, but I don't want to be the one to ask, for fear of scaring her away. She helps me send a text to Levi and is way too happy to do so. I let him know that we'll talk when I get back home, which is exactly a week after Dominance Day.

Working as Amaya's valet is going about as well as it can. I'll be lying if I said it's not hard to resist kissing her after every match. She's constantly fighting with Val for me to interject in more matches so I can get some action in the ring. Val isn't budging, and it no doubt has something to do with Andres. Amaya hasn't really spoken to him since the award show.

Her mom calls pretty often, and Amaya always steps away to take those calls in private. I don't take it personally. I know her dad's still a sore subject, and considering I used to be the loudest voice against the Acosta family, it's probably best we leave family talks off the table, for now, at least.

Aiden, on the other hand… I had no idea he could be more of a pain in the ass than he already is. I keep my word to Amaya, not telling Mariana that Aiden spilled the beans, which caused the night that changed my life forever. She was ecstatic when I told her what went down between us, and I made her promise not to make it a big deal when she flies down to watch us fight during Dominance Day.

Tonight's the final match before the pay-per-view, and the crowd is already buzzing with excitement. Most of the audience will be back for the big event, and since we're in Vegas, I'm expecting a loud and rowdy kind of night. Just the way I like it.

Amaya has really come into her own as a heel. Don't get me wrong, she has always walked into the arena like she owns it, but it's a different energy now when she steps out behind the curtain and into the spotlight. She gets to be more herself, not having to fake a smile for the camera, letting her fiery personality shine. Amaya struts down to the ring with a smug smirk. She's insulting hometowns, mocking other wrestlers' injuries, and rolling her eyes at every underdog story. She even made a kid cry sitting at ringside for holding an *I heart Tashi* sign, and I've never felt prouder of anyone in my life.

She was amazing before, but as a heel, she is pure magic. She's cruel and calculated. You're not supposed to root for her, but deep down, part of you *wants* to, because she's so good at being bad. Tonight, she is being pure *evil*. She is tossing Geneva Cross around the ring like a rag doll.

Amaya hits her finisher, not bothering to hook Geneva's leg. Instead, she sat on her chest, flipped her hair, and checked her nails while the ref slapped the mat.

"One. Two. Three"

The crowd boos, and she smiles as she blows a kiss to the camera. I meet her in the ring, celebrating her win as if it's my own. My arm hangs over her shoulder as I whisper in her ear for no one else but her to hear.

"Can you pin me like that later tonight?" I ask, half-teasing, half-serious.

She raises a brow. "You want me to sit on your chest?"

"A couple of inches higher, Red."

She punches my shoulder and can't help but grin as we walk backstage, away from the chaos Amaya just caused.

36

Amaya

I can honestly say my life has never felt as perfect as it does right now. Amaya Acosta, the heel, just *works.* There's a power in it, a freedom I didn't know I was missing. Life as a baby face started to feel like autopilot.

Predictable. Safe.

I was falling out of love with wrestling, but this? I finally feel proud of where my career is headed. Not only is my career thriving, but I might have a girlfriend?

Ravyn and I haven't put a label on it. I might not know where we stand, but I know we feel like a real unit, together in this space; it feels easy and warm and electric all at once. We're doing what feels good for us. And for now, that's enough. But the idea of defining it? Terrifying.

I haven't been in a serious relationship in so long, let alone dating someone I work this closely with. Every bone in my body is telling me to brace for impact, like I'm waiting for the moment the rug gets pulled out from under me, for our perfect little bubble we're in to pop. I just have a bad feeling that everything is going to come crashing down on me because shit always hits the fan in your life when you're at your happiest. That feeling intensifies as I check my phone and see a text from Val, wanting me to meet in the meeting room set up in the arena. She and I haven't been seeing eye to eye lately. I send Ravyn a quick text, letting her know she can go on without me to the hotel, before heading towards Val's temp office.

My phone buzzes, and it's Ravyn.

Silver: Don't be stupid. I don't mind waiting for you. Good luck with Val. 💋

Tashi is here, laughing up a storm with Val, and as soon as I enter the room, they go silent.

I don't like that at all.

"Have a seat, Amaya. I have good news."

Val looks way too cheerful for my liking.

I do as Val asks and pop a squat next to Tashi.

"So, your father and I have been talking." Val continues.

Yup. Not going to like this at all.

"You're going to win the match on Dominance Day."

This is good news, I should be delighted. I want to keep this title. Not just because it's what's expected of me, but because I've earned it. I've bled for it, sacrificed for it. I hate that I'm torn. All I can think about is *her*. Ravyn deserves it, too, and if I'm being honest with myself, she deserves it more than I do. She's putting up with all this valet shit, and it can't all be for nothing. It's her time. Everyone sees it. *She* sees it. What can't Val?

I sigh before speaking the words I know will send Val into a spiral, "Val, I think it's time."

"Oh, no, Amaya. You've done everything in your power over the past couple of months to make my job impossible. You're sticking to the script on this one."

I try to argue, and Val isn't having any of it.

"In the triple threat match, you're going to betray Ravyn. You're going to side with Tashi, claim that you've seen the light or some shit, so that you can become baby face again. Tashi will be your valet for a couple of weeks, and then you're going to try and become a tag team. You'll be double-belted. EWC Women's champ and a tag team champ. We haven't figured out all the logistics, but I have faith it's going to all come together."

This is complete bullshit. I don't want Tashi as my valet, let alone my fucking tag team partner.

"No offense, but I don't want to do any of that. It doesn't make sense for my character right now."

Val stands up, leaning on the table, towering over both Tashi and me, "You're character is what I say it is, Acosta."

I have to find a way out of this. Ravyn deserves more than this, and I refuse to be the one to betray her. I won't be another person who loves her and does her wrong.

Realization hits me like a ton of bricks.

Holy hell. I love Ravyn.

There's no way around how I feel. I believe in her. I want her to have everything she dreams of. I want to be by her side for the ups and the downs. It's all because *I love her.*

"Amaya, you're about to set a record for the longest reigning EWC Women's Champion. Do you really want to throw it all away for Ravyn?" Tashi asks.

It's been my dream to break this record. Should I step away so that Ravyn can have her dream? I don't know when I'll be able to hold a title for this long again.

Do I fight to keep what's mine? Or step aside for the woman I love?

Either way, someone walks away hurt, and I'm scared it's going to be *us.*

37

Ravyn

"Hey, sis." Aiden slings an arm over my shoulder as I make my way towards the women's locker room.

"Do *not* call me that." I shrug him off without breaking my stride.

"Why not? You could be my sister-in-law one day."

"You're jumping the gun, per usual, Aiden."

Still, the idea of having *Amaya* as my *wife* gives me butterflies. Why does that thought feel so good and so terrifying all at once?

"When you know, you know," he said, all smug.

"Oh, yeah? Is that how it was for you and Mariana? Oh… wait." I shot him a sideways glance, my sarcasm slapping him in the face.

"Our love story is still being written, okay?" his hand covers his heart.

"Aiden, don't get me wrong. I don't *completely* hate the idea of you and Mariana."

"You don't?" His voice jumps a few octaves.

"Then again, that might just be because I *do* hate her with Ethan."

A smirk makes its way onto his face. "So does that mean you'll put in a good word for me?"

"No can do. Mariana made it *very* clear. Her love life is off limits, it's the one thing I can't meddle with."

"But—"

"I pinky promised, Aiden."

He steps back as I make it to the locker room door, his hand raised up in surrender.

"Fine, I'll win her over without your help."

Aiden starts to walk away, but I stop him.

"Hey, can I ask you a question?"

"Can I call you sister?"

"No." I roll my eyes.

"Fine, shoot."

"Why are you so into my best friend? You barely know her."

"I can't explain it. It's not just that she's hot, which, yeah, obviously, but it's more than that. The more I talk to her, the more I'm around her, I feel... grounded. Something about her feels familiar, like I've known her in another life."

Holy shit, does he love Mariana? I thought it was just a silly crush, but...

"I know I sound ridiculous," Aiden said, cheeks turning red.

"No, you don't. I've *never* heard Ethan talk about her like that. He talks about her more like she's a prop, not his girlfriend."

"Yeah, well... she *thinks* she loves him," he shrugs, bitterness in his tone.

I scoff. "I thought I loved Levi. It was just puppy love. I love him as a friend now, but back then, he felt like home. Now, when I think of home, I think of..."

I froze. My heart stopped mid-beat.

Aiden's grin stretches, slow and smug. "Oh. My. God. You *love* my sister."

I love Amaya.

Aiden repeats, "Oh Dios mío. Amas a mi hermana."

"Listen here, pendejo. I swear to God, Aiden, if you open your *fucking* mouth—"

"Yeah, yeah, you'll powerbomb me into oblivion. Blah, blah, blah."

"I'm being serious, Aiden."

"Fine, I pinky promise."

I narrow my eyes. "We both know your pinky promises mean *nothing* when it comes to keeping secrets from your sister."

He stands there, mouth gaping as he realizes I know his dirty little secret.

I turn and disappear into the locker room to take a shower and overthink the fact that I've fallen for Amaya Acosta.

217

38

Ravyn

My shower didn't help. My body's clean, but my mind's in chaos. I'm spiraling, trying to trace the exact moment it happened. When *she* became something more. When did *hate* turn into *love?* I guess between the years of knowing each other and the past months we were forced to spend together, there's been a hundred small things in between that have added up to something I can't ignore anymore.

The way she delusionally laughs when she's exhausted after a long day. The way she remembers the smallest things about me, like how I hate pickles. Which is perfect because she loves them. The way she looks at me is like I'm the most important person in her world. We haven't put a label on this, haven't defined what we are. I tell myself I'm fine with it. If it's not broken, don't fix it. It feels light, easy, like we're figuring it out without any pressure. But now? Now I wake up hoping she's by my side. I miss her when she's not around in a way that's painful. Isn't that love? God, I hope I'm not wrong. I thought Levi was my endgame, but there's a difference between loving someone and being in love with them. How I feel about Amaya. This feels different, deeper, real.

Even if we haven't said it. Even if I'm unsure if she feels the same. I'm in love. I know it with every fiber of my being. I need to find her.

I throw on my hoodie and rush out of the locker room. The arena is a ghost town, yet I can't find Amaya anywhere. I bend down to adjust the ankle brace I put on earlier. Of course, my ankle wants to act up the day before one of the biggest matches of my life.

Medical room, that's where she is.

Amaya's shoulder's been bothering her, so maybe she's in there picking up something to help. Val hasn't talked to me yet about tomorrow's match, but for the first time in a long time, I feel good. Like *really* good. Maybe, *finally,* this could be my time. Just as I round the corner, I hear two voices, Amaya and Tashi.

What the fuck?

My gut tells me to turn around, to keep walking. I know I should mind my own business. Hell, I *really* should. Yet, something keeps me planted in place, my feet becoming one with the floor beneath me.

The door is slightly ajar, just enough that I can hear their conversation, sneak a peek inside, but not enough for them to see me. Tashi's voice is sharp, low, and urgent. Amaya sounds off. Maybe she's just tired? I should knock. I should interrupt. I should leave and pretend I didn't hear anything.

Don't do it, don't do it, don't—

I stay. I'm listening now, fully committed to whatever secrets they clearly don't want anyone in on. Tashi grabs Amaya's arm, and I have to stop myself from barging in.

"You've been in this business long enough to know that this isn't personal, Amaya. It's *just* business."

"I don't know, Tashi. It's more complicated than that."

"You're telling me what you have with Ravyn. Whatever it is, is it worth losing your title?"

"How did you–"

Tashi rolls her eyes, "I'm not blind, Amaya. Now, is it worth losing your title?"

Amaya stays quiet.

Why isn't she defending me, defending us, what we have?

Tashi sighs, "Amaya, it is so simple. Attack Ravyn, pin Ravyn, Retain championship."

She wouldn't.

"Are you listening?" Tashi asks.

Amaya finally speaks, "I hear you."

"Good."

Maybe she would.

***

My heart feels like it's been shattered into a million pieces. How could she do that to me? After everything we've been through, after I let my walls down, after I struggled to accept the feelings I had towards her. All of the thoughts and insecurities I've had since childhood keep replaying in my head.

Everyone that you love leaves.

Everyone that you love disappoints you.

Everyone that you love chooses you second.

Everyone that you love hurts you.

I'm an idiot to think that Amaya Acosta would choose me over her fucking career. Thankfully, Mariana flies in tonight, and I text her, letting her know that I'll be staying with her tonight. She agrees, no questions asked. I'm frantically going through our room, making sure that I pack everything that's mine so I can get the fuck out of here before she comes back. Amaya calls me nonstop, probably looking for me in the arena, but as soon as I heard her and Tashi, I bolted.

I should've known. God, I should've known.

A soft click from the hotel door breaks my concentration.

Dammit.

"Ramona, why is the deadbolt on?"

A precaution, one I should've taken with my heart.

"One second."

I shove the rest of my belongings in my suitcase, clothes wrinkled, shoes mismatched, none of it folded. It doesn't matter. I just need to leave.

My hand lingers on the cold metal of the door handle, and it's the only thing that feels real. I open the door, and the look on her face breaks my heart even more. Amaya looks confused as she looks me up and down, noticing my suitcase packed and ready beside me.

"Where are you going? Do we have to move rooms?"

"No, you can stay here, but I'm leaving."

I try to go around her, but she blocks me in.

"What's wrong?"

I scoff, "Don't. Don't pretend like you give a shit."

"Ramona—"

"No. You don't get to call me that anymore."

"I'm so confused. Just talk to me."

"You're confused? How do you think I feel? You made me believe that you could be my safe space. I confessed things to you that no one knows. I let you in, slowly at first, but dammit, then I fell headfirst, and I started to believe I didn't have to brace myself all the time. How silly of me to think that maybe this time... maybe *this* was real."

"It is—"

"Please stop talking, Amaya. Let me get this off my chest so I can go."

She stands there frozen, and I have to look away; the tears forming in her eyes are too convincing.

"I showed you all of me, my messy parts, my cracked edges, the pieces I've never admitted to anyone, let alone myself. Was it a game to you? Was any of this real? Or was it just a part of a plan you and your father cooked up once your dad brought Tashi into the EWC?"

Finally, the words are clicking in Amaya's head. She knows that I know her plan, her betrayal tomorrow night.

"Silver, just let me explain," she begs.

"No. You don't get to call me that either. God, the worst part isn't even the betrayal. It's that you made me believe. You made me hope. Do you know what I've told myself since I was a little girl? My depressing mantra. Everyone that you love leaves. Everyone that you love disappoints you. Everyone that you love chooses you second. Everyone that you love hurts you."

Amaya's green eyes are red, the tears are slowly running down her cheeks, but I won't fall for it. She's just upset that she got caught.

"I hate myself for letting you pass the walls I built to survive. Most of all, I hate that you proved my mantra true."

This time, when I try to pass her, she doesn't stop me.

39

Ravyn

Not a single tear escapes as I make my way to Mariana's hotel room. My body is on autopilot as I navigate the Vegas strip, trying to avoid the billboards with Amaya, Tashi, and my face on them.

Mariana opens the door, a look of concern on her face. "I hope it's okay that we have a party crasher?" She moves her body out of the way so I can see Eddie sitting on the bed.

I'm not sure if it's because Amaya and I are over or the fact that the two people in my life came together to be there for me, but I finally break down in tears right in the middle of the hotel hallway.

They both rush towards me, and I let my body collapse as I feel everything all at once. They help me into the hotel room, one on my left, the other on my right, arms around me like anchors. I'm breaking, and they're holding up the pieces. No fixing. No questions. Just warmth. Just helping to hold me together until I can hold myself together again on my own. My face is buried in Mariana's shoulder, the tears coming harder, and I'm not sure if I've ever felt this kind of pain in my life. It feels good to let it out, because for the first time in what feels like forever, I don't have to be strong. My sobs soon become sniffles, and my breathing begins to even out, and that is when I lift my head off of Mariana's shoulders and look between her and Eddie.

Eddie breaks the silence, "Do you need me to kick her ass?"

"Don't worry. I'll do plenty of that tomorrow night." I replied.

"Your phone has been ringing nonstop since you got here," Mariana said.

"Chuck it over the Hoover Dam for all I care." I scoff.

"Consider it done." Mariana tosses my phone to the other side of the room.

"Can I chuck you over the Hoover Dam since I had to hear all about your juicy love affair from Mariana instead of straight from the source?" Eddie pouts.

"Next time, I'll make sure I make a newsletter about it." I roll my eyes.

Eddie gasps, clutching his chest like I personally wounded him. "A newsletter? Wow. So I've been downgraded to *email blasts* now?"

"I'm sorry, okay," I whine.

"I'll forgive you. Only because I know you've been busy. Rumor has it that eating pussy is a lot of work. I wouldn't know, of course." Eddie picks at his cuticles, acting as though the most obscene thing didn't just come out of his mouth.

Mariana and I just stare at him, both our mouths gaping open before bursting into a fit of laughter. The tears coming from my eyes are now out of amusement instead of agony, and I'm so close to peeing myself from the laughter.

"God, I love you guys." I wipe away my tears with the back of my sleeve.

Mariana rubs my back. "Do you want to tell us what happened?"

* * *

The sound of loud banging at the door wakes us all up, and even though I did zero drinking last night, I feel completely hungover. My eyes are swollen and my throat raw.

I turn on the light, and all of us groan.

"Who the hell is banging at your door like that?" I question Mariana.

"How the hell am I supposed to know? Go check." Mariana throws a pillow at my head.

224

She has never been much of a morning person.

Another loud bang at the door makes me jump.

"For the love of God, Ravyn, if you don't answer the door, I will become an angry gay. Do you want to deal with an angry gay?" Eddie groans.

"I'm going, I'm going. No need to get hostile."

I rub the crust out of my eyes as I make my way to the door, peeking through the peephole to make sure it's not some crazed fan who's found me. What I see is *much* worse.

"Mariana, who did you tell that you were here?" I ask, my voice a whisper to make sure he doesn't hear me on the other side of the door.

"Here, as in *Vegas*, or here as in *this* hotel room?"

"Mariana," I warn.

"Ethan. I obviously had to tell him my hotel room and number for security purposes."

Fucking Ethan.

"Does he happen to still talk to Levi?" I ask.

"I'm not sure; I didn't ask. Why?"

"Because he's at your *fucking door* right now, that's why."

Both Eddie and Mariana's heads snap up like a pair of startled meerkats.

"No fucking way," Mariana hisses, hands flying to her hair in a desperate attempt to tame the mess that was her bedhead.

Eddie narrows his eyes at me. "Ravyn, no offense when I ask this, but *what the fuck* do you have going on in your coochie that this man is obsessed with you?"

"Ugh, *not now*, Eddie!" I groan, frantically rifling through my suitcase, trying to find anything that screams *"emotionally stable"* and not *"I've been having a crazy love affair with a woman I thought I hated while I've been sending you dry texts after we had sex and it all fell apart and last night I cried myself to sleep."*

Another knock.

"Coming."

Hold it together, Ramona. You got this. You are strong. Just tell him everything. Okay, not everything. He can go without knowing about how you faked it and how Amaya gave you earth-shattering orgasms. Yeah, don't tell him that, that's just cruel.

I swing open the door, and Levi looks like shit. His eyes are rimmed red and have dark circles. His stubble's a little too grown out, and his hair is a mess. Levi sighs deeply as he looks at me.

"Rami. We need to talk."

"I know."

I close the door behind me, joining Levi in the hallway and trying to ignore the shuffling of feet I hear on the other side.

Let them eavesdrop; less work for me later.

He stands there in the doorway, shoulders slouched, shirt wrinkled. One hand raking through his hair, slow and shaky, like even that small of a motion took effort.

"I know you said we would talk when you got back home. I'm not sure if you can tell, but I'm a wreck." He gestures toward himself with a half-hearted, self-deprecating smile that doesn't quite reach his eyes.

"You? No. You look great, just like the first day I met you," I said, trying to offer a shred of levity, even if it sounds like a lie dressed up in comfort.

He lets out a low, tired chuckle. "I'm far from my teen years, but thanks for trying."

His eyes dropped to the floor for a second before he looked back up, suddenly more serious. "Listen, Levi—"

"No, please. Let me go first." His hand lifts slightly.

I nod, motioning for him to continue.

He exhales through his nose, slow and deliberate. "It feels like ever since I've come back into your life, all I've done is apologize." He lets out another soft laugh, the sound is more bitter than amused. "I just want to apologize for that night after the bar. I got caught up in the moment."

My chest tightens. "It's not all on you. I was there too, and if I remember correctly, I started it."

"I should've stopped it. I shouldn't have let it get that far, because Ramona, I didn't want to blur the lines of our friendship. I should've known better."

I reach for his hand, and he takes it. "I'm hearing a lot of 'I's.' It takes two people to have sex, and I'm just as much at fault as you are. We're only human, Levi, please don't beat yourself up about this."

"How could I not when it's clear that you've been ignoring me", he whispers.

"I—"

"I'm not an idiot. I know when I'm being blown off."

I bit my lip, looking away, full of shame.

"I also have eyes and can feel vibes," he adds with a weak smile. "That night at the bar, I could sense something between you and Amaya."

My eyes dart to the window, to the floor, to anywhere that isn't him.

"You admitting you have feelings for her won't hurt mine. It's okay if you like her."

More like love, but that doesn't matter anymore.

"I just want you to be happy, Rami," he said softly.

I swallow hard, heart pounding loud enough to drown out the silence between us.

I was happy.

"I'm going to stay in Florida, maybe fix my apartment up to feel like home. I would love a redo… *again*. Friends *for real*, this time."

My arms wrap around him, and I don't have to say anything. He knows the answer.

"Now that we've got that out of the way. Want to catch your friend up with what's going on with you and Amaya?" he arches his brow.

Before I can answer, the door behind us swings open, and both Eddie and Mariana are on the other side.

"Please step inside our office." Eddie smiles

"*Our* office." Mariana snorts, pushing him aside. "It's *my* room and *I'm* the one with a psychology degree."

"Oh, really?" Eddie arches a brow. "When did you get that diploma?"

"Technically, I don't have it *yet*, but it's coming very soon!" Mariana rolls her eyes.

Levi lets out a laugh, "Hello to you two, too."

I groan, dragging a hand over my face. "You two are *so* embarrassing."

"You love it," Mariana said with a wink, grabbing both of our wrists and tugging us inside before either one of us can protest. "Now, hurry up. I'll order room service, and we can catch Levi up on how tragic your love life is."

40

Amaya

Last night was the longest night of my life. I didn't eat, I didn't sleep. I cried so much that I physically can't produce any more tears. How am I supposed to be excited for wrestling's biggest night of the year when the one person I want to celebrate it with is not talking to me?

I tried calling, texting, and even sending messages through social media. Mariana won't answer me, Eddie's also MIA, Reina answered only because she has no idea what the fuck is going on, so I sobbed my eyes out over the phone with her, and she called Ravyn for me, and still no answer. I got as desperate as to message fucking Levi.

Ravyn told me she grew up with no one in her corner. Well, now she has a whole army, and they won't let me get anywhere near her. She didn't even give me the chance to explain, to see my side of it. Maybe Tashi and Val are right, maybe I shouldn't throw away my shot at making history. I've been driving myself crazy thinking of all the ways I could do what Val wanted me to without hurting Ravyn, because even though it feels like my heart was stomped on, I still love her, and I don't want her to get fucked over. She's been through enough. I grab my phone and dial the number of the one person I swore I would never call for relationship advice.

"You fucked up, didn't you?" Aiden questions through the speaker.

"This is why I don't call you. This was a mistake." I hang up.

Aiden tries calling me back, and I hit the decline button, throwing myself onto the bed.

There's a light tapping on my door.

No, he didn't.

"Go away, Aiden," I yell.

"I tried to be a gentleman and knock. You've left me no choice."

There's a click, and then the door opens. Aiden waves at me from the doorway.

"Aiden, what the fuck?"

"The secret's out."

"How do you have a room key?"

"Well, you know how you always lose your room keys?"

I gasp at the realization, "You do *not*."

Aiden rubs the back of his neck, looking sheepishly at the floor. "Yeah, I swipe them from you so that I always have a copy. It's for security purposes, just looking out for you, sis."

"Did Dad put you up to that?"

"Nah, the one thing he can't control is how crazy of a big brother I get to be for my baby sister, Maya."

He calls me by my childhood nickname, and I can't help but smile.

"I always know you're about to impart some wisdom on me when you use that nickname. You use it to soften me up before you hit me with the cold, hard truth."

"Have I become that predictable? I'm going to have to switch up my strategy."

The bed sinks under his newly added weight, but I don't move. I stay on my back, staring at the ceiling. Aiden's waiting for me to talk, to let him know what went wrong, but I lie there a little longer, letting the comfort of his presence fully sink in before I speak.

"She left. Ravyn overheard a conversation I was having with Tashi about what Val wants us to do during the match, and she lost her shit. Rightfully so, if I were in her shoes, I would be pissed too."

"What's Val's big master plan?" he asks.

So I tell him everything. I talk to my brother in a way I don't think I ever have before. My mouth is moving faster than my brain can process the words coming out, and I'm telling him all about Ravyn and I's story, about the fight with dad, about how being a heel makes me feel.

"Did you know about the baby face clause in our contract?"

"You really think I took the time to read that long ass contract?"

He starts to speak and then pauses, as though he's trying to pick his words carefully, and I think it's the first time I've ever seen Aiden think before he speaks.

"Lately, I've been asking myself the question, 'When did I stop thinking for myself?' I can't remember the last time a decision I made was because *I* wanted to make it. I've trusted Dad so much, believed in his vision, let his voice echo in my head louder than my own. Somewhere along the way, I stopped asking what *I* wanted. I stopped listening to *my* gut and blindly followed his lead. I let his dreams become the guide I use to live my life. I convinced myself that his approval matters more than anything else in the world."

I crawl over to Aiden, curling up beside him like I used to when we were little. As he wraps his arms around me, something in me softens, and for a moment, I feel like a little girl again, safe with the one person who's never asked me to be anyone else but his little sister.

The tears came quietly, without warning. I'm shocked that I have more to give. Aiden reaches and begins wiping them away.

"Hermana mía, I'm telling you this because I love you and I want to see you happy. I'm not just his son, and you're not just his daughter. Yes, we're Acostas, but we're our own people too. You have to do what's right for you, *fuck* the consequences."

"I want to get her back," I mumble.

"So you'll do just that. Ravyn loves you, Maya; she'll forgive you."

"She what?" I adjust myself, making sure I'm making direct eye contact with Aiden.

He mutters under his breath, quick and sharp. "Mierda, Ravyn me va a matar."

"Aiden, you know I hate it when you speak Spanish to me. I don't understand what you're saying!"

He gives me a smug look, "Well, whose fault is that, Ms. 'I don't care about Spanish class. I just want to wrestle like daddy.' "

I groan, throwing my head back. "I was ten!"

"Old enough to know better. I mean, even Mariana knows Spanish, and she's a gringa," he said, grinning and clearly enjoying himself.

"So I've heard." I roll my eyes.

The tension in the air lightens, and it feels like we were kids again.

"Aiden, come on," I growl.

"Fine, but I promised Ravyn I wouldn't say anything."

"Did you make a pinky promise?" I ask.

He blinks, "No."

I smirk, "So then it doesn't count. Now talk."

41

Ravyn

The air backstage is electric and thick with adrenaline. Wrestlers are pacing on the concrete floor, stretching and hyping each other up. It's the biggest night in wrestling, and for some, it's the biggest night of their careers. A majority of the matches tonight are title matches, mine included. I make sure to stretch my ankle out so there's no casualties tonight. Val made sure to pull me aside to remind me of my place in the match tonight. She told me not to win, but said nothing about not kicking ass in the process.

One by one, I watch as my colleagues make their way through the curtains and into the roar of the crowd. Their entrance music hits, the spotlight hits them, and then they're gone, running down the ramp to fight their hearts out in that ring. I'm sitting on a bench in the corner, making sure my breathing is steady and slow. I haven't seen Tashi or Amaya yet, and I don't want to. I don't want their head nods or the forced small talk. No words. Just action. The matches come and go, and before I know it, it's time for the main event, for our triple threat match.

Tashi passes me without a second glance. She's wearing red gear with gold embellishments. Her name's embroidered in bold, sharp lettering, and her boots are matte black, laced up to mid-calf with gold eyelets and soles. Tashi's big, beautiful hair is in a wild halo of tight brown curls. Her entrance music vibrates through the walls, and off she goes. The crowd cheers as soon as they set eyes on her.

I feel her before I see her. There's a shift in the air, a sudden weight in my chest. I look up, and there she is, talking to a producer. Everything in me clenches.

Amaya's gear is navy blue and gold. The top has a gold mesh accent along the sides, letting just enough skin show. Her high-waisted trunks have a wide, metallic gold waistband; her ass, of course, looks amazing in them. Her red curls are braided back tightly on one side, the rest pulled into a high ponytail that swings with every step. I turn away before our eyes can meet.

Focus Ravyn. Don't let your emotions get the best of you in that ring.

She starts walking toward me, and instantly, my leg begins to bounce; nervous energy pulsing through me. I don't have to look up to know she's standing in front of me now. Her floral scent reached me first, soft and familiar. It wraps around me, and I'm hit with the memory of her getting into my car for the first time; my car smelled like her days.

Amay's hand gently rests on my knee, stopping the movement with nothing more than her touch. I freeze, the warmth of her palm spreading through me, the memory of what those hands can do making me ache for more than a gentle touch.

"Don't be anxious," Amaya speaks softly. "You're going to be amazing."

I give a stiff nod, jaw tight, still refusing to meet her eyes. If I open my mouth now, I know my voice will betray me, be shaky, and crack. Mr. Acosta rolls in, and I'm the one who notices him first. I can tell how unhappy he is to see her speaking to me before the match.

"Amaya, a word?"

Amaya turns around and just shakes her head, and her father.

Oh shit.

"Come here, now." His voice is stern.

"No. I love you, Dad, but I'm not a little kid anymore. Thank you for showing me the ropes, for helping prepare me for my career, but it's *my* career, not yours. I'm going to wrestle my ass off, like I always do, but it's going to be on my terms. I'm an Acosta, but I'm so much more than that. I'm going to create my own legacy."

Her entrance music starts to play, yet she stands still, staring at her father.

The boos are getting louder, yet she stays in her standoff with her dad until he leaves.

"Amaya, get out there." A producer yells.

She leans down, whispering in my ear.

"I will *not* leave you. I will *not* disappoint you. I will *not* choose you second. I will *not* hurt you. *All* because I love you. Pin me tonight and get your belt."

42

Amaya

Fuck being an Acosta. I'm done living my life to please my father. He can yell at me all he wants in the morning; hell, Val can even fire me, I don't care. I'm living my life for *me*. I'm doing what *I* want to do, what *I* think is right, and dammit, Ravyn winning that belt is the right thing to do.

Who would've thought that Aiden would be the right person to call during a romantic crisis? Guess there's a first time for everything. He told me that Ravyn loves me, she was going to tell me last night, and instead she told me all the fucked up things she tells herself. How no one she loves ever loves her enough to stick around or pick her first. I won't be added to that list of people. I want to be the person she turns to, the person she knows with all of her heart will never do her wrong.

Is telling Ravyn I love her right before a triple threat match on Dominance Day the smartest thing to do? No, but I can't hold it in any longer, and I want to let her know that I have no intention of winning this match. Val will be furious, but I tried to reason with her; she's left me with no choice. I would rather ask for forgiveness than ask for permission. Now here I am, in the middle of the ring, waiting for Ravyn to come down that ramp and beat my ass for the title belt. If this isn't a grand gesture, I don't know what is.

Ravyn stands tall at the front of the LED Screen, her music bumping, her name in bold colors behind her. She wears her signature color, black. Her gear looks painted on, moving with her like a second skin, and her eyes have a fire in them. Just beneath the edge of her top, black ink climbs her arms, the tattoos that I love to trace with my fingers as we lie in bed. She's wearing black combat boots laced with silver cords. Her jet-black hair is pulled into Dutch braids, with her two silver streaks framing her face like sharpened edges. She looks breathtaking, and there's no one else I'd rather lose my title to than her.

"Are you ready?" Tashi whispers to me as Ravyn makes her way down the ramp.

"The question is, are you ready?" I raise an eyebrow.

She has no idea what's coming, sorry, newbie.

Ravyn slides under the ropes, and the energy in the arena cracks like thunder. All three of us are ready to give the crowd the best wrestling match of their lives. We each take a corner of the ring, our eyes locking in on one another, the tension's so tight it feels like the ropes of the ring might break. The bell rings, and the fight for dominance begins.

Ravyn lunges first, going straight towards me. Tashi slips in between us, dropkicking Ravyn right in the ribs. She stumbles back into the turnbuckle, and chaos ensues.

Tashi might still be going through with Val's plans, but I'm not.

I grab her by the arm, whipping her across the ring towards Ravyn. She clotheslines Tashi and then turns her attention to me, wrapping her arms around my waist. "What do you mean, I'm pinning you tonight? Did Val change the plan?" Ravyn whispers in my ear before launching me into the mat.

I try to catch my breath as Ravyn hovers over me. Tashi comes for Ravyn, launching herself off the ropes. She leaps, wrapping her legs around Ravyn's neck in a swift hurricanrana that flips her clean across the ring.

Shit. She's about to pin already.

I get myself up as the referee starts their count, "One. Two."

Ravyn kicks out. Tashi is distracted, so I perch myself on the top rope and, with no hesitation, I fly towards her. A clean moonsault that should keep her down for a little while, so Ravyn and I can talk.

I lunge at Ravyn, pulling at her braids. "I'm sorry, Ravyn, but there can only be one champion," I say loud enough for the audience to hear before punching her in the gut.

My hands don't leave her hair as I drag her to the corner of the ring and position her back to be on the turnbuckles. I slap her on the chest, and the crowd starts to count, "One."

I get close enough to Ravyn's ear so she can hear me, "Val didn't change anything. I'm telling you to pin me tonight. I'm giving up my title." I slap Ravyn again, and the crows chant, "Two."

Ravyn looks thoroughly confused, and as I raise my hand to slap her again, Tashi grabs me by the arm and twists.

Fuck, my shoulder.

Tashi places my arm behind my back and applies pressure.

Double fuck.

She hooks my head and drives me down towards the mat face-first, my arm still behind my back. My screams of pain flood through the arena. The referee comes to check on me, and I assure them I'm fine. Tashi's looking down at me, and I can tell that it's finally clicked for her. Which means she's about to make it harder for Ravyn to win this title.

Ravyn spears Tashi, knocking her down. She mounts her and lets her fists and elbows rain down on Tashi. Once she's sure Tashi's down, she comes over to me, and what she does next is pure evil. I scream out in pain as she positions my ankle in an ankle lock. A position I know well since it's my favorite to use on her bum ankle. Ravyn knows I won't break. She flips me onto my back, repeatedly kicking my stomach.

Bending down towards my ear, she murmurs. "Why are you giving up your belt? Why are you sacrificing everything for me?"

I catch Ravyn's leg and use mine to sweep her standing leg out from under her. I take advantage of her being down, running to the ropes and using the momentum to leg drop Ravyn across her chest.

"Did you not hear what I said before I came out here today?"

Now it's my turn for kicks.

"I will not choose you second. Title included."

I go to kick again, and Ravyn uses my move against me, catching my leg, and I hit the mat. Neither of us is paying attention to Tashi, and she uses that to her advantage. She launches herself at Ravyn, the perfect diving crossbody, and Ravyn joins me on the mat.

Tashi goes for the pin. "One. Two. Thr—" Ravyn kicks out.

That was too close. I'll be damned if Tashi gets this belt.

The crowd roars, half in disbelief, half in awe. Frustration's mounting now. Breathing heavy, bruises forming on our skins, hair coming loose from ponytails and braids, eyeliner smeared with sweat and grit. This needs to end before we shred each other to bits. Val's already going to be pissed, no need to add gasoline to the fire by going over our match time.

Ravyn and I lay on the mat, looking at one another.

"Because you *love* me?" she asks, her question a silent whisper.

"*All* because I love you," I repeat.

Ravyn gets up, staring down at Tashi like she's the bull and Tashi is the red flag. She attacks, grabbing Tashi by her hair and dragging her to the turnbuckles. Ravyn headbutts Tashi, causing her to fall. She is kicking her like her life depends on it, which in a way it does. I'm content with lying here and watching, but we have a match to finish, and time is up. It's time for the big finish.

I walk towards Ravyn and swing, but she dodges it. Grabbing my arm and twisting it back just like Tashi did earlier. Ravyn uses her other hand to grab Tashi and drags both of us to the center of the ring. She grabs both of our heads, one in each arm, and places us in a front facelock. She jumps, driving both Tashi's and mine heads into the mat simultaneously.

The crowd is going insane, screaming louder for Ravyn than they have ever done for me. She grabs me by the nape of my neck, "The reign of the Acostas is over," she screams, and the chants from the crowd are loud and clear.

"Ravyn. Ravyn. Ravyn."

It's like music to my ears.

"Thank you", she whispers. "Oh, and I love you, too. In case you were wondering."

My heart feels like it's about to explode, and I know I made the right choice tonight.

"You better. Now finish this so I can brag that I'm dating the new EWC women's champ."

She looks over at the turnbuckles.

"From the top rope?" she asks.

I nod, "From the top rope."

Ravyn grabs both of us, giving us both her signature Ravyn's Rapture, and because my girl loves a little extra flair, she climbs to the top turnbuckle. She executes a perfect Corkscrew Moonsault on top of both Tashi and me, hooking both our legs, and the referee starts their count.

"One. Two. Three."

43

Epilogue

Ravyn

"We're going to be late." I groan.

Nobody knew it yet, but tonight was a big night for me and Amaya. I want everything to go perfectly, just like it has been for the last six months.

My title reign has been going strong. Val was, of course, livid at first, but she got over it once she saw that Amaya and I were in love, plus it didn't hurt how fast my merch was selling once I was named champ. Amaya had to face the wrath of her father, who was now walking with some help, but his anger didn't last long once her mother got in the middle. They're still working on their father-daughter relationship, and I'm still working on getting him to like me instead of calling me *"the reason his daughter lost her championship."*

Hating Tashi is my new number one hobby, since she's made it well known that she thinks Amaya and I should retire already and let the new meat get the titles they deserve.

Wait your turn.

Aiden is still desperate for Mariana's love and affection. They're actually becoming good friends, though, too close for my liking, because if she thinks she can replace me, she has another thing coming. I keep telling him not to lose hope, but honestly, I'm getting worried that Ethan is going to propose soon, and she's going to say yes.

Reina, well, is Reina. No new updates on her life, that woman is a real enigma.

Mariana is due to graduate in the fall, and we're all very excited and happy for her. She just has to complete one extra-curricular activity, and then she's done. Aiden said he could get her a sweet gig at EWC, and she checked with her guidance counselor, who gave her the green light. It'll be nice to have her around more.

"Amaya, please, for the love of all that is holy," I yell from the bottom of her staircase.

Levi has a girlfriend now; her name is Mia. She's sweet, and I'm happy for them, especially since Amaya was getting just a tad jealous when I would hang out with Levi solo.

Eddie's still killing me at the gym, which feels extra rude considering he's also the reason I need extra time in the gym; he shows up to our place like a walking snack aisle.

"Can you even hear me, or am I talking to a wall?" I yell some more.

Amaya emerges at the top of the stairs. Looking as gorgeous as ever, wearing a fitted forest green satin top and a pair of dark jeans.

"I can hear you just fine, babe. I'm just choosing to ignore you. I'm almost done, I just have to put on my shoes." She walks down the stairs, heels in hand.

"Okay, a little pep in your step wouldn't hurt."

"I'm sorry. You try getting dressed with one arm!" Amaya points to her arm, which is currently in a sling. Dominance Day really didn't help her bad shoulder, and she had to have surgery. She's been out of EWC due to the injury, but I know she's going to train even harder once she's medically cleared.

"You're right, I'm sorry. Let me help." I bend down, strapping her heels on for her.

"Thank you. You know, just because you live with me now doesn't mean you get to boss me around."

"I thought you liked being told what to do," I smirk.

"I do, but I don't like being rushed. Plus, you were in no rush earlier when my mouth was on your—"

"Hey, yo. Your brother is in the kitchen and can hear *everything*."

"Who invited him again?" Amaya groans.

"I had to, you know, he would've found out. Mariana is stupid enough to trust him with her location now. At least this way, there's no way he can surprise us."

Aiden walks into the living room, and our eyes widen.

"Holy shit, Aiden. You're hair." I shout.

His colorful locks are gone, now replaced with a haircut that's short on the sides in a clean, tapered fade, while the top was left longer, swept back in smooth, effortless waves.

"What did you do?" Amaya shrieked.

"You look like you could be a member of a boy band." I grimaced.

"It's just a haircut, relax." Aiden shrugs.

I grab the keys from the coffee table. "We do not have time to discuss Aiden's midlife crisis. Everyone in the car, now."

"Where are we even going?" Amaya asks.

"You'll see." I sing, a mischievous grin tugging at my lips.

***

Amaya

"You must be mental if you think I'm stepping a foot inside there again." I cross my good arm in front of my chest.

"Come on, baby. You love Karaoke." Ravyn pouts.

"This is true, but I love it anywhere *but* here." I stare at the sign that hasn't changed since the last time we were here.

Guys' Night!
Sing it Loud, Sing it Proud!
Drink Specials All Night!
Bring your friends and show off your best karaoke skills!
Prizes for Best Performances!

Let's make some noise!

"Aww, sister, you know this place holds a special spot in my heart. It's where I first met Mariana," Aiden said, stretching his arms behind his head.

Immediately, Ravyn knows he isn't referring to me. She narrows her eyes. "Aiden, how many times do I have to warn you. Do not call me that."

He turns to her with that smug half-smile we all know too well. "Just accept it, Ravyn. Let it happen."

"Silver, the last time we were here, we almost got into a full-on bar brawl." I sigh.

"I would think that you would want to come back and show off by making out a little."

"Gross," Aiden grunts.

"You, go inside," Ravyn growls.

"Yes… *sister*." Aiden dodges Ravyn's purse by only an inch.

"Amaya, everyone is waiting for us, and I have a surprise for you. You love surprises."

Dammit, I do love surprises.

"Fine, but if we see Larry, I call dibs on throwing a drink in his face." I stomp towards the front door.

"Deal." Ravyn chuckles.

She wasn't lying; everyone really is here. Mariana, Levi, Reina, Aiden, Eddie. We make our rounds, saying hello to everyone and catching up. I look over at Ravyn, and I can't help but smile. My girl has everything she's ever wanted. She's a champion, she's in love, and she has a family that will never abandon her. I've stayed true to the words I promised her months ago.

"So Rami, what's this surprise?" Levi asks.

"Yeah, Ravyn. We're dying with anticipation here." Reina takes a sip of her beer.

"Is no one else curious as to why the *fuck*, Aiden cut all of his hair off?" Eddie questions.

Everyone turns to face Aiden.

"I think I speak for the whole group when I say. No, not really." Reina shrugs.

"Well, I like it." Mariana smiles, her fingers combing through Aiden's new haircut, and Aiden just about faints at the compliment.

"We're still waiting, Rami." Levi pushes.

"Fine, I'll go get it. Wait right here," Ravyn said, pushing back from the table with a smirk. I watch her walk away, and my eyes can't help but linger.

"You like that ass, Amaya. I help sculpt it and keep it nice and toned, so… you're welcome," Eddie winks at me across the table.

I roll my eyes, trying to hide my grin.

"Ugh, you guys are so annoyingly adorable," Mariana groans, pouting dramatically. "I'm jealous."

"What do you have to be jealous about? You have Edgar," Aiden said, tilting his head at her.

"You know his name is Ethan. Anyway, we broke up," Mariana replies, way too casual for the emotional bomb she just dropped.

"YOU WHA—" Aiden starts to shout, shooting forward in his seat, but Reina cuts him off sharply with a hiss.

"Shhh! The first act is starting."

I do a double-take, blinking hard to make sure I wasn't hallucinating. I wasn't. Ravyn's on stage, microphone in hand. The spotlight catches the shimmer in her eyes as she stares right at me.

My heart is fluttering, my breath is catching somewhere between my chest and my throat.

"I hope this song speaks to you," she said, a message meant only for me.

Then she turns slightly toward the booth and raises a hand. "Hit it, DJ!" The beat drops, and an instantly recognizable and upbeat song floods the room.

Ravyn opens her mouth and sings. "This was never the way I planned, not my intention. I got so brave, drink in hand, lost my discretion."

She's singing I Kissed a Girl by Katy Perry, and she's dedicated it to me.

I looked towards Mariana and Reina. Both are looking at me because I guess they remember that night, too. I'm not sure why, but Mariana's eyes are glossing over like she's about to break out into tears.

"Ugh, I still hate this song," Aiden mumbles.

"Aiden, shut up. You're ruining the moment." Mariana slaps him on the arm.

"Ah, just like old times," Aiden whispers.

I look back up at Ravyn, and our eyes find each other again. She's waving at me to go on stage with her, and so I do, because where Ravyn goes, I'll always follow. The DJ hands me a mic and I sing along with her, side by side, and watch our friends join in at our table, even Aiden. I close my eyes, feeling the music and enjoying the moment, singing a song with the girl of my dreams. Suddenly, all I hear is my voice; Ravyn's is missing, and when I open my eyes, I see why.

Ravyn is down on one knee. The lights are changing from a harsh spotlight to soft and twinkling. The song changes into something slow and romantic, and all I can focus on is how badly Ravyn is trembling. Her propped knee is bouncing, and I place my hand on it.

She takes a deep breath, "I didn't write a big speech, because every time I tried, it just came out sounding smaller than how I feel about you."

I can feel my heart racing. She reaches into her pocket and holds out the most beautiful ring I've ever seen, but she could have handed me a ring pop, and my answer would still be the same.

"I've fought a lot of battles in my life. I've built a lot of walls, and yet you've fought through them all to be with me," she said, voice low now, almost breaking. "I used to tell you that hating you was at the top of my favorite hobbies list. The truth is that loving you is my favorite hobby."

"Even before wrestling?" I question, an eyebrow raised.

"Yes, even before wrestling, Red." Ravyn laughs. " I will *not* leave you. I will *not* disappoint you. I will *not* choose you second. I will *not* hurt you. *All* because I love you. Amaya Acosta, will you marry me?"

"Yes, of course, Ramona," I whisper, only for her to hear. I make my voice louder and scream, "Yes!"

I nearly knock her to the ground as I throw my arms around her. The bar erupts in a roar, cheering, hollering, glasses filling the sky as the whole bar toasts to us. Laughter and applause ripple through the crowd as our friends rush the stage with open arms and tearful grins. They surround us in a flood of affection, hugs, high-fives, and shouts of "Let me see the ring."

"Wait," Aiden shouts, making us all pause.

"Does this mean I can call you sister now without you threatening me?" he smirks.

"NO." Everyone yells in unison.

I might have lost the championship, but what I've gained is something no belt can ever replace.

Acknowledgments

I can't believe this book is in your hands.

This story was born during a *WWE* event I attended in Puerto Rico in 2023. My family and I were sitting in the crowd, and the air was electrifying. I couldn't help but wonder what it would feel like to be a professional wrestler. And, because I'm a hopeless romantic, I also found myself wondering who might be dating whom behind the scenes. Right then and there, in that buzzing arena, I took out my phone and started typing notes for what would become this book.

Writing this story has brought me so much joy. It let me combine two of the things I love and gave me the perfect excuse to attend more wrestling events and call it *research.*

I see myself in both of these characters. Amaya and her want to find her voice in all of the noise of what others believe she's supposed to be. Ravyn, who makes her friends her family. She finds out that it's okay to be authentically yourself, and that love doesn't have to look a certain way or be with a certain sex. Love is love.

I want to thank my husband, Louis. We both grew up watching wrestling, and finding our way back during the pandemic has been such a gift. Nothing brings me more joy than spending time with you at these events. I love the booing, cheering, and laughing together. It's number one on my list of favorite things to do with you.

To my sister-in-law, Annie. Thank you for your advice and sapphic book recommendations. I've always wanted to write a sapphic love story, and you helped me do this genre justice.

To my editor and dear friend, Allison: Yes, the front desk agent was named after you! That hospitality job brought us together, and I can't imagine my life without you in it. Thank you for always being excited when I text you about another new book idea. Your support means everything.

To all the indie bookstores that support local authors—thank you. Because of you, I got to see *my* book on a shelf, in a store, ready to be discovered. You help stories like mine find their way to the readers who need them.

And finally, to *you*, the reader. I'm not sure what brought you to this book, but I'm so glad you're here. I hope you love book one of the *Wrestling with Love series* as much as I do.

I'll see you for book two. It's time to explore Mariana and Aiden's story.

Tamara Lemus discovered her passion for writing at a young age, sparked by the gift of journals from her mother. Later, she branched out onto the online writing scene by writing *Harry Styles* fan fiction on *Tumblr*. Her love of reading started when a little book titled *Twilight* entered the world. As life became more demanding, reading fell to the back burner, but the moment she picked up a book again, she was hooked once again. Today, Tamara enjoys diving into fantasy, romance, and thrillers. In her free time, she loves to travel, explore new cuisines, and spend quality time with her family and her beloved fur baby Xena.

Also by Tamara Lemus

Runaway Fae

Corvina Morticia Umbra is the sole heir to the Shadow Court throne, a court that is famous for her Papi's cruel and wicked ways. Ever since she was a little girl, she feared the crown. She wants nothing to do with becoming a queen, but when her Papi becomes ill, her coronation isn't far behind. In desperation, she flees her home of Aebriera. The portal to the human world awaits, and on the other side, she finds Dante, a human male Corvina finds herself drawn to. As her life in the mortal realm becomes easier, her past starts to haunt her. Truths come to light, and Corvina now has to choose between the life she's longed for and the life she was born into.